MARSEILLE NOIR

EDITED BY CÉDRIC FABRE

Translated by David and Nicole Ball

Published by Akashic Books
©2015 Akashic Books

Series concept by Tim McLoughlin and Johnny Temple
Marseille map by Sohrab Habibion

ISBN-13: 978-1-61775-295-7
Library of Congress Control Number: 2014955090
All rights reserved

First printing

Akashic Books
Twitter: @AkashicBooks
Facebook: AkashicBooks
E-mail: info@akashicbooks.com
Website: www.akashicbooks.com

This book is dedicated to the loving memory of our friend
Salim Hatubou, who left us on March 31, 2015.
—The Authors

ALSO IN THE AKASHIC NOIR SERIES

FORTHCOMING

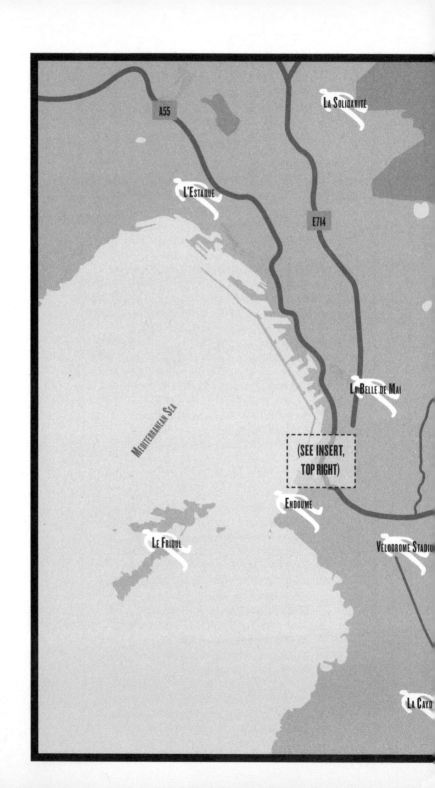

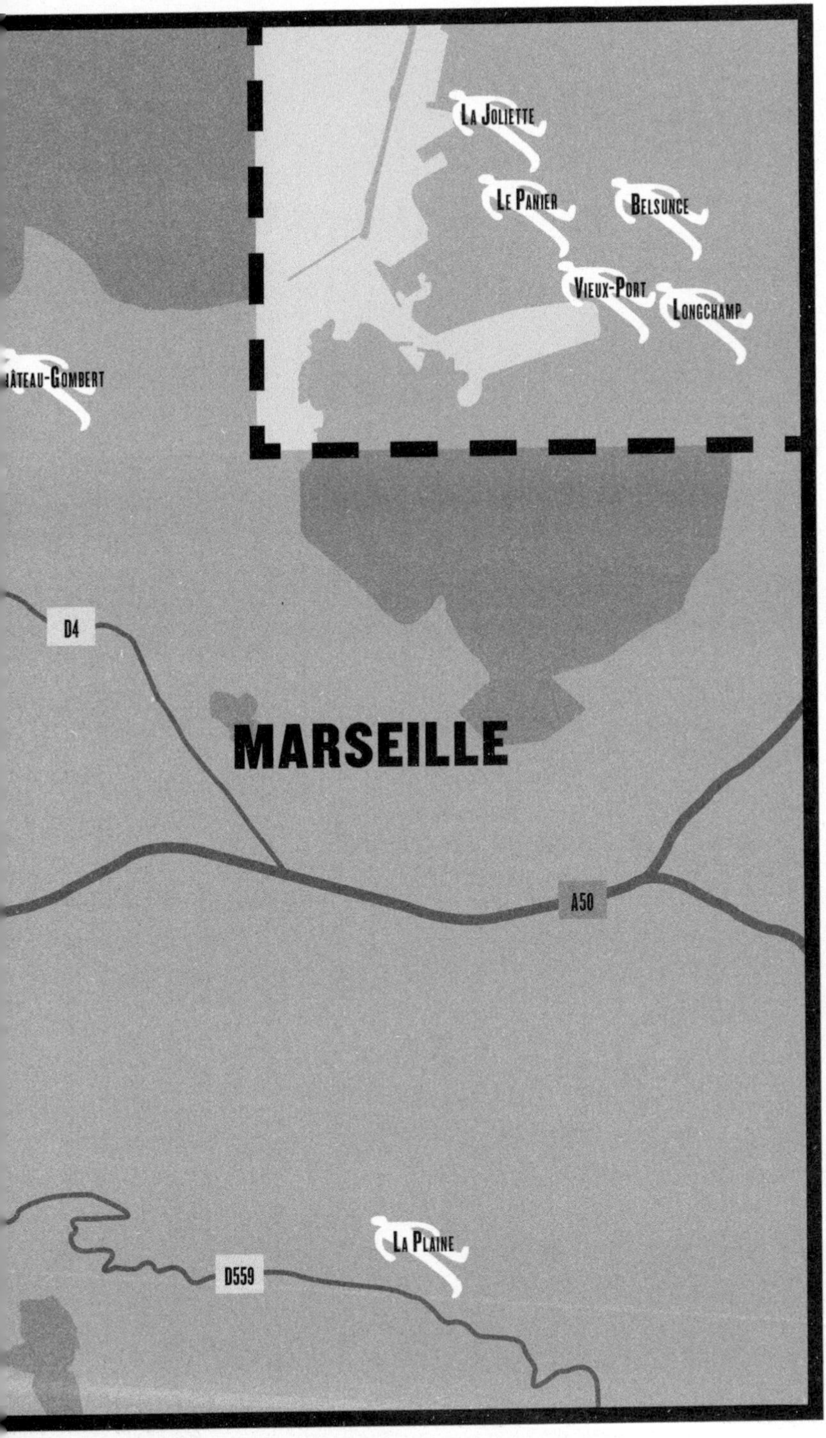
La Joliette
Le Panier
Belsunce
Vieux-Port
Longchamp
âteau-Gombert
D4
MARSEILLE
A50
La Plaine
D559

TABLE OF CONTENTS

INTRODUCTION
Marseille Calling

In 1900, after fifty years of unprecedented growth and modernization that radically transformed the city, Marseille was the queen of the Mediterranean, tirelessly drawing its power from the vast French colonial empire. In the eyes of the writer and reporter Albert Londres, it had acquired the status of an "imaginary court in a universal palace of trade." Its decline began in the 1960s, when France lost its colonies, and this accelerated with the oil crises of the following decade.

Marseille's past glory is still visible through its industrial remains: old, abandoned oil refineries, soap and brick factories you come upon at a bend in the road between L'Estaque and Callelongue. Today, moving through the city from one end to the other can feel like a dive into a socioeconomic slump, with its decrepit villages and its housing projects in constant decay and an unemployment rate sometimes over 50 percent.

A postindustrial city might be defined by the distance that separates it from its golden age, because it's at the heart of that space-time—when a page of glorious history has been turned—that the mythologies and fantasies, the resentments and nostalgias that play a part in shaking up and rebuilding its identity, are formed. For if its changes are sometimes blindingly obvious, its permanent features become more tangible. "Marseille, always bound for elsewhere," wrote the French author and songwriter Pierre Mac Orlan. Unfortunately, the horizon seems—let's say *momentarily* to remain optimistic—out of reach, and the city is still trying to figure out a future for itself . . . And indeed, it does keep transforming, sometimes for the best, if only in its outward appearance. It was named the 2013 European Capital of Culture, and our dream is that a stimulus like this will be the opportunity for a new chapter. A city of tragedy—it is partly Greek—Marseille does, however, have resources, and can count on its formidably dynamic youth.

Marseille is a "world city"—which makes one think of London more than Paris, in many ways—a crossroads for the people of Europe and the Mediterranean, a city that welcomes all migrants and exiles. It is a city that embodies the rabble-rousing, tough-guy side of the whole French nation. People like its cocky humor and its accent as much as they fear its spirit of rebellion. In fact, its identity is often reduced to a sports slogan, *Proud to be Marseillais*, which also reflects a feeling of abandonment and helplessness. Here socioeconomic struggle brings people together and unites them just as much as the wins of the Olympique de Marseille soccer team. It has the aura of noir, an aura that its residents often love as much as they hate, enlightened—or blinded—by that southern light. "You can't understand Marseille if you're indifferent to its light. It forces you to lower your eyes," said Jean-Claude Izzo, the extraordinary novelist who finally gave Marseille back its voice after decades of almost no decent literary fiction.

Fooled by clichés that it was partly responsible for creating, Marseille sometimes portrays itself with an unconscious, disorganized strategy to constantly scramble its image. The city is never where you think it is. Local elected officials have often denounced "Marseille bashing" in their speeches, promising to improve its image before they make a commitment to fix its problems. While the cover headline of a Parisian weekly recently read, "Marseille, a Lost Territory for the Republic"—the vast majority of its people respect the laws of the Republic, vote, and pay their taxes, thank you very much—the *New York Times* declared it was the second must-visit destination, after Rio and before Nicaragua. Marseille is frequently reduced to the capital of delinquency and corruption in France. But for journalists looking for this raw reality, it is often difficult to grasp and define, since it is composed of a multiplicity of fictional fragments.

Marseille's violence has become the violence of a closed city, wedged between the sea and the hills and thus often turned against itself. The killings linked to drug deals are blown out of proportion; and the reality of the ever-increasing economic gap, between the north and south and the violence it results in, is neglected. Of course there is organized crime . . . Michel Foucault said it's on the margins that the center is constructed. And local organized crime has been connected to politics for a long time, going back to the German occupation of France during World War II when the Guérini brothers chose the side of Gaston Defferre, an important figure in French history who went on to become the longtime mayor of Marseille. And the image of Marseille as a city of thugs goes back even further: it was in the second half of the nineteenth century that the city acquired the reputation of being dangerous, when crime was becoming "organized" little by little, and it continued all the way to the famous "French connection" of the '60s and '70s.

Today the crime tends to be disorganized, fragmented, more violent: the kids mowed down by gunfire are often under twenty-five . . .

In such a context, how can culture be given the place it deserves? Before Marseille was labeled the European Capital of Culture, we were already patching together garage rock concerts, beach parties with deejays, art shows, theater and dance performances, all with a do-it-yourself spirit. Each one in his or her own corner, more or less; private resourcefulness that held little interest for politicians. People deplored Marseille's constant reluctance to honor its own artists, musicians, and writers—an old tradition. You had to *leave* in order to succeed. The writer André Suarès, strolling through the neighborhoods of Sainte-Marthe,

Saint-André, and Saint-Julien, said that we have always pro-
duced saints when poets were needed. Marseille writers are still
not highly regarded, neither here nor elsewhere. They're accused
of "doing their Pagnol"—a reference to Marcel Pagnol's folksy
plays that have become classics—before they're even read, and
they remain largely unknown.

Yet how can one write about this city and its people any
other way than through fiction? Reality here seems so completely
unbelievable. If elsewhere the crime novel can claim a kind of
"socio-realism," in the tradition of Zola or Vallès, here the genre
can rapidly turn into social surrealism. Because here, a gang of
youths can "rob" a downtown parking garage and manage it for
months under the nose of the police, collecting money and raising the gates manually, before anyone finally intervenes; because
here, too, when we try to honor a poet like Rimbaud (who died in
Marseille) and we can't find an available stretch of an avenue or
alley to bear his name, we settle the matter by baptizing a space
in the Saint-Charles train station the Arthur Rimbaud Waiting
Room—inaugurated by none other than Patti Smith.

For all these and many more reasons, Marseille provides magnificent material for writing. For a long time, when it still had its
eye on the sea, it was in fact a veritable "open city" for writers on
shore leave.

"Marseille belongs to whoever comes from the open sea,"
observed the poet and novelist Blaise Cendrars. Stendhal, Zola,
and Mérimée wrote of its excess, its fiery personality, and its cos-
mopolitanism. It welcomed some of the greatest globe-trotting
writers: Joseph Conrad, Albert Londres, Pierre Mac Orlan, Blaise
Cendrars, Walter Benjamin, Mary Jayne Gold, Claude McKay,
Anna Seghers, Ousmane Sembene . . . all lost travel writers and
novelists, advocates of a vagabond literature that turned Marseille into one of the capitals of "world fiction" well before the
English defined the concept. The literary journal *Les Cahiers du
Sud*, which was founded by Jean Ballard in 1925 and lasted into

the mid-'60s, was a brilliant illustration of this. At the same time, poets and lovers of literature were growing up in the city, from Victor Gélu to Louis Brauquier, as well as André Suarès, all largely forgotten today. It's not surprising that it became a capital of rap and slam poetry, for Marseille knows, intimately, what "popular culture" means . . .

Thus, approaching the city through the genre called "noir" seemed to make sense—even if this genre, supposing that it actually exists, encompasses different realities, since each author is free to define it from his or her own perspective. A number of the writers who agreed to contribute to *Marseille Noir* don't write crime fiction or any other type of "genre fiction." Some grew up outside of Marseille and have just settled in the Phocaean city; others were born here and then left for other horizons. They come from diverse cultures—and sometimes languages—but all of them participated in the construction of this fictional cartography of Marseille—or is it a monograph?—with their own imaginary visions. All have their own re-creations, or even their own distorted memories or selective amnesia . . . We had no intention, of course, of spotlighting some school of writing or literary movement, nor of speaking with only one voice, nor of coconstructing an exhaustive or realistic portrait of our city. Rather, our goal was to present different ways of seeing.

This anthology is neither a comprehensive survey nor a compilation, and still less an enumeration of the emblematic places of the city. An anti-guidebook? Maybe. If *Marseille Noir* does have any homogeneity, it's mostly because the authors put Marseille at the heart of their stories, because the city here is omniscient, omnipresent, and recurrent—a character in its own right. Some stories resonate with each other and we marvel at the discovery that sometimes it is in the interstices, in invisible points of junction between two stories, that magic exists . . . for we're betting that in literature, everything is a matter of secret, mysterious correspondences.

In this collection, we have retained crime fiction's predilection for a literature rooted in a specific place, as well as its obsession with the power of the connection between the individual and his or her environment, between the individual and the community.

Some authors chose to infuse humor into their dark tales, as when Philippe Carrese, who began writing a series of crime novels about Marseille in the mid-'90s, depicts ordinary *cagoles* (sluts) and *cacous* (show-offs), eternal victims of themselves and of the city that made them. A comical tone is also found in Serge Scotto's writing, as he relates the tribulations of a bohemian apprentice in the iconic neighborhood of la Plaine at the end of the '80s, an island of punkness in a city which was then turning to rap.

At times the city seems to circle around the Vieux-Port, where fishermen have given way to yachtsmen, and narrow streets swarm with exhausted, bitter characters who can't cope anymore, because behind the flashy façade, the world is an open-air garbage dump, as Pia Peterson shows us. François Beaune sets his story on the 49 bus, with exhilarating verve, where he presents a Marseille that can test one's patience and lead to angry outbursts. Minna Sif, whose story takes place partly in Belsunce, the cosmopolitan heart of Marseille, describes a city woven like a net that imprisons its prey, a city of wandering and waiting that can feel like the last stop. In some stories, the city appears almost as a hopeless dead end for bad boys on the lam, like the characters of René Frégni and Emmanuel Loi, who, each in his own way, present stories of vengeance and gangland killings, the stuff local legends are made of. For Marseille loves these urban myths—especially if they're rooted in cult places like Vélodrome Stadium where François Thomazeau sets his story, or Endoume, through which Christian Garcin walks us, with a pinch of nostalgia; or Le Panier, an underworld mecca, revisited here in an insolent, surprising way by Patrick Coulomb.

Salim Hatubou's political police procedural, which stretches from a housing project in the North End to the far-off Comoros, is quite different from the usual stories of drug dealing. Besides, the dealer isn't always the way you imagine him, as you see when you follow Rebecca Lighieri's character in a theoretically harmless location, the zoo. And, moving away from the swarming heart of the city, we land in Le Frioul for an outing in the form of a macabre, grandiose farce penned by Marie Neuser.

Finally, this anthology is an homage to Marseille: "It's a mess after my own heart," as Cendrars said. For Marseille also cures us of our obsession to be in control of everything, to get results, to be showered with praise. Because here, where we know how to cultivate a certain sense of self-mockery, we hope we've learned at least one essential thing: we know the foreigner is above all oneself.

Cédric Fabre
Marseille, France
September 2015

PART I

MYTHOLOGIES

THE JOSETTES REALLY LIKED ME

BY CHRISTIAN GARCIN

Endoume

I never knew which one of Ange Malatesta's four sisters was the craziest. I don't know anything about the symptoms of dementia, psychosis, schizophrenia, or any other mental illnesses, so I certainly wouldn't dare to diagnose them, but I do know they were all nuts. Besides, they took turns in a mental hospital, sometimes even together. They were interchangeable, and that probably didn't do much for their mental stability. To begin with, their names were almost identical: Josiane, Josette, Jocelyne, and Josephine. People called them "the four Joes." They were as alike as four peas in a pod—same height, slightly thin, kind of pretty too, wavy, almost curly dark hair, big black eyes, usually wearing the same flowery dresses all bought together at the same time—so actually, I never could determine who was the youngest and who the oldest. And yet I would see them almost every day on the little dead-end street where we lived, near rue d'Endoume, whenever they weren't in a "special home," as their mother called it. She had a strong taste for euphemisms.

Their mother was Madame Malatesta; I never knew her first name. She had bright red hair, sometimes even blue, which, in the Endoume of the sixties, was considered bizarre. She had given birth to them at closely spaced intervals, so that the eldest was only about three years older than the youngest.

Their father Claudio was a mason. He was rarely seen, and when he was, he would usually be wearing a sleeveless undershirt and a cap, with a cigarette between his lips, his hands in his pockets resting just below a slight paunch. I don't think I ever heard the sound of his voice. I was afraid of him. Ange said that nobody at home was allowed to ask him questions or interrupt him when he talked. Rumor had it that he drank pretty heavily and beat his wife and kids. I had no trouble believing that he drank; I'd seen him stagger before climbing the stairs to their apartment. As for the rest, Ange never talked about it, so I think it was just neighborhood gossip.

I have no idea if there was gossip about my own father. If there was, it probably wasn't very far from the truth, which was that he worked with the mob. That, however, nobody in the neighborhood was supposed to know: theoretically, everybody took him for what he claimed to be—an honest salesman of wine and spirits. Sure, he was a mobster, but a small-time mobster, someone who never threatened anyone. Or not very often—or, let's say, not on a regular basis. Who in any case had never stolen, or killed anyone. He had connections to the Corsicans, who controlled the slot machines in the bars and cafés. He was a collector. Otherwise he was a very nice, sensitive, and generous man who loved his wife and son. I was an only child.

He was born into the mob, he'd always lived in it, and he saw no other way of earning a living. He would finally get out one day in 1970, feetfirst, a bullet in his belly and another in the liver after a drive-by shooting in a bar on boulevard des Dames. He had the bad luck of being there when it happened, although he was only doing his job—that is, collecting a payoff. Two young hoods on motorcycles fired wildly through the plate-glass window, killing the manager, who was actually their target, as well as two customers plus my father, who were not. But that's another story.

Ange and I were the same age. In the Malatesta family, he was the youngest, five years younger than his youngest sister. He was very dark too—the family was Sicilian—with big eyes lined with long black eyelashes. He laughed a lot, and loved to sing the hits of the day at the top of his unbearably shrill voice. It irritated his sisters and the whole neighborhood too. I particularly remember a Mexican song Henri Salvador had adapted, "Juanita Banana," where Juanita sang an aria (from *Rigoletto*, I would learn years later), which Ange would sing for days on end in a voice that literally pierced your eardrums.

We lived at the bottom of the path leading up to Roucas Blanc, almost on rue d'Endoume, in a little dead end of gray tar, next to a plumber's workshop where I would sometimes play with the boss's son, a little blond kid named Denis Fornasero. On the other side there was a grocery store run by a gentle, mute Algerian couple, Leila and Saïd Bijaoui, who didn't have any children; I learned later that they'd had a son who was killed in the Algerian War. Maybe that's why their eyes looked so very sad. The Malatestas lived right across the street, as did the Fabrizios (their son René was more Ange's friend than mine and he sometimes invited Ange over); there was also the Ollives, the Nicolaïs, the Mattéis, the Lacépèdes, and the Pagès—all families I knew less well, since they didn't have any kids my age. A little farther toward boulevard Tellène, there was the Girard family. Their son François was ten years older than me. He played in the Endoume soccer club and was pretty good. He called himself Francis, I never knew why. A good-looking guy, blond with light eyes, who could get any girl he wanted. He kind of fascinated us, Ange and me.

I never knew exactly what the mental problems of the four Joes were, but I remember that one afternoon when we were playing in our street (Thursday was then the day off from school), Ange told me, looking dejected, that the day before, when he happened to be alone at home with his sisters a little before their mother got back, one of them had suddenly started to crawl over the dining room rug, crying and spitting like a cat, while another one danced naked and another meticulously tore apart the leaves of their plants, humming a tune of Luis Mariano's under the watchful eyes of the last one, who was sucking her thumb and stroking her hair. When their mother got there, she called an ambulance and three of the sisters left the house. So only one remained that day: I'll call her Josette for convenience, though I'm not absolutely sure she was really the one.

Josette liked me and so did the three other Jo sisters, although she never remembered my name. And in fact, since the four sisters were interchangeable in my eyes, I'd be better off using an original grammatical form when I talk about Josette, fusing the singular with the plural: "Josettes liked me," for example. Or, "Josette liked me, although they never remembers my name." However it may be, this girl was like a condensed version of the four, as if Jocelyne, Josiane, Josephine, and Josette were suddenly put together in one body, which I had decided, with all the confidence of my nine years of age, to call Josette.

At the time I was going to the elementary school on rue Candolle, on the other side of rue d'Endoume—just like Ange, but we weren't in the same class. As for the Jo sisters, they were old enough to go to lycée (at that time high school and junior high were combined), but I'm not sure their condition allowed them to attend school at all. Today, I no longer remember. What I do remember is that a little later that same Thursday afternoon, I found myself alone with Josette. Her father was at a construction site, her mother probably at the hairdresser's, the three other sisters in the psychiatric unit of La Timone Hospital, and the brother had gone to his neighbor René Fabrizio's to look at his collection of Norev car models. (René was a tall, skinny kid with pale skin and a freckled face who spoke very fast and was crazy about cars.) My parents weren't home either. My mother was out that day visiting her sister, who'd just had her appendix removed at La Conception Hospital. As for my father, he was rarely there anyway.

So I was alone at the Malatesta's, with Josette. I was reading *The Secret of the Unicorn* while she was silently playing with her hair on the flowery couch in the living room with a magazine she wasn't reading on her naked knees. She was staring at me in a strange, slightly sorrowful way. I pretended not to see anything when she slowly raised her dress to the top of her thighs, which were brown and slender. From the corner of my eyes, I caught a glimpse of the white, scalloped bottom of her panties. I didn't react when she walked over to me either, swaying her hips in an exaggerated way. But I was vaguely terrified: she was tall, and I was only a shy, embarrassed little boy. She kept on twisting the long locks of her shiny black hair between her fingers. She sat down right next to me. She smelled nice: shampoo and milk soap. I pretended to go on reading *Tintin*, and persisted in not reacting when she began to cry silently, murmuring some words I couldn't quite understand. Then she stroked my thigh. The Bird Brothers were trying to kill Tintin in the underground passages of Moulinsart, but I wasn't really paying attention to that; I was just mechanically turning the pages as if nothing was happening. Josette put her head on my shoulder while continuing to stroke me through my shorts. She murmured other words that I couldn't understand. Her hand slipped into the opening of my shorts. It was soft. I felt my little penis rising. She took it carefully between her fingers, kept on stroking it gently, and then leaned over toward it, surrounding it in a humid sheath. I closed my eyes and forced myself not to move an inch.

That's when Ange came in. Josette jumped back and began to whimper. Then she sprang up and ran into her room. As for me, I was paralyzed, like a rabbit caught in the headlights of a car. But I did have the presence of mind to drop *The Secret of the Unicorn* on my thighs. I'd been squeezing it against my chest, right above Josette's curly hair. Ange froze and gave me a dark look that scared me a little. I had never seen his eyes like that, intense and hostile at the same time. In fact, I had never known him to be so serious; usually, anything would make him laugh. I was confused about that look I'd never seen before; he was suddenly rising above his age, our age: it was a grown-up look, not the look of a nine-year-old child. Then he put his keys down on the little table at the entrance and said nonchalantly, "What's her problem now?"—and without waiting for an answer, he became a little boy again and told me about René Fabrizio's collection of Norevs.

At that time Endoume was a village. I'm talking about East Endoume, the Roucas Blanc–Saint-Victor–Corderie side, not to be confused with West Endoume on the Corniche side, which was the hip part of the neighborhood. In fact, Marseille was less a city than a patchwork of villages, each one with a clearly defined identity. In general, each of these villages ignored the existence of the others. It was useless to speak of La Belle de Mai to the residents of Sainte-Marguerite, of Canet to the people of Endoume (East or West), of Montredon to the people of L'Estaque, of the Aygalades to the people of Saint-Barnabé: at best these were places where they'd never set foot, and at worst they considered it useless, even degrading, to go there. Only the Canebière and the Vieux-Port, which made up the tiny city center of what was nonetheless the second largest city in France, were common to everyone—or almost everyone.

A quarter of a century later, that hadn't changed much. The village of East Endoume still had its own character, the small shopkeepers hadn't yet seen their shops bought up by national chains, and life there was rather pleasant. The residents of the little dead-end street, however, were not the same. I still lived there, but alone since my mother died; I never got married. On the other hand, the Malatestas had moved away long ago, like most of the other neighbors except for the Fabrizios. Their son René had the same passion for cars he had as a child, and now worked as a sales executive for Renault in La Capelette.

As for me, I had taken over from my father. It was the end of the nineties. Around twenty years earlier, there had been the famous "French connection," which a movie with Gene Hackman had made famous all over the world. The Endoume mob was active in it, particularly our neighbor François Girard, a.k.a. Francis, a.k.a. Le Blond or Hay-Head. He was still a handsome guy, still a lady-killer, and still loved soccer. But at the very beginning of the eighties, he'd been accused of ordering the assassination of a well-known judge who'd had the unfortunate idea of digging a little too deep into the scandals linked to this French connection, and he got life. They made a movie about that too.

The mob was changing a lot during those years. Besides, at some point there was no longer a single, unified "mob," just bosses fighting each other. Their methods were more violent than before and summary executions were the rule. The great upheavals at work in society at the time, the sudden rise of laissez-faire economics, the increasingly aggressive sales techniques, the way the workforce was managed—*management*, as they said, using the American word with a French accent—and the first notions of "flexibility," "adaptability," and "downsizing" that would flourish after 2000 were nothing else but the good old system of shameless exploitation of the most vulnerable. A brief parenthesis of four decades marked by concern for working people, roughly from the Liberation to the second election of Mitterrand, had more or less put a brake on the system, but now all that was washing over the deepest levels of society, multiplied a hundredfold and in the most violent ways, in the small, medium, and of course biggest spheres of organized crime. In Marseille, the Corsicans and the Arabs, who at first had more or less agreed to divide the territory (the Corsicans downtown with the slot machines and the old mafia-like system for bars, restaurants, and prostitution; the Arabs in the North End with the flourishing drug business—and prostitution too), were now becoming greedier, and each tried to take over market shares from the territories and businesses of the other, which led to endless gangland killings. You'd think the young generations—mine was already over the hill—had seen too many ultraviolent American movies. I was becoming an old schmuck: my credo was, *It was better in the old days*. I was barely over thirty, but I was already thinking of taking some sort of early retirement.

When I talked about it around me, I was made to understand that it was not wanted. But I kept at it and was told to talk to Raymond Burr.

Raymond Burr was the actor who played Robert T. Ironside in the 1970s TV series: a paralyzed cop in his wheelchair, surrounded by his sidekicks—a young dark-haired guy, a blond girl, and a black guy, all neatly dressed with well-combed hair. Raymond Burr was also the nickname of a baron of the Damiani branch of the powerful Altieri family, who ran part of the city. Raymond Burr was mostly in charge of the Endoume-Corderie-Catalans sector, going up toward Notre-Dame de la Garde. He was said to be utterly devoid of scruples. Some claimed his nickname came from his temperament, others said it was because he was paralyzed and in a wheelchair, which still others denied. Me, I had no idea: I'd never met him.

They gave me an appointment with him on a Monday at six p.m. in the back room of Chez Fernand, a bar that was then on the corner of rue Perlet, not far from the former movie theater, Bompard, where I had seen *Planet of the Apes* as a child and a whole lot of noir films—including Jean-Pierre Melville's *Le Deuxième Souffle*, with Lino Ventura, which I saw twice. It never stopped playing because of its last scene, which took place nearby, almost at the corner of rue d'Endoume and boulevard de la Corderie, right at the beginning of rue des Lices.

It was only the beginning of June, but it was already very hot. I had walked there and was sweating in my shirtsleeves, with my beige blazer in hand. When I opened the door of the bar, Fernand nodded hello and pointed with his thumb to a door that said *Private*. I nodded back and went into the bathroom first. Splashed cold water over my face. Then I put on my blazer: I was known in the profession as an elegant, clean-looking man and I wasn't going to start looking slovenly just because it was ninety-one lousy degrees in the shade. I took a comb out of my inside pocket, grazing the small metal Jesus I'd taken with me as a precaution, and straightened my hair. When the result seemed more or less acceptable, I went back to the bar without looking at Fernand and opened the door marked *Private*.

Two guys were standing there, cigarettes in their mouths, near an antique chest of drawers that could have belonged to my great-aunt Thérèse, the one who'd lived in the colonies for twenty years and was involved in diamond trafficking in the Congo. A big fan was turning, bringing a few breaths of welcome coolness. I knew the two guys: Milou and Doumé, two inseparable gunmen, one tall and thin, the other short and fat. Don Quixote and Sancho Panza, you might say. More precisely Emile Leccia, a.k.a. Milou, also The Radish (I never knew why), and Dominique Franceschi, a.k.a. Doumé (nobody ever took the trouble of finding a real nickname for him). They looked at me without moving a muscle.

There was also a third person, sitting in the shadow: Raymond Burr, no doubt. I noted the two big metal tires of the wheelchair, which possibly explained the origin of his nickname. He moved forward a little and his face came into the light. He was bald and puffy, dressed completely in black. A character from a Scorsese film.

"So, you want to hang it up?" he said in a weak voice, a little too soft, with what seemed to me a slightly fake Corsican accent. And he shot me an intense, dark look, in complete contradiction to the tone he'd just used—the look of a Dalmatian eagle, the nickname for Josip Skoblar, the greatest shooter ever to play soccer for the Olympique de Marseille.

Except that the guy facing me wasn't Dalmatian but Sicilian. My eyes widened.

"Ange?"

"Ah . . . so you do recognize me," he said slowly, still with the same fake accent. "That's good."

It was a statement of fact, both satisfied and surprised. And yet, no, I certainly wouldn't have recognized him without the look he'd just given me, exactly the same look he'd given me twenty-five years earlier in his living room, just after his sister Josette or whatever her name was had introduced me to forbidden pleasures for the first time. How could I have recognized the slim kid with a high voice who liked to laugh in this fat bald guy slumped in a wheelchair? I was stunned.

"Go see if it's nice out," he said curtly to the two thugs who hadn't taken their eyes off my face or their cigs out of their mouths.

The Radish and Doumé left slowly, with a walk a bit too studied to be natural. I knew them well, one couldn't make up for the other: both equally violent and simpleminded. Total morons. I turned my head to Ange. His expression had changed: less hard, but not the like the child I'd known. A look that had seen it all, slightly weary, both disillusioned and determined. But he still had his long black eyelashes.

"What happened?" I asked, pointing to his wheelchair.

He told me disdainfully that when he was twenty-five and still living with his parents near La Pointe-Rouge, he wanted to show off for a few pals and especially a few girls—among them, one he really liked despite her excessive blondness and her unfortunate tendency to chew gum with her mouth open. On a July day, before the whole little group, he dived off the rocky peak of the Saména inlet. But he'd misjudged the depth of the water and crashed on the rocks that were sticking out of the water a few inches. He'd been stuck in a wheelchair ever since.

"No luck," he concluded. "But what can you do? Two years later I married the blonde with the chewing gum. I taught her to keep her mouth shut and made her go back to her natural hair color. In fact, her hair is as dark as mine. Well, like mine used to be," he smiled, stroking his bald pate.

I didn't know what to say. "And . . . your sisters, they're okay?"

He gave me another dark, implacable look and remained silent for a few seconds. I withstood his gaze without blinking. We were right in the middle of the final scene of a spaghetti western; all you needed was the harmonica. Finally, he spat out: "Two committed suicide, one's locked up."

I pretended to think about this. "Oh God, no . . . But . . . there's one left, right?"

He nodded slowly. "You got it. Yours."

"Excuse me?"

"Josiane."

I shook my head and knitted my brows. I didn't understand at all. "What do you mean, Josiane? And why 'mine'? What're you talking about?"

He sighed. "You want to hang it up, right? Let's say that's a go. But under certain conditions. Okay," he added, "I'm thirsty. Pastis?" He rolled his wheelchair over to a low piece of furniture and opened its door, revealing about a dozen bottles. "Ricard, Casanis, 51? I even have some Pec, if you like."

"51, thanks. Ange, I don't understand a thing you're saying."

"Ice?"

"Sure. Ange, could you be more explicit, please?"

He filled up the glasses and motioned to me to help myself. We clinked glasses. The ice cubes gave off their delightful little crystalline noise.

"It's been a long time, right?" he said, smiling. "How long? Twenty-five years?"

"Around that, yeah. Here's to you."

"How's your mother?"

"Died ten years ago. Cancer. How about you, your parents?"

"Same thing. One year apart. Cancer too. I know you never left the street. René Fabrizio's still there?"

"Yeah, he sells cars. Predictable. I think his dream is to run for city council." We began to laugh. "But how about you?" I went on. "How did you end up working for the Damiani-Altieris?"

"It's a long story. I'll tell you about it some other time. Anyway, I'm here. And *I'm* the one who decides whether you retire or not," he declared in a harsh tone.

I didn't answer. The conversation was taking a different turn.

"I don't want you to leave the business," he said, more gently. "We need reliable, discreet personnel. You're the perfect fit. But if that's what you really want, I'll see what I can do. Let's say it's in memory of the little street we grew up on. I trust you, I know you won't go blabbing your head off if you retire. But there's a price to pay."

I could see where he was heading. "And that price is . . . ?"

"I told you: Josiane."

I pretended not to understand.

"I know," he sighed, "you never could tell my sisters apart. Not you or anyone else, for that matter—not even my mother, sometimes. And as for my father, forget it. Everybody called them the Four Joes. When I heard that, I used to think of the four Daltons in *Lucky Luke*, and since one of them is called Joe, I couldn't hear anyone talk about them without instantly having the image of Joe Dalton in front of my eyes, the little nasty, nervous guy. And I felt for them. But anyway. I was the only one who could tell them apart. For me, they didn't look all that much alike."

He sighed again.

"Okay, that's all past . . . Jocelyne and Josette committed suicide, one by throwing herself off the Fausse-Monnaie Bridge, the other when she managed to escape from her room during one of her many stays at La Timone. She climbed up to the roof through the service stairway and jumped off. One three weeks after the other, after our mother died. Since then, Josephine's been hospitalized full time with no chance of getting out. Seems she's incurable. Sometimes they put her in a straitjacket."

He stopped talking abruptly, as if he were short of breath.

"Jesus, a straitjacket, you hear that?" he said in a dull voice. "My sister in a straitjacket!" He took a handkerchief out of his pocket and wiped his eyes.

I let a few seconds of silence go by out of decency, then said: "And . . . Josiane?"

"Josiane? Let's say her condition is a little less worrisome. All four of them went downhill as they got older, but her a little less than the others. Sure, she's losing her marbles, but it's not too serious yet. In any case, she's the only sister I've got left, and I want to do anything I can to prevent her from being locked up in a mental hospital, but I can't take care of her full time. And that's what she needs. I don't want a home nurse either. I'd hate to have someone I don't know snooping around my place, you just never know. So you see, I'm kind of stuck." He refilled our glasses. "You know, she still talks about you sometimes."

"About me?"

"Actually, she doesn't say your name because she certainly forgot it, but sometimes she talks about my buddy from the dead end, the one who lived across the street. Other than my parents, me, and my three other sisters, you're the only one she mentions from time to time. But by the way," he narrowed his eyes, "you see which one of the four we're talking about, right?"

"Uhh . . . yeah, I think so."

"You *think* so?" he snapped. "For chrissake, she gave you a blowjob in my house! You son of a bitch. She was the most gentle of the four, the most sensitive. She's pure, she's fragile. *Very* fragile! I swear, when I saw you getting a blowjob in our own living room, I almost killed you. If I'd been ten years older, I don't think you'd be here today!"

I shrank back. "But Ange . . . come on, I was a kid, just like you. It didn't mean anything, I . . . I was caught off guard—I was only nine, I mean—"

"Bullshit! You dishonored my sister. *Basta!*"

The last word cracked like a wet whip. That's when I fully realized how Sicilian he was. They don't kid around with things like that in those families.

"I kept that inside myself for twenty-five years, can you imagine? Never talked about it with her, ever . . . Anyway, she might've forgotten it the very next day, but you, I could never make you pay for it. Not that I didn't want to—believe me, I did! But I remembered our games in the street. And then after my accident, I became a little more sentimental too. If I hadn't crashed on those fucking rocks, who knows, you might not be here today. You'd have gotten a bullet in your head one day without knowing why."

I breathed in deeply. "Ange, what're you driving at?"

He stared at me again with his Sicilian-eagle look, a look that came from far away, a look heavy with tens of centuries of shepherds, of sailors, of wiry, dark, austere peasants for whom honor was the cement of life, whose curses and revenge never stopped, passed from one generation to the next, until the debt nobody really remembered anymore was finally paid, usually in blood and tears.

"You have to take care of Josiane," he said. "You owe her that much, at least. That's the deal if you want to leave the business with my blessing. The only one I'm offering. Otherwise, it's simple: you're gonna get it."

Twenty years went by. Marseille changed somewhat, on the surface: the renovation of La Joliette to attract rich tourists, the promotion of our historical heritage, the destruction of the horrible high-rise parking garages and bypasses that used to disfigure the downtown area, even the architecture of the new museum near the cathedral—all that's very good, quite a success, I must admit—but it's only on the outside; it's a trompe l'oeil. Inside, nothing's changed, or almost nothing. In any case, the ordinary people of Endoume are still the same.

On the other hand, what used to be called "the mob" is practically gone: modern, cynical free-market society got the better of it—and in this respect, yes, from my point of view, yes, it *was* better in the old days. Today, there are just a few bosses scattered here and there throughout the city and the suburbs, and they're more and more vicious. But when all is said and done, maybe they haven't changed that much. The rules and methods are just more violent and arbitrary, that's all—although, relatively speaking, no more so than those of society as a whole. In fact, one might wonder what miracle could have prevented that generalized violence in human relationships, that extreme tension in the workplace, even in the streets, from spreading to all sectors of society, including what used to be called "the mob." Like employees and executives, gangsters had to show "flexibility": most of them turned into more or less respectable businessmen. New markets popped up. New rackets. New networks. You had to adapt. Ange was able to do it. He moved upward, and got much richer. But the "worker bees," the invisible people, guys like me, they don't see too much difference. The Milous and Doumés, for example, are still just as dumb, servile, and violent. Francis Girard, a.k.a. Le Blond, a.k.a. Hay-Head, and now called The Old Guy, was let out in 2005 for medical reasons, then arrested again in 2009 for dealing drugs. Today he's still locked up in Baumettes prison.

And for the rest, life goes on in town just as it did before. Like before, city hall tries to shove the poor out of the center of the city and it still doesn't work. Like before, though not much more than before, the gangs are killing each other off slowly but surely and that has no more effect on the daily life of the people of Marseille than it did before, even if the media makes a big fuss about it. As ever, it's too hot, as ever the wind blows too hard, as ever everybody speaks too loud and gets mad too fast but it doesn't last, it smells just as bad in the summer, the streets are just as dirty, and on the whole, it doesn't make a very good impression. It's always been like that. All the clichés keep getting trotted out: Marseille is the city of excess, and that's supposed to be what makes it as irritating as it is endearing.

In Endoume, it seems nothing has really changed, aside from the franchise signs that replaced the little shop signs of my childhood, and the disappearance of Fornasero's plumbing business right next to my place, and Bijaoui's grocery store. I work with René Fabrizio: I sell cars for the Renault dealer in La Capelette. Nothing exciting, but still, it's better than harassing bar owners to pay back their bets, and risk finding myself on a stretcher with two pieces of lead in my belly like my dad.

No, actually, something did change: for the last twenty years, Josiane's been living with me.

She was happy to come back to the little street of her childhood. When we got there together, she clapped her hands and cried out in joy, like a little girl. She even flew into my arms, but even this didn't cheer me up. I felt cornered, humiliated, reduced to nothing. I never would have thought I could live with someone I hadn't chosen, especially someone who is relatively nuts. And yet I have. True, I didn't really have a choice. I wouldn't say we form a couple, but we live together without any clashes. When Ange wants to visit his sister, he calls me and we agree on a time when I can leave the house, because he doesn't want to see us together.

Josiane's really more than "borderline," but Ange was right: she's gentle, sensitive, and very emotional. Incapable of caring for herself. Unfit for life in everyday society. Still beautiful, despite her age. Supple as a liana, slim, elegant. Easygoing. Silent, available, and discreet. Often miles away, her eyes lost gazing at the ceiling for hours on end, or contemplating an invisible spot while talking incomprehensibly in a small, plaintive voice. She never asks anything of me, except to be home from time to time. I do in fact like her. Her presence is soothing. And now, after twenty years, I've grown attached to her. Through René Fabrizio, I found a kind of nurse who keeps her company when I'm not there, during the day when I'm working or in the evening when I feel like going out to see friends or flings. Sometimes she has a fit and starts crying and twisting her hair—graying now, but still prettily curled—between her long, slender fingers.

Then she mumbles and walks over to me, gracefully swaying her hips.

I never saw Ange Malatesta again.

EXTREME UNCTION

BY FRANÇOIS THOMAZEAU

Vélodrome Stadium

I t happened four times. André would come get me at Grandma's on Wednesday mornings and take me to Vélodrome Stadium. On the way, in his big, brand-new German sedan, we wouldn't exchange a word. He'd light up a cigarette, lower his window, stick out his arm, and cough all the way. At the stadium, a flunkey would open the gate for him and we'd park smack in the middle of the empty parking lot in front of the main entrance that said *Jean Bouin*. When there was someone there besides the guard, he'd politely say hello to André, lowering his eyes. Occasionally some bolder guys would throw out a, "Hi, Dédé." And he'd cough to answer them.

Then he'd pull me into an empty part of the stands, never the same one. We'd set our butts down on the blue seats, strangled by our scarves, with the tramontane wind howling at us. Way up in the stadium, above the railing where the crowd looks like it's going to spill overboard on the nights when there's a game, the seagulls would protest our presence. There were only the two of us, except for the raw-boned silhouette of an old guy in denim overalls leisurely pushing his lawnmower along the bands of light green grass. Once we'd sat, we'd stay there for a long time without saying anything, long enough for André to finish his Marlboro. Then he'd turn to me, look me in the eye, and start talking. He said anything that came into his mind: he liked Andalusian resorts in the fall, nightclubs at dawn—"when it's time to stuff your cash in your pocket before you go home to bed," nameless roadside hotels, empty stadiums frozen in silence. Hideouts.

"That's what my life is like, see."

I didn't see anything, but André seemed happy to be there. Grandma had told me to be good. And try to be nice. So I acted as if I was happy too. He'd pass me potato chips in crumpled packs in the colors of our soccer team, the Olympique de Marseille. And I'd suck in the sickening foam of my cans of Coke.

"You want me to tell you a story?"

And every time, we were in for a good quarter of an hour. You'd think André was telling me a story before tucking me in.

The first time was in November and the cold was pinching my cheeks the way old ladies do to chubby babies. Dédé told me the story of a boxer. The way he was talking about him, with his fists squeezed against his chest, I had the feeling he'd known him. He was staring straight at some vague spot in the stands across the field.

"Ray was great, see, a real champ. Good-looking too. A class act. You should've seen his mother Marie-Jeanne, the way she watched him. Like he was a little diamond her husband gave her. A pure fighter, a thoroughbred, with a dark look that put ice in your veins. His opponents were always afraid of him. The first time I saw him fight, it wasn't far from here, in Huveaune Stadium, down below toward the Prado. At the time, boxing used to draw big crowds. There were thousands of us cheering him on. He should have been a Carpentier or a Cerdan. But then . . ." André stopped talking and pulled a Marlboro from his pocket without even taking out the pack. As if he was drawing a gun. "How old are you?"

"Thirteen."

He nodded like he was taking stock of his dead memories. "Ray was hardly ten years older than you when he died. He could've become the strongest, the greatest. But then . . . boxing. It's a tough life. It stops without warning. And his life stopped with Chickaoui, an Algerian tough guy they called Damage Man.

It didn't go well. It was fierce, violent, real butchery. As I'm talking to you, I can still hear the punches pounding Ray's face. And I can still see the sweat and the blood spurting out all the way to the first row." André raised his eyes, you'd think he was looking for a friend beyond the stands, out in the hills maybe.

"It was in the stadium down on Prado. At that time there were still bulls there. The animal they sacrificed that day was Ray. He fell, he lost his mouthpiece and his belt—Champion of France. But he was still alive when the audience stood up. You can imagine the silence, like right now . . . Ten thousand people getting up together. Without saying a word."

No, I couldn't imagine it. I'd never seen a boxing match, never seen a bullfight.

"The next day when we learned he was dead, a huge crowd from all over Marseille flocked to the hospital. And the day of his funeral, there were four times as many people as there were at the fight. Jesus, did his mother cry. I swear, we were all crying . . ."

The seagulls started screaming again. André straightened up. A strained smile crossed his face. More like a scar. I wondered if he'd been a boxer himself. He sure had the physique for the job.

"Anyway . . . that's why this section is called Ray Grassi. It's in his honor. In honor of the boxer who died that day . . ."

He shoved his fists into his pockets and got up. I don't know if it was the cold or the early hour, but he was clearing his throat as if a cat had slipped into it and was trying to get out.

Every time, we went for a pizza. There was a pizzeria in the stadium. And they knew André there. People called him Dédé and watched him out of the corner of their eyes as if they were afraid of I don't know what. He would go behind the bar and help himself to peanuts and glasses of pastis as if he were at home. The pizza was pretty good. I'd always order a "Royal." He would smile at me as we ate and we'd laugh because we realized we both left the black olives at the edge of the plate. And then André would drive me back to Grandma's.

* * *

The second time was just before Christmas; he gave me a present. A blue-and-white Olympique de Marseille scarf. It wasn't so much a luxury because we were freezing our butts off, even more than the first time. I even think it snowed the next day. It was so cold the gulls stayed nice and cozy in their nests. Me, all I thought about when André was telling me one of his stories again was the pizza. We had climbed up the bleachers facing the stands we sat in the first time. In fact, I was trying to find the row we were in before. I was telling myself that André should be taking me to an actual game. What with the action and all, it would have been a lot warmer. And well-known as he apparently was, we would've been treated to the VIP booths. I had asked Grandma if he was the owner of the Olympique de Marseille. She'd shrugged and spat on the ground.

This time, he talked about a little guy with a mustache who could run faster than anyone else in the world. Dédé was tracing big circles around the stadium with his finger, as if he was still seeing a track there.

"And the worst was, he smoked, can you believe it? Yes, Jean Bouin smoked. But that didn't stop him from beating everybody," he said, lighting a Marlboro. "I didn't know him, of course. It was in 1912 that he won the silver at the Olympics. Behind a Finn who beat him at the finish line. But I knew a guy in le Chapitre who'd known his mother well. And especially his stepfather, who was a real bastard. A guy named Galdini, who skimmed money off his back, made him run for the bread and then dropped him as soon as he could screw the mother without Jean bugging him. Oh, sorry . . ."

I motioned that it was okay, he could talk, I was young but I knew a thing or two.

"Jean Bouin. He left home at sixteen. About three years older than you. To break all the world records, see."

I asked André why Jean Bouin had a stepfather and he answered that his real father died when he was one. A little like me . . . my mom died practically when I was born. And I never even had a stepfather.

"A lot of time, orphans make good," Dédé said. "It makes you want to fight."

I wanted to ask what he knew about that, but I'm not a moron. I understood they named our part of the stands Jean Bouin because of his achievements. And I also understood that André wanted to tell me something but couldn't bring himself to do it.

"So how did he die?"

"In the First World War, at twenty-eight. They said he ran to the front with a French flag under his arm yelling, *Vive la France!* It looked good in the papers . . . Actually, he and his buddies were wasted by French artillery fire. *Friendly fire*, as they say today."

That time I ordered a tiramisu at the pizzeria. I wondered if we would go through every section in the stadium, but I didn't ask. I knew grown-ups had their own absurd logic. They gave a lot of importance to a whole bunch of stuff that didn't have any. Memories. Regrets. And I had the impression that André liked things to be done a certain way. He yelled at the waiter because he was too slow bringing over the spicy oil.

As for me, I didn't like sports much. Grandma signed me up in a Judo club a few years ago, but I didn't stick with it. Just a soccer game from time to time on the little square. But even that . . . I wasn't good enough and I didn't really like it that much. I thought of that because I had the feeling André was going to ask about it. But he didn't. He was a man who talked a lot, but didn't say much of anything. I said so to Grandma and she answered, "That's Marseille for you: here, they talk a lot, but they never say what counts."

The third time, we were at the beginning of the new year. I was going on fourteen. André didn't open the window but that didn't stop him from coughing. On the other hand, he didn't light up a cigarette until we got to the stands. He savored the first puffs of his Marlboro as if they were his last.

That day, he explained to me why we in Marseille hated the Parc des Princes.

"Nothing to do with the Paris-Saint-Germain soccer team, son. Nothing. It goes back to 1927, see, at the time when the most popular sport was bike racing. That's why this stadium is called Vélodrome—velo's short for velocipede, you know. People came from all over to see the guys racing on the track. They were stars! In Paris, in the Vel' d'Hiv, you had the Six Day race. It lasted all night and Paris celebrities flocked to see it—Gabin, Mistinguett, all the stars. You had to see and be seen at the Six Days . . ."

"What about the bikers, did they race for six whole days?"

"No, they took turns. They only raced evenings and nights. Everything stopped at sunrise."

André sighed and tossed his butt aside.

"But for the hard-core fans, the real show was the middle-distance race. The guys used to bike at top speed behind motorcycles that droned like mad. People called them 'the butterflies.' The middle-distance racers were really crazy. They went up to sixty miles an hour or more, faster and faster, until one of them finally cracked and picked up his foot. You see the stakes? How do you know when and how to stop? . . . The guys who couldn't do it got killed."

"Like Gustave Gamay?"

He looked disappointed. "How do you know?"

I turned around and pointed to the name above the entrance. "It's the name of the section."

He burst out laughing, then his laughter degenerated into a fit of coughing that echoed along the rows of seats. "You're a little wiseguy, that's what you are."

He shot me a hard punch in the shoulder and it hurt. He'd been a boxer for sure.

"Yes, Ganay. He was the best middle-distance racer. A dare-devil who worked as a stagehand at the Alcazar. That guy was no chicken. And then one night in Paris at the Parc des Princes, he went too far too fast. Like a poker player who raises the ante without the cards. A last bluff. He slipped under his bike and the butterfly dragged him all around the track. You can just see the victory lap . . ."

And so, according to Dédé, it was from that day on that we in Marseille hated the Parc des Princes. Why shouldn't we? It had robbed our champion cyclist from us. I didn't dare ask if Ganay took steroids.

André let his eyes wander over the hills again. Under it all, he seemed like a sad guy. He turned to me and looked me straight in the eye. I saw something like reproach.

"It was an accident, understand . . . An accident."

It was cold, but I ordered lemon ice cream anyway.

The last time André came, I could tell it would be the last. He was shivering despite the fact that spring was coming in. It must have been close to the beginning of March. The sun was early. Dédé's features had hollowed out and his complexion had taken on the color of Grandma's cigars. He didn't smoke at all. Not in the car and not afterward.

I almost asked him what sport the Chevalier Roze had starred in, the one who gave his name to the last section of stands. But he didn't give me a chance. And this time, we didn't even go up. We stayed down below, in front of the entrance to the stands.

"The Chevalier Roze, see, was a nobleman who'd acted heroically during the Great Plague of Marseille in 1720. He took a team of convicts with him and they threw all the corpses that were rotting in the streets into old abandoned wells. He caught the plague, but he survived. A miracle!"

At least one of them didn't die. I thought about it so hard that André laughed and said: "You were starting to think this goddamn stadium was a graveyard, weren't you? Well, that's not completely wrong . . ."

His face darkened and his hand mechanically groped for the packet of Marlboros that was no longer in his pocket.

"It's such a graveyard here that they built a purification plant under the stadium that produces the best water in Europe. That's what it takes to administer extreme unction to our dead."

I never saw André again. I asked Grandma why he didn't come around anymore. And she answered the less I knew, the better.

On July 28, 2000, Patrice de Peretti, the most famous fan in Vélodrome Stadium, died of a coronary aneurism. A sad end for "Depé," known throughout all the stands in Europe as the emcee of the MTP, the Marseille Too Powerful fan club. For years, rain or shine, winter or summer, in Turkey or in Denmark, he harangued his troops. Stripped to the waist, always. On the radio they said Olympique de Marseille fans wanted to rename a section in his honor. I had to go to the stadium before it was too late. I took the Prado, sped my BMW up to the gate where I used to enter with André. The same flunkey came to the gate. I lowered the window and said: "Back in the day, I came here in the morning a couple times with Dédé, you remember?"

His face lit up. "Dédé! Yes, of course."

He pulled open the gate and let me in. I parked right in the middle of the empty lot. There were more people working than usual because there'd been a championship game against Troyes the night before. They had to spruce up the field, pick up the trash. I walked around the arena to get to the north stands. During the night, members of the MTP had sprayed Depé's name all over the walls of the Ray Grassi section. They even rubbed off the boxer's name to replace it with the name of their martyr, carried off at the age of twenty-eight by his love for the club and for ganja. A second death for the former featherweight. His section was now the Depé section. With the can of black spray-paint I'd brought, I added an accent on the first "e," erased the foot of the "p," and completed the letter. Then I admired my work. The Dédé section. To make my own homage.

I walked back to the car. The flunkey held the gate open for me respectfully.

"How long ago did he die?"

"Seventeen years . . ."

"That doesn't make us any younger. You were . . ."

"Thirteen."

"He always talked about his kid, his little guy . . . Always." He shook his head and sighed heavily. "When you lose your father, you never recover, ain't that right?"

I didn't say anything. I had no idea. I started up the BMW. Opened the window and lit up a Marlboro. I could see Notre-Dame de la Garde. The Holy Mother up there on the top of her hill was giving me the finger. I drove toward the sea in the summer heat.

SILENCE IS YOUR BEST FRIEND

BY PATRICK COULOMB

Le Panier

1

The music woke me up. Like it does about three times a week. The streets aren't wide in this neighborhood. Often just alleys, but elsewhere, venturing even into the broadest ones would be thought of as taking your life in your hands. I have noisy neighbors who only have a very vague notion of time and politeness. They wear me out too. Between them and my students . . .

I'd collapsed on my couch when I got back from school. Fell asleep right away and slept like a log. When the music woke me up, for once it was at a decent hour, so I wasn't going to complain. Actually, it was the right time to go out, take a little walk, maybe get a bite in one of the new joints around here. I live in Le Panier, the heart of the city, but it's also becoming its belly, a neighborhood crammed with trendy little restaurants. Geographically, it's a hill overlooking the sea, a labyrinth of alleys where it's hard for cars to get through, a challenge to the past, in continual flux but always anchored by the perpetual movement of the sea and the immigrants who hang onto it, wave after wave. The men and women who live here come from Africa, Europe, and Asia; they're black, white, and yellow, Arabs and Europeans, people of the land and islanders, poor and rich. Well . . . rich, that's pretty new. Before, the few rich people of the neighborhood were more or less members of the thugocracy. Since I moved here, I've become one of the many specialists on the subject. Like a true geography teacher, I've tried to understand if there was some kind of determinism or fate, if there was any link between a land that welcomes immigrants and the birth of organized crime, and if Le Panier could be seen as a neighborhood with a curse on it, branded by that fatality. I think the answer is yes.

I shook myself awake, got up, looked in the mirror, and slipped a book in my pocket—I always take a book with me—and walked briskly to the place de Lenche. The old Greek agora, from the very beginnings of the city: a square that slopes downward, looking over the nearby sea, full of cafés and restaurants, with a theater, as if Greek tragedy had taken root here for all eternity, God knows why. Tragedy begets violence and, in this respect, eternity is not an illusion: what is more eternal than violence? . . . Before the Vieux Quartier, the Old Neighborhood, as it was called for a long time, was razed to the ground by the Germans and the Vichy government in January 1943, it was the dark side of Marseille, a huge bordello where sailors from every sea refueled on fresh meat, a labyrinth of every kind of trafficking, the dead end for every naïve fool.

I walk up and down the ghosts of streets that are no more and I hear shots from the 1930s, I can make out the knives cutting the throats of people who didn't pay up. I go further on in time and am close to the sixties, when the neighborhood, finally rebuilt, was still used as a base for thugs from the French connection. At that time, Le Panier was a kind of Hell's Kitchen looking over the Mediterranean, with its Dagos and Corsicans as powerful as the Gambinis and the Corleones . . . I walk in the blood of the past and the walls and cobblestones speak to me and scream violence, violence, violence.

I know, everything has changed, it's now full of health food stores and artists of all kinds, art galleries and clothing stores, there are even Canadians who make bagels. It's no longer Little Italy or the Bowery, it's Soho or Greenwich Village. On a smaller scale, of course, with streets so narrow you can hear your neighbors belching across the way. So just imagine, when they turn the music up to the max . . .

I decided not to think about it anymore. A kid bumped into me as I turned a corner going up the stairs of the Accoules. I felt around in my pockets, nothing missing. You get paranoid fast in this neighborhood when you think about the past too much.

When I got back to my place, silence had finally filled the night; it must've been midnight, the hour of crime. At least.

I finally slept well that night. I dreamed of Carbone and Spirito, of Francis the Belgian and Gaëtan Zampa, firing away like mad, bumping off the dumb, aggressive kids in my class of seniors and my inconsiderate neighbors in the same bloodbath. Calmly, I'm telling you. As long as I was only whacking them in my dreams. I'm a calm man, everybody tells me nobody's more laid-back than I am. But only if I've had a good night's sleep, I say.

At school, it didn't get any better. I'm *too* laid-back, that's just it: they take advantage. Whoever tries to insult me most takes the prize. I've had it up to here with those little shits who won't listen. When I talk about history they laugh, and when I teach geography they show me their backs. As if it didn't matter; but here in this damn city more than anywhere else, they really should take an interest in the past. Just like they should know how the world works, the history of migrations, understand Marseille's role in this human maelstrom. They come from all over, they've got roots in their Elsewhere. They're all islands in their own heads, villages, but they act as if this has no connection to what I teach them. I could help them decipher who they are and why, help them find their way, but no, these morons would rather piss me off by making fun of my name: "LaMarca la Marquise! LaMarca la Marquise!" Yeah, that really cracks them up, and I'm not even gay, just single and vaguely intellectual. But all they see in me is a guy who's not quite a man—contemptible. Just goes to show how mixed up they are.

Back at my place it's no better: the morons across the street go on thinking they're at a nightclub every other night.

I'm tired, I'm telling you. Knocked out.

And it's been going on for months.

2

I don't know if I'm dreaming or awake. I've got a book in my hand, a book like a weapon. A nice big weapon. A nice fat volume. At least six hundred pages. Yes, pages instead of punches. Bigger reach. Harder. Hit him, keep on hitting.

No, I really have the feeling that this time I'm not dreaming. I hit and hit again, I crush his throat under the thick spine of the book—a crime novel, in fact, what could be more fitting? I really think the guy's dead, right there at my feet. I feel his pulse, nothing. I press my ear to his heart, silence. I wait. Nothing comes, no movement, no breathing . . . I took first aid classes long ago, I can recognize death when it's there.

It's here.

It's crazy. I couldn't have done that. Not me. I'm a calm guy, so calm. Nobody's more laid-back than me. I'm the coolest, the most accommodating. Everybody says so. I didn't kill anyone, it's just impossible. Impossible.

But there's no doubt about it, the guy here isn't moving. He's slumped right there with his back to the wall as if he had too much booze, all limp and soft, flat as a crepe, motionless. I can't believe it.

What is this book anyway? I still have it in my hand. I read about fifty pages of it. Or tried to. With that racket, no way I could really read. *Random* by Mathieu Croizet. Heavy . . . I noticed on the back cover that the author is a lawyer. Hey, I could call him. The guy at my feet . . . we killed him together, right? If I need someone to defend me, I couldn't do better than a lawyer for an accomplice.

I can't believe it! Shit, man, wake up. Can't say I was crazy about you, but that doesn't mean I'd waste you like that, smash your throat with a big fat thriller. This is ridiculous.

Jesus, what the hell am I doing here? I came to ask the guy to turn off his fucking music. In this apartment, I'm telling you, they have a party three times a week. Like they're the only people in the world, like their place is a nightclub, the assholes. For months it's been like that; I completely lost it, lost hold of who I was, that calm cool cat, he split, like he's not in me anymore.

I went downstairs at two thirty. I'd been pretty nice; after all, I hadn't called the cops; I'd been patient, telling myself they were bound to stop sooner or later. And I saw them coming out of the building across the street one after the other, completely smashed on booze and weed. Yelling in the alley. Then disappearing into the night in a straggly single file. But that fucking music was always turned up to the max, I could hear it as if I was on their goddamn couch swilling whiskey-Cokes with them. I put my boots back on and walked out with the book in my hand, my keys in my pocket and my nerves on edge. I rang a bell at random. Some moron opened the door. I walked up to the floor above, to where the music was coming from. The door was half open. It's funny, but on the landing of their floor the music wasn't as loud as at my place. I shrugged. Assholes. A shaggy-haired guy opened the door all the way, laughing stupidly.

"Hi, man, you're late. Everybody split already."

"So why don't you turn off your music? Let me tell you something, I live across the street and it's starting to fuck me up, hearing your music all the time. Some people have to work, you know?"

"Hey, man, take it easy. It's not late, nobody's here now. It's all cool!"

I looked at him, stunned. He's telling me, *me*, it isn't late? He's telling *me* to be cool? *Me*, the most laid-back cat west of the Canebière? I began waving the book around in my hand and it hit his shoulder, but not too hard.

"Hey, man!"

"What, what's the matter?" I said.

I couldn't control my right hand anymore, and this time I smacked him right in the face with the book, intentionally. He backed away.

"You're gonna stop your fucking music now, okay?"

The guy wasn't moving anymore, his smile frozen across his face. Then the asshole started up again. "Hey, cool, man, be cool," he said while trying to close the door.

I blocked it with the tip of my boot and pushed—the door with one hand, the joker with the other. And I walked in.

"Okay, deejay, where's your fucking sound system?"

He'd collapsed onto the floor. Waved, pointing to a wall. I gave the hi-fi a good solid kick and swept it all away with a backhand chop of my book. His gear crashed to the floor, a nice wooden, well-varnished floor. Silence returned at last. You could hear a garbage truck going by down below, probably around the rue Caisserie. Urban bliss regained. If you perked up your ears you could almost get the backwash of waves in the Vieux-Port. Almost.

I was going to get the hell out, but he stood up and staggered toward me, half dazed, half mad.

"Hey, man," he said. I wondered if he had any other words in his vocabulary. He started to push at me weakly, but apparently the weed and booze weren't giving him superpowers . . . I pushed him away but he kept at it. I banged him once on the head with the book so he'd stop, then another. He kept going, the asshole. So did I. *Bang, bang, bang!* I began hitting harder, harder and harder. Man, it felt good. Until I saw him knocked out against the wall.

"Asshole," I muttered. "Fucking asshole." And I shrugged.

I pushed the book down over his throat, the spine against his glottis. I pushed hard, I wasn't myself anymore, I hit, harder, I heard him gasping for breath, gurgling, I was beside myself, I crushed the book down even harder to make him swallow his trachea along with his birth certificate. Wasn't moving anymore. Not at all.

This time he was really dead. It's insane. I couldn't have done that. Not me. I'm a calm guy, so calm. The most laid-back cat in the world.

Okay, so I hadn't touched anything in the asshole's room, I'd done it all with the book. All I had to do was get rid of it. No see, home free; I felt pretty calm, considering. Although not seen—that remained to be seen, as a matter of fact. The only hitch in this whole thing. They'd think one of his buddies had knocked him off, or several of them, under the influence. Of booze, weed, or whatever. I didn't feel an ounce of remorse. I told myself that would surely come later, there was a chance I'd totally screwed up my life. We'd see. Then I thought I heard the stairs creak. I froze for a moment, I thought I saw a shadow go through the door and walk up to the floor above. I shivered violently, feverishly, and then I came to, made sure I didn't touch anything, and left. The stairs creaked again. It was time for me to disappear. I left the door half open and went out, crossing myself and hugging the walls.

I walked around the block, then around another. To tell the truth, I was sort of dazed myself, and I walked without thinking much about anything. I went by the Vieille-Charité and the Hôtel-Dieu. When it's not all narrow streets, the neighborhood is full of beautiful seventeenth-century buildings . . . I meandered through the streets to wherever the night led me. I walked by the famous Chez Étienne pizzeria, founded by a Sicilian immigrant. Closed at that hour, of course. Too bad, I really would have liked to get rid of my anxiety by biting into a pizza covered with anchovies, tomato sauce, garlic, and olives. Then I walked up to the place des Moulins. The streets were quiet. I avoided clacking my boots. I sat down on a bench. Thought things over. I had just killed somebody. The asshole surely had parents, a girlfriend, but no children, no, too young and obviously the type who doesn't give a shit; that, at least, was good. I wanted to light up, but I don't smoke. I looked at the windows on the square. All dark. It was close to four. I still had the book in my hand. I took a look at the author's mug on the jacket. A lawyer who writes novels, you don't see that every day, most of them just blab. I memorized his name just in case, then I moved down the narrow streets, crossed the passage through the Pouillon buildings to the waterfront, on the Vieux-Port. There I threw the book into the water. It swelled and sank fast. Exit the murder weapon. Exit a piece of myself too.

Then I walked back home.

I fell asleep in the peaceful silence, telling myself it sure had been a strange night.

To be honest, I'm not sure I slept all that well. When I woke up I saw myself again at that asshole's place, closing out his case with the lawyer's big thriller. I felt feverish and made myself coffee. Heart racing two hundred miles an hour. On the other hand, I was kind of pleased. A little like Dexter on TV: the feeling of a job that had to be done, and from then on you have to face the consequences, avoid making a stir, be discreet. Anyway, what could I have done? Complaining to the police again about my neighbor disturbing the peace would have been useless, I might as well piss into the wind—I had finally realized it simply wasn't their problem.

But when a neighbor of the asshole discovered the body—like an idiot, I'd left the door open—I'm the one they came to see first. Routine questions and all that, but with pretty mean insinuations, like they were well aware that I didn't like the neighbor's noise and, "Sir, we've seen other cases like this, respectable accountants, nice little teachers too, who went postal for the most trivial reasons," and maybe I'd decided to act on my own . . .

"Accidents can happen so fast, Monsieur LaMarca," the inspector said as he checked my name on a card.

I shrugged, with a cup of coffee in hand. I answered nervously that I was in a hurry, work can't wait. "The music stopped around two and I went back to sleep. End of story. I'm certainly sorry for that gentleman, but honestly, I can't say I'm going to miss him."

"What do you do for a living?"

"I teach history and geography. In fact, I'm supposed to be at school in less than an hour."

"What high school?"

"Pierre Puget."

"Oh, I see."

He saw *what*? I wondered. He was acting official, that's all. But he let me go, to continue his investigation with the neighbor upstairs—Djibril—a Comorian who'd just created a start-up. Djibril didn't give a damn about the neighbor's music, he spent his nights with headphones over his ears, immersed in his own music and his wooly theories about making it big through computer science. He was developing tourist apps for Marseille and the Comoros; he'd just launched a guide to the Panier district for cell phones, with QR codes and the whole digitized shebang, and in fact he wasn't doing so badly. He wouldn't have much to tell the police; I could rest easy as far as he was concerned.

It was Friday, 10:35. I took off for school on my scooter at top speed, half to make time, half out of pure nervousness.

3

Three days later, the cops called to summon me to the Évêché, the police headquarters of Marseille, which is right behind where I live, at the border of Le Panier and La Joliette. I walked there around six thirty. It was nice out for that time of year, but I didn't really have the heart to appreciate the weather. I wasn't exactly anxious, but still, not 100 percent calm either. Who would be, in my shoes? The same inspector—from the CID, I learned that as I read his name, *Kevin Gandolfini*, on a prominently displayed plaque—received me in a room crammed with cabinets overflowing with papers. But his desk was all shipshape, a computer, a notebook, a pen, and a pair of Ray-Ban Wayfarer sunglasses. That made me smile: I had the same glasses at his age; it just goes to show how generations often replicate themselves.

"Monsieur LaMarca . . . sit down, sit down."

He pointed to two wooden chairs which must have come from the Emmaüs charity stores and deserved to go back there.

"I asked you to come because there are new elements in the investigation and I have a few questions for you."

Yeah, right . . . He looked me in the eye as he said this and I must admit I was worried stiff, even though I didn't flinch. The guy was playing cat-and-mouse with me and wanted to claw me a little before he swallowed me up.

Gandolfini still hadn't taken his eyes off me. "You didn't tell me everything Friday morning, Monsieur LaMarca."

"What was I supposed to tell you?"

"Tsk, tsk. Well, for instance, you're sure you went back to sleep when the music stopped?"

If you don't know what cold sweat is, I advise you to live through this kind of moment. No doubt Gandolfini was going to play with me a little and then reach the obvious conclusion: if I wasn't home, it's because I was tearing my poor neighbor to shreds across the street. I had learned his name in the meantime. At least I could now put a name to my crime: Antoine Julien.

Despite the fear gnawing at my insides, I told the cop he was right, it's true that I was on edge that night and I decided to calm myself down by taking a walk. I told him about the quiet of the narrow streets free of cars at night, the sweetness of the sea breeze. You could even say I put on a lyrical, romantic show, and I ended by explaining that if I hadn't said anything about it Friday morning, it's because I was afraid he'd misinterpret my wanderings.

There was a long lull in the conversation. My eyes were riveted on the tips of my shoes, his were still fixed on my humble person.

"See," he said, "you can do okay when you want to . . . You did well not to continue your lie of omission, Monsieur LaMarca. It would have made you extremely suspicious, because guess what? You were seen at 2:35 a.m., walking down the Montée des Accoules . . ."

I smiled inwardly at the paradox of "walking *down* the Montée"—the "ascension" des Accoules—and at the fact that at two thirty that night, I was beating up my neighbor in his apartment and certainly not walking *down* the Montée des Accoules . . .

"Monsieur Romuald Lopez, a homeless man who was lying there, recognized you. He knows everybody in the neighborhood and he's absolutely positive. So, I wondered what you were doing outside even though you stated that you never left your apartment. You get my drift?"

"Mmm," I said, close to fainting.

"Now, it so happens that at 2:25 a.m., Monsieur LaMarca, your unfortunate neighbor Antoine Julien was facing his murderer because that's exactly when he sent a distressed text message to a certain Diego, a heavy he was doing business with, saying, and I'm reading: *fuk crazy guy here y* . . . 2:25 a.m. on one side, 2:35 on the other, for the moment I've got to think you probably weren't at your neighbor's place at the time of the crime, even though it's only a matter of a few minutes. So unless things change I'm not holding you. But you have to remain at the disposal of the police, and of course do not leave Marseille."

I shut up and blessed the lenient nature of Inspector Gandolfini. But what followed would turn out to be something even more pleasant.

I left the Évêché free as a bird. I stopped on place de Lenche to have a beer and nibble on some peanuts. The usual crowd was hanging out there—a few artists, a handful of tourists, and some neighborhood people you wouldn't want to associate with. Maybe even that guy Diego was around, busily planning a couple of nice illegal jobs. Diego . . . to tell the truth, that name rang a bell. From my experience in rummaging around in the history of the local milieu, I'd picked up a lot about the past, but also the present. Diego, Diego . . . I went back home fast. I had to review my personal archives right away.

I found him under his real identity, Jean-Louis Younger, in an article from a few months back that mentioned drug dealing. He seemed to be the local kingpin. A promising suspect for the police, surely more interesting than an innocuous little teacher like me. But I couldn't leave everything to chance, better to give it a little help. Younger had gotten six months with probation, so he was around somewhere. It was up to me to show he was the guilty party. A call to my friend Blanco, Chief Inspector Blanco, was imperative. The conversation with Gandolfini had given me a good kick in the butt, a shot of adrenaline. I forgot my qualms, my feelings of guilt. Now I had to get out of the mess I was in, avoid being identified as the real perpetrator. So I called my friend Blanco. We'd gone to college together, but not for long. He'd stopped after he got his degree in history and took the exam to become a police inspector. And passed it. We'd kept in touch, not very regularly but always in a friendly way. Blanco was appointed to Marseille. I called him to meet over a pizza the next day.

On a little square just above city hall, a discreet family restaurant beckoned. The waitress took us up to the second floor. Blanco looked in good shape, his ironic smile still fixed at the corners of his thin lips. He didn't really appreciate my trying to get information about an ongoing investigation out of him, but I was sure a good pizza and a few glasses of wine would activate his vocal cords. Blanco was a chatterbox who didn't know he was one.

According to Blanco, Jean-Louis Younger sent one of his emissaries over to poor Antoine Julien to collect a debt of tens of thousands of euros and it went wrong, so wrong Julien died. Younger could get sent down for accessory to murder, illegal drug trafficking, and criminal conspiracy—and this time, no probation. The cops would be delighted to collar him, without being too fussy about the exact timetable of other possible perpetrators. From Blanco's smirk when he said that, I clearly understood he'd be ready to hang the murder on Younger's man without batting an eyelash. The emissary in question answered to the name of Crazy Toto, which in local talk marked him as a troublemaker, a guy with a bad temper. Only problem, this Toto was nowhere to be found at the moment: there were reports of him in Paris, in Cadaquès, Spain, and some even said he left for Turkey to bring back a shipload.

Blanco winked at me with his famous smile, and explained that he knew exactly where to find Toto: in a furnished room on rue Paradis. He suggested I reserve a table at the restaurant of the new MuCEM (Musée des Civilisations Européennes et Méditerranéennes) that had a sea view and a three-star chef, for he was definitely going to get me out of the fix I was in.

I didn't try to understand how Blanco knew so much about this case. I knew he had some weight in the local police but between the official hierarchy and deals with the unions, I could never tell with any certainty what kind of real power my friend actually had. I didn't even ask him about Gandolfini. Like a good chatterbox, he's the one who spilled the beans, and this time without the smile: "Gandolfini's going to have to back off, he's not on this case anymore, he's out, ba-da-bing! He's mixed up with some murky debts at the Casino Barrière de Cassis and the Inspection Générale de la Police Nationale—the police of the police—are all over him. He's now persona non grata at the Évêché. They asked me to take over some of his current cases. So it's simple: tonight we didn't see each other and I'll call you for that invitation when your case is cleared up. Don't worry, as soon as I get my hands on Toto, it'll be a done deal. We've been trying to get Younger for a long time and now both of them will spend a little time behind bars . . . And don't bother to try to find out how we'll do it, we've got the text message and he'll tell us the rest."

A new wink, back to the smile, two glasses clink. It's like the case was already closed.

4

A few months later, everything was okay. Crazy Toto was convicted and just like Blanco had predicted, the police were able to get to Younger, a.k.a. Diego, and send him down for accessory to murder. Nobody bothered me anymore, and though I wasn't very proud of what I'd done, I was glad I could continue living in total freedom. The neighborhood was quiet again and the death of poor Antoine Julien was forgotten. His apartment had finally found a new buyer. A Swede had moved in, attracted by the new trendy aspect of Marseille, which was making the whole city and Le Panier in particular one of those spots on the planet that attracts rich Anglo-Saxons and Germano-Scandinavians longing for authenticity. On place de Lenche and rue des Pistoles, English and French were replacing Arab and Berber in daily exchanges, Corsican and Italian having long been assimilated into the local yet very international French. Okay, I'm exaggerating a little but not much: my taste for geography might make me overestimate the number of different nationalities who go by under my windows, and I keep dreaming of a world where coming from somewhere else wouldn't be a stigma but a subject for joyful curiosity.

But do I have the right to dream? I'm a murderer . . .

I began to read Confucius—I'm trying to learn how to be really Zen. Luckily, it's a very thin book with a hard cover, the better to resist the treatment I inflict on it daily. "Silence is a friend that never betrays you," said the Chinese sage. So I keep silent.

The Swede I mentioned, my new neighbor, had moved to Marseille to train the new ice hockey team and had a hobby that seemed likeable at first: he loved the tango. So much so he played tangoes on his violin from morning to night on the days he wasn't on the ice. Everything went fine for a few months. But when his team started losing, he began to play out of tune. Terribly out of tune. And very, very late.

So last night, with my nerves completely on edge, at two thirty in the morning, despite my close acquaintance with Confucius, I went over to explain that he'd better stop his music. I put my book in my pocket and felt the cover. It seemed good and solid. I'm sure you understand.

Silence is a friend that never betrays you.

THE DEAD PAY A PRICE FOR THE LIVING

BY RENÉ FRÉGNI

Château-Gombert

> *Murder is not what I want to talk about. I want to speak of joy, suffering, and love.* —Knut Hamsun

> *When I look at dogs, I miss wolves.* —Victor Hugo

I didn't come back to the suburb where I grew up to pick olives. I came back to kill a man.

I'm going to crush that man like a rat. He is a rat. He was my childhood friend.

During the eight years I've just spent behind bars, he took everything from me. All my savings and the little money my mother left me. I invested everything in that restaurant with him, without even going through a lawyer. I thought he was my brother. A brother . . . he took my wife.

At first she'd come to see me three times a week in the visiting room of Baumettes prison, then twice. After eighteen months, she only came on Saturday afternoons with clean laundry and three St. Victor cookies. She would stare at her hands; I didn't touch her anymore. A quick kiss on the cheek. She could hardly wait for the guard to show up so she could rush back into the street a half hour later.

After the trial, she stopped coming altogether. I was transferred to the penitentiary in Arles. That's where I learned she was sleeping with him. I beat the hell out of a guard and they dragged me off to the hole. I lost six pounds and the little confidence I had in human beings.

For years, I killed that man every single day. I would imagine them together. I could hear her moaning and shouting the way she did with me for almost ten years. She would fall asleep against that man's belly and thighs. A breast in that man's hand, the left breast, she only falls asleep on her right side. For years, I loved to fall asleep with that pretty breast in the cup of my palm. She disgusts me.

As for him, I killed him mornings, afternoons, evenings, and especially at night, in my dreams, in my nightmares, with my eyes wide open in the darkness of my cell, lit only by the searchlights shining on the outside walls.

I grew up with that man, on the same street, in the same school, we ran side by side through the same hills, in the same playgrounds, we kissed our first girls together on the sand of les Catalans Beach. He beat me at foosball a hundred times, I slaughtered him a hundred times at boccie. We never stopped laughing, even on that day when we were fifteen, hiding together in a garbage can with the cops on our ass. As soon as I turned my back, he took everything from me. I'm going to crush him like a rat!

I found this job so I could spy on him and kill him whenever I decide to. I want to see terror filling his eyes and twisting his guts, see how much he regrets his mistake before he disappears.

All day I pick olives, a stone's throw from the village. We always called this suburb of Marseille "the village." It's not like any other neighborhood. When I was a kid, there used to be over a hundred truck farmers here; there must be only two or three left. Château-Gombert has remained a village curled around its church.

At noon, I have the day's special at a café right across from our restaurant. I still dare to say "our". . . Alone at my little table, hidden behind a curtain, I watch. Nobody can recognize me. I wear a cap, glasses, and a mustache. I tell the young waitress I'm picking olives on chemin de Palama.

My hands are red with cold and scraped by branches. From time to time, I see someone I knew in school come in, a shopkeeper, a troublemaker . . . They don't even notice me. I could be Portuguese, Moroccan, a seasonal worker. Who still picks olives here? Aside from poets and madmen. All my old buddies are hiding out in the city or selling drugs and anything that falls off a truck.

On my street, nobody made it and nobody gives a damn. "Take it easy . . ." That's what they've been saying from morning to night ever since they were born, with a pair of boccie balls in their hands. "Take it easy . . ." Their fathers used to say it, their grandfathers too, in every bar in Marseille. You can hear the clack of boccie balls all around the memorial to the war dead and, for some time now, behind the church, where we used to fight over *Lui*, *Playboy*, and *Penthouse* when we were twelve, all those blond girls perched on their high heels or leaning forward under the weight of their heavy breasts that made our pants tight and our mouths dry.

I came upon the ad last week in *La Provence*. Mademoiselle Niozelles was looking for someone to pick her olives in Château-Gombert. The name jumped out at me like a cat: *Château-Gombert*. I jumped on my bike and was the first to arrive. It wasn't even eight in the morning.

We decided to share the crop. That's what's been done here forever. Mademoiselle Niozelles is a widow, but she's still young. She would have given me ideas if I hadn't come here with five years of hate in my belly. She's a schoolteacher who owns about a hundred olive trees around her little pink house with a dovecote next to it. We had coffee in her kitchen. There is a lot of discretion and sensitivity in her eyes. She didn't ask me a single question. I had the feeling she could see my life palpitating under my skin. Her students must love her. She's calm and luminous like this month of November.

I got to work the same day. I hung a basket around my neck,

on my belly, and we went to get a little ladder under a shed before she left for school.

"It's a very good year," she said as she walked away, "I don't remember seeing so many for ages. It must've rained at the right time."

I like that expression she uses, *belle lurette*, "for ages." I didn't think a teacher would use it. Mademoiselle Niozelles doesn't look like a teacher, she's like wild grass. She's like no one else.

The olive trees are planted on narrow terraces held up by little walls made of stones as white as bones. They're literally collapsing under the weight of the olives, as if to say, *Give us some relief, we can't take it anymore.*

They're still green, full of water, hard, and so strongly attached to the branches that you have to really tug to get them to cascade down into the basket. They're Aglandau olives, perfectly oval. On the trees with the best exposure, they're already purple, you can see the oil under the skin. I notice that a little farther on they're as big as plums. I'll keep those for the days when I'm tired or the mistral is blowing. I'm going to pick all these olives and then I'll kill the man who filled my blood with poison.

I watch the sun turn around the village. It's a fine day, calm and blue. From here, in the midst of the hills, all the houses are golden. I spot the façade of the one I grew up in, the windows of the kitchen and our bedroom. I say "our" because I slept in my parents' room for a long time and so did my sister. I liked to sleep near my mother's breath. Who now lives in that house where I was so happy?

My parents are far away, and yet here nothing has really changed and my childhood is everywhere. When I got here I spotted two or three irrigation basins, the last surviving farms, and the canal we'd dive into every summer at the risk of drowning. The iron wheels of the trolley and the canal were my mother's two nightmares. We used to swim with the current and grab onto a huge sluice gate at the last minute. If we missed it, we couldn't get out: the walls of the canal were slippery with mud and much too high. We'd be trapped like a rat.

One day Maurice missed it, he was carried away in the current and sucked into the pipe. He disappeared into the tunnel under the road. They found his body two days later in another pipe at Plan-de-Cuques.

Perched in an olive tree, I see the canal gleaming. It twists and turns through the fields, disappears between the houses that didn't used to exist, gleams again for a moment, very far off between two concrete giants, and loses itself in a vertical Marseille where the setting sun is exploding a million windowpanes. For three minutes, they fill up with blood.

Like every day, I take a break from picking at noon. I empty my basket of olives into big green plastic crates and go have lunch at the little café. I have my own table. The young waitress shows me to it with a little smile and a knowing look. How could she imagine that I'm lying in wait for a man so I can rip his heart out? A guy who orders the day's special, has his coffee, and leaves discreetly to go out into an olive field can only inspire confidence. I always tip her two euros.

I can see the three other cafés on the square from my observation post. At the Bar du Centre we used to play foosball every night and howl with laughter, at Terminus we'd watch soccer games on a big screen, from the sidewalk seats of Café de la Poste we'd watch the girls go by as we sipped our milk grenadines.

A lot of stores' signs have changed. The little Casino grocery has become *Newspapers Tobacco*; an electronics store has replaced the butcher's; the wine merchant is gone. The Chez Georges barber shop has become a real estate agency. The Mazet patisserie, where I had the best rum baba in my life, is still there; the photography studio owned by the Cayrol family is still there too. Those are the two village institutions. Only the Cayrol son could recognize me despite my mustache and glasses. He has the portrait of each of us in his mind's eye at every stage of our lives, in every class. He's the village memory. If he turned up, I'd run straight to the bathroom or hide my head behind a newspaper.

It's not the Cayrol son who I see all of a sudden, but the traitor. Yes, him, Franck, the man I've been waiting for, over a week now, the man I'm going to kill.

I don't know if I said his name was Franck. For me, he doesn't have a face anymore, no name, no past. He's already dead.

He comes out of a magnificent gray Mercedes with black leather seats, double-parked right in front of my eyes. He walks into our restaurant on the other side of the street and comes out almost immediately. He starts the car and then walks back in three minutes later. I've never seen him so well dressed—in a navy-blue Lacoste jacket. A prince! For eight years, I was in hell.

I pay for my meal and take a short walk around the village. I have no problem spotting the luxurious Mercedes. He parks it on boulevard Fernand Durbec, where we grew up. I've got him.

I walk by our restaurant again. It's no longer called Le Petit Farci but La Coupole. Why La Coupole? No idea. I think it's pretentious, stupid, and it doesn't make me hungry. It makes me think of some kind of meeting, or a sect.

I take a look at the menu of the day, written in chalk on a huge slate standing on the sidewalk.

Tartare of salmon with lemon juice and dill
Sea bass with basil and garlic pistou
Opera golden square cake
Orange and lemon cream

I'm staggered. I walk on. He went into semi-high cuisine and apparently it works. He doesn't drive a little Twingo. He loves money like a shark loves blood. He's got the money, he'll have the blood.

To think that I held up a truck coming out of the Seita tobacco factory with two hundred thousand euros' worth of cigarettes to buy myself a lousy apartment. The one I'd just spent eight years in measured fifteen square feet and stank of moist bread, disinfectant, and misery. And this piece of shit drives a Mercedes, dresses like a cabinet minister on vacation at Cap Ferret, and he's screwing my wife.

I can see the steely eyes of the DA behind his glasses again: "Armed robbery, attempted homicide. We recommend fifteen years."

I try to calm my hands by dropping olives into the basket. They vibrate all afternoon.

One evening when I was seven or eight, I climbed onto my mother's lap and she began to read me *The Count of Monte Cristo*. For months, every evening I would sit on her lap as she read me the extraordinary story of that man locked up in the bowels of a dismal fortress for fourteen years. She read me the story of that man's suffering and then his escape and his implacable vengeance on every one of the traitors who'd sent him away to rot in a cell below sea level.

For me, Edmond Dantès was the greatest, most beautiful man in Marseille. Justice wasn't judges, DAs, and jailers, it was that man who'd learned philosophy underground and who defended life.

I saw him everywhere: in the streets, in my dreams, on the school blackboard. My mother's voice reverberated throughout my body every night. I would put my head on her warm bosom and listen to the story of Edmond Dantès; I could hear my mother's heartbeat, hear the sea pounding against the dark rocks of Château d'If.

I was in a field a few hundred yards from the kitchen where my mother used to take me on her lap every night, and I heard her voice, I felt all her gentleness, the enormous strength of her love. What had happened to me?

I picked olives all afternoon in the beautiful blond light in the hollow of the hills. I was alone and I was telling myself that if I didn't have to kill a man, I would probably feel happiness right here, behind the pink house of Mademoiselle Niozelles.

I worked till night fell. As soon as the sun disappeared, the clouds became big red birds; a minute later, the birds were black.

I loaded my crates into Mademoiselle Niozelles's old Renault van and drove them to the mill.

Every two or three days, I bring my olives to this modern mill; they weigh the contents of my crates, they give me a print-out that details how many kilos my crop has increased every day. From dawn to nightfall, I can sometimes pick up to seventy kilos. When they're violet and big as plums, my basket is always full.

I went home to a steep little street in the shadow of a church—downtown, as suburbanites say. I took a scalding shower and sawed off the butt and the double barrels of the twelve-caliber my father had hunted with all his life. I slipped a cartridge of buckshot into each barrel and went to bed. I fell asleep even before my head hit the pillow. And if I wanted to make a bad pun, I'd say I fell into a leaden sleep.

The next morning, I arrived at Mademoiselle Niozelles's house with the daylight; her shutters were still closed. The grass was soaking wet under the trees. I chose the first olive tree the sun strikes on the highest terrace. It caught fire before my eyes and I felt the warm fingers of the first rays of sunlight on my shoulders.

Never had I been so calm. In the saddlebag of my old bike there was my father's twelve-caliber and in its sawed-off barrels, two cartridges capable of ripping the head off of a hundred-kilo boar. The sky was clear, the horizon limpid on the Allauch side, and the Pilon du Roi was glittering above the hills.

Again I worked hard all day. At twilight, I put my olive crates away in Mademoiselle Niozelles's garage. I grabbed a dark coat hanging on a peg among other old work clothes. It must have belonged to Mademoiselle Niozelles's father or husband. It smelled of grass and old dust.

I parked my bike at the very end of boulevard Fernand Durbec, in front of the elementary school I'd gone to for almost ten years.

The gray Mercedes was there, more or less in the same spot as the day before, right in front of the little movie house where I'd seen so many films long ago, every Thursday, with Laurel and Hardy, Fernandel, or Charlie Chaplin. The narrow theater had been closed "for ages," as Mademoiselle Niozelles would have said. Now you could read above the entrance: *Marseille Department of Sanitation.*

I pulled up my collar. The night was very dark now. I started walking down one side of the street, then the other, without ever taking my eyes off the gray Mercedes. Through my pocket I could feel the twelve-caliber I was holding under my coat, against my thigh. I had put on thin leather gloves so as to leave no trace in Franck's car.

The mistral had risen—people were going home with their heads buried in their necks, nobody was looking at anybody else. There was only the hoarse sound of the dead leaves scraping over the asphalt of the boulevard.

Just once, I made a little detour by the restaurant; only three customers were sitting at a table near the bar. The whole village was deserted. It was really the first evening of winter. All there was in the streets was silence and dogs.

I saw him come out fast on the first stroke of nine. He wasn't looking at anything either. Toward what warmth was he rushing with his head down? From afar, he unlocked his car and jumped in. I unlocked the safety of the rifle with my thumb.

Just as he was about to close his door, he caught a glimpse of me. He turned his head and saw the two dark eyes of the sawed-off shotgun looking right into his eyes. My ice-cold blood was beating through my whole body.

"It's you?" he managed to utter. His mouth remained agape. In this suburb where I'd spent so many years, he was the only one who recognized me.

"It's me, Franck. Eight years later. Seemed long to you?"

"What are you doing here, Charlie? I heard you got out . . . I was glad to hear it. Why didn't you—"

"Shut up, Franck! Put your hands on your head! You move one centimeter, I rip it off. There are two loads of buckshot inside and you know I'm quick."

He did exactly as I asked. I opened the back door and sat down behind him. Now he had the two barrels on the right side of his head.

"Close the door and start the car!"

"Charlie, you're really fucking up now, you're gonna go back there for twenty more years."

"Close your door! I won't say it again!"

He obeyed immediately.

"Start the car!"

"Charlie, I'll give you all I have—the car, the restaurant, everything . . . the house. We'll go have a bite, Charlie, and I'll give you everything."

I pushed the double barrel against his temple.

He turned the key and put the car into reverse with a grinding sound. His whole body was vibrating now. He glanced to the right then to the left; the village was even more deserted, dismal.

"Take Palama and stop when you get to the canal."

He did it. In an instant, the car was filled with the smell of fear. A ghastly stench I had only smelled in prison—from a pedophile they'd mistakenly put in my cell who had inmates waiting for him in the corridor to cut him up. A smell every man or beast recognizes right away, even if he's never encountered it. A primal smell, wild and revolting. The age-old odor of instinct.

"Park over there."

I heard his ring clacking against the steering wheel, maybe

his teeth clacking too. Years of terror had taken over his body and there was nothing he could do about it.

"Please, Charlie," he stammered, "please, please, anything you want . . ." He was almost screaming. "I have the money from the cash register!"

"Pass me the keys."

He gave them to me over his shoulder. I got out of the Mercedes and opened the door.

"Get out!"

He was now incapable of doing anything. He almost fell as he tried to get out of his seat. His legs couldn't carry him anymore. I saw long threads of drool shining in the moonlight.

"Climb up on the bank!"

He slipped on the grass three times. His sweat was stinking up the night. We found ourselves on the little dirt track that runs along the canal.

He began to drone out disconnected phrases that helped him make his way through the night. He seemed drunk.

"Remember, Charlie . . . We . . . we . . . we used to swim here when we were ten . . . You'd dive off the bridge . . . you . . . And the soccer team, Charlie, the goal you scored in Endoume . . . at least forty yards out. I did something dumb, Charlie, you're my only friend . . . Smash my face in if you want, but spare me, please, please, I'm a schmuck, but I'm your friend . . . I'll give you everything . . . Tomorrow morning, we'll go to the bank and I'll give you everything! She's the one who came to see me, Charlie, I swear, I tried to help her, I—"

"And you helped her into bed."

"People say all kinds of things, *please!* You're going to do something crazy, Charlie. You'll be sorry all your life. Your whole life, you'll see what you did! You're not a killer, Charlie, you're the most—"

"I'm not killing anybody. You're going to commit suicide. In two days, they'll find your body in the spot where they found

Maurice's body. Remember little Maurice? You're going to go through the pipes all the way to Plan-de-Cuques."

He fell to his knees. His joints were failing him, each of his tendons, every nerve in his body. Terror was twisting his face, shiny with drool and snot. His mouth was a horrible wound and a long sawing sound was coming out of it.

"You're not just a bastard, you're a coward, Franck. I remember what the lawyer René Floriot said about his client, Dr. Petiot: *He walked to the scaffold as if he were going to the dentist.* Think of Dr. Petiot. Stand up and look me in the eye!"

I stuck the double barrels to his forehead.

"Get up and climb onto the wall. I'm giving you a chance. You remember the sluice fifty yards from here, on the other side of the canal? We hung onto it hundreds of times. If you can grab it, I'll let you live; if not, you go through the pipe."

"They'll arrest you, Charlie, you'll go back there for life . . . Please . . . please . . . please . . . don't do this!"

"I'm wearing gloves and a coat that's not mine. I didn't even sit on the seat next to you. No prints, no DNA. You committed suicide. I've been thinking of this moment for years. I've already lived through it ten thousand times. You've already died ten thousand times. Even if they question me, they won't have a thing." I held out his car keys. "Put them in your pocket!'

He obeyed. If I'd told him to eat his shoes, he would have eaten them.

"Now jump, or I'll blow your head off! It's your last chance."

He huddled up on himself. I turned the rifle toward the canal and pulled the trigger. The report pummeled the night. It banged against the hills, rolled through the valleys, hit the rocks of the Barre de l'Étoile.

With the terrible wind that was now blowing and the blackness of the countryside, I was in no danger. No shutter creaked open on the other side of the fields, behind the rows of cypress trees.

Suddenly, he uncoiled like a spring and threw himself into the canal.

I leaned over the dark water. He was thrashing around, breathing noisily, groaning, suffocating, beating the water like mad to reach the other side of the canal. Fifty yards.

I had given him a chance. I turned on my heels and ran off toward the village. I heard him fighting awhile longer in the icy water and then there was nothing but my partner in crime, the wind, on this little piece of land where we'd been happy so long ago.

The next morning I went back to work. The sky was extremely pure. The wind had fallen during the night. I hung the coat back up on its peg in the garage. Mademoiselle Niozelles heard me and invited me to come up and have a cup of coffee in her kitchen.

I told her: "I'll be done this evening. If you want to go to the mill with me, we'll have the exact weight of the crop. You can stock oil all over and there'll still be some left."

She agreed. She was holding a little red steaming mug in the hollow of her hands. She must have just come out of the shower; her wet hair was sticking to her forehead. I'd never seen her so fresh, so pretty.

Around six that evening, I loaded the last crates into the van and we went off to the mill.

Since the beginning of November I'd picked 1,378 kilos. They told us the oil would be ready toward the end of January.

I asked Mademoiselle Niozelles if she would go out to eat with me to celebrate this beautiful crop. It was Saturday night. She said yes.

"What do you feel like eating?"

"Foie gras, Sauternes."

She was so simple and natural it threw me off balance. I said, "You know what I call you in my mind?"

"No."

"Belle Lurette."

"Well, in *my* mind I call you Geronimo. Every morning, I'm happy when I hear Geronimo's motorcycle."

She took my arm and we left. I didn't dare look at her. On my right cheek I had all the sweetness of her smile.

The stars are never as beautiful as the night when a widow turns toward life again.

PART II

WANDERINGS

I'LL GO AWAY WITH THE FIRST MAN WHO SAYS I LOVE YOU

BY MARIE NEUSER

Le Frioul

T he small boat slowly leaves the safety of the port, chomping at the bit. No sooner has it brushed against the last dike than it will abandon its elephantine pace and bounce over the swell with childish glee, thumbing its nose at the haughty sailboats, and, with the wind at its back, speed toward the white island.

On the deck, the benches are empty. Cold and spray have discouraged anyone from sitting on them. Anyone. Not quite the word: in reality, you can count the passengers on the fingers of one hand. The time for the detour by Château d'If has passed: the site has closed its doors, winter schedule, last shuttle for the archipelago. Instead of the day's tourists, the boat, putting on a Breton air, is only taking the residents of the island. Behind the portholes, several people dazed by their day's work on the continent are returning toward their solitude, pitched to and fro by the waves.

You are among them.

You. And I, in your suitcase.

You don't look at anyone. And as if to thank you for so much discretion, no one really looks at you either. A man, yes, a man glanced at you stealthily, because you're a pretty woman. No. The man corrects himself. He tells himself pretty's not the word, you're not pretty. Pretty is a word that implies freshness, luminosity, youth, something innocent or carefree. Instead, you look like a flower about to close for the night. Your features are drawn, your eyes are puddles of oil and their outlines are blurred in the harsh neon lighting. And yet I know how beautiful you are, I do. How beautiful you were before the catastrophe. The man realized it too; he tells himself that if you hadn't looked so sad, so out of it, he would gladly have been flirting with you. But he tells himself that you've reached the end. You don't flirt or even just chat with someone who's reached the end. You don't want to be contaminated by the end.

"Be quiet. Get out of my head and leave me alone. Enjoy your last trip in silence."

You did everything right, my love. The boat, the crossing, the island . . . Like in Venice, to the Island of the Dead. You did a good job with the symbols to celebrate our farewell.

"Be quiet. Leave me alone."

I don't know if I should feel sorry for you. You're so silly on this boat with your rolling suitcase. Another person noticed you, precisely because of the suitcase. Nobody crosses over to the island with a suitcase. People generally land there with beach things during the summer months. And even in the Indian summers, which can sometimes go on forever. Or in hiking shoes and a backpack to tromp over the stony ground. But never a suitcase. You didn't want anyone to notice you? You screwed up, baby. You made this crossing on the last shuttle, the one that's almost empty, with your lovely eyes like faded violets and your little suitcase. They'll remember you.

"I had . . . how can I put it . . . something else in my head."

Try not to talk out loud to me, my sweet. People are looking at you. The person who just noticed you because of the suitcase is wondering where you can possibly be going. There's no hotel on the island, maybe just a single furnished room.

"I could be someone going to her yacht anchored in the marina. To spend a few nights on it?"

That's exactly what the woman watching you just told herself. To spend a few nights or go sailing . . . Risky. The weather reports said there'll be a mistral blowing at a hundred miles per hour in the next few days. Very few yachts go out to sea in conditions like that, in fact none at all, because everybody knows the Mediterranean can turn itself into a coffin without warning. And I'm sorry, but seeing you so frail, so tired and alone, sitting next to your rolling suitcase, nobody thinks you bear the slightest resemblance to an adventuress on the raging seas. No, darling. You make people uncomfortable. You're a weird stranger entering a village where everybody knows everybody, where everybody spies on each other and picks each other apart, at an hour when only residents return.

"Please, get out of my head! I came here because I'm looking for silence, darkness, and solitude. Our last night is worth at least that, don't you think? No other place in the city offered me that privilege—a night of silence and darkness, next to you."

And then what? What do you intend to do with me?

"With what remains of you?"

With what remains of me.

"I'll improvise. I'll offer you to the sea. You wanted some kind of symbol, you've got it."

How about you?

"Maybe I'll follow you. Yes, it would certainly be better like that. You said so yourself. I've reached the end."

Hey, look. With the twilight creeping toward Château d'If, it looks more than ever like a sand castle. We're brushing past it. We're ignoring it. We keep bouncing over the whitecaps until the boat slows down and the sailors moor it to the dock. One of the men even helps you slide your suitcase down the gangplank. He must have found me heavy. Do you think he suspects something? No. Nobody could possibly imagine this.

"Of course. Just yesterday, I couldn't have imagined it either."

We're going by the final hikers getting ready to board for the last crossing of the day, the one that goes back to the Vieux-Port. In a few minutes, Le Frioul will be totally cut off from the city for the next twelve hours. Don't worry, you'll find the solitude you long for. Look: no one's paying the slightest attention to the woman with the suitcase, not even noticing the little hypnotic music of the wheels over the concrete of the dike. Careful . . . careful . . . there! It's done. Everybody turned left toward the houses and restaurants. Except you. They all forgot about you, and you kept going right. Toward the desert.

"Not toward the desert, no. Toward the places we loved. The beach, the inlets a little farther on. We used to plunge our bodies into that water slightly colder than elsewhere and, under your rather pitying look, I would pick up those pink stones, like pyramid-shaped candies, and then polish them and pile them up in candy boxes."

You always were a pack rat. I wasn't pitying you. You amused me. I found you beautiful, and so childish. I would watch you walking up and down the beach, your supple little body, so tanned it looked like you'd slipped into it like a dress.

"My body?"

Yes, your body. Which clothes your soul.

"But as for bodies, you preferred hers. We wouldn't be in this situation today if you had been content with mine."

That's only a matter of physical bodies. Now, just when you're beginning to struggle to climb this road, pulling your suitcase behind you, you tell yourself it's a body that brought you here—mine. Nothing's harder than getting rid of a body, right?

"The problem isn't getting rid of a body, but getting rid of a body one loves. And you know that: I'm not here to get rid of something, but to push us very gently out of life, you and me."

Do you really mean to take this road? You know it leaves the populated area behind as it moves along the coast. Reckless, isn't it? You leave behind you the ugly buildings that were once modern and today are only yellowish, the terraces of the restaurants hibernating with all the sadness of summer resorts in January, the empty tourism center and the building they made for the pilots with its facade like an ocean liner. You seem determined, you don't have the slightest remorse . . . The streetlamps are still projecting reassuring halos, but soon we'll be in complete darkness. What have you gotten yourself into? You were always afraid of the dark. When I wasn't there, you'd sleep with the TV on and the sound off so the glow dancing on the walls could give you the illusion of perpetual daytime.

"I wasn't afraid of the dark, I was afraid of loneliness. In your absence, everything became terrifying. But tonight I'm not alone. You are near me. I like having you near. Besides, the sky is clear, bleached by the wind, dotted only by the moon. The night will not be dark, it will just be cold."

And you plan to pull me along behind you like that, to where . . . ?

"I don't know, François. I didn't make some grand plan. I want to enjoy not having a goal, having this time free from the hands of clocks. I feel truly free for the very first time in my life, free of all that shit that makes us aware of our human condition. I'm no longer afraid of death or night or what tomorrow will bring. I'm no longer afraid you'll leave me. I feel in complete harmony with the present. I almost have the feeling that it's a privilege. Very few people ever get to know this empty, slightly numb serenity and it makes me feel like tasting it, chewing it, absorbing it through each one of my senses. The road is hard, you are heavy, and that's good. I'm thirsty and soon I'm going to be hungry, but that, too, is good. I know very well that you're inside my head as I talk to you and—"

I'm in your suitcase, Caroline. Not in your head.

"You're not entirely in my suitcase. In my head, you are complete. It's better that way. It makes communication easier."

Since you're raising this subject . . . why didn't you make me disappear completely? You had the time. You would have spared yourself a lot of trouble . . . It all started off so well . . . Cutting me up into little pieces to put me into the blender—a brilliant idea! You always had a practical mind.

"When you're in a jam, you jump at the first idea that comes into your head. Modern appliances are surprisingly efficient. French quality, *oui, monsieur!* Once I started I found it pretty easy to do. In fact rather fun, I must admit. Your legs, which dared to run to her . . . Your arms, which dared to embrace her . . . I was so angry, and that did me good. But your face . . . your face, I just couldn't. It was too much for me."

And yet it's my face that did it all. My eyes, which veered from you to her. My mouth, which betrayed you. My tongue, which conveyed the lies—

"Stop it. Spare me the nauseating details. Yes, of course it was your face that offended me, when it was still giving me those casual as-if-nothing-had-happened looks and everyday smiles when you'd just given her a quick fuck. It's not that I didn't feel like wiping it out, turning it into a mush of bones and blood, and that's exactly what I was getting ready to do . . . but then I just didn't have the heart. Your face, which I still loved so much—"

What about my torso? My hips? My penis? That, you didn't eliminate, and yet that's what started it all.

"Same thing. That stupid love. It was still too strong, you no longer deserved it, but it kept me standing up. Once arms and legs had been blended and thrown into the toilet, I looked at what remained of you, of fifteen years of life together, and I was struck by a sort of astonishment that kept me from going on. I actually felt bad when I realized what I'd just done. Flushing you down the toilet like diarrhea. Is going from mad love to diarrhea really the normal order of things? I couldn't bring myself to chop up the face I had loved so much, your chest where your heart had throbbed for me, just for me, for so many years, your penis that had thrust for my pleasure alone for so long. No, I couldn't. That's when I decided to take us to the island. Think it's absurd as much as you like. For me, it was the obvious choice."

And now you're stopping. You're hesitating. Are you going to retreat?

"No. I'm taking a last look at this spot. It always amazed me. There are places you can never understand and this is one of them."

This empty lot?

"Yes, empty's the word. Empty, as if nature itself never knew exactly how to fill it. Even the few prickly pear trees sticking up here and there look lost. They didn't even dare grow too tall, for fear of being decapitated by the storms. Everything looks lost.

Even that old boat dumped on the scrub, tilting over as if the earth were heaving. It seems to miss the time when they took it onto the water. It's been forgotten here since . . . I don't know. I always saw it here. Year after year, it lets itself be eaten away by the salt, slipping from dirty white to the gray of a rainy sky, stung by moss and seagull shit, and the rough lances of the grass that ended up splitting its belly."

A bit like our own story, don't you think? From luminous white-ness to disemboweling.

"Please don't. We never went through rain."

Not true. We never went through a storm, but a permanent drizzle kept us wet.

"Because you let go. Because you could no longer take me on board for wild times and sweet pleasures. You'd just answer my loving words with a smug nod before going back to whatever you were doing. It's easy to speak about drizzle when you let my light go out for lack of *I love you*'s. Be quiet. Let me look at this land. I've always thought nothing illustrated the word desolation quite so well."

Or a big hodgepodge, like this whole city. Remember? You used to say it yourself: Marseille isn't a city, it's an agglomerate, a haphazard conglomeration of arbitrary constructions, a swarming space between entrance and exit signs without anything ever having been thought out. You used to rail against its total absence of harmony, its dislocated, disfigured, patched-up face, glued back together any old way, like you'd treat the broken head of a china doll . . .

"Yes . . . I also used to say that if people thought Marseille was beautiful since from some neighborhoods you could watch the sea, it was because it had failed in its vocation as a city. Saying a city is worth something because the nature around it is pleasant is totally absurd. But do you really think we're here to discuss urbanism? I would so much like to devote these last hours with you to talk about love."

Even though you just killed me?

"The logical consequence of my love."

You're being cynical.

"True. It wasn't supposed to be like this. What I expected from the two of us was a child. It was the desire to see us grow old together, loving even the passage of time on our skin. I was beginning to look tenderly at your brow gradually receding, your belly getting soft."

I loved the wrinkles around your eyes. The scars of your perpetual smile.

"Vile flattery. It didn't prevent you from finding a younger woman with eyelids as smooth as the belly of a fish. And if I used to smile so much, it's because you made me happy, because I felt like a queen. A queen doesn't pout if you forget to say I love you to her. I even managed to keep smiling after I found out."

Maybe that's the mistake you made. If you had screamed and cried, if you'd made a scene by smashing the dishes and slapping me silly, I would surely have left her.

"I don't think so. You keep lying even when you're cut in half. You had organized your new life. You were on your way out. How could I ever imagine you'd be so stupid? Why would you wait till you're hurt to get us back on an even keel . . . No pun intended."

Ouch! You're shaking me. I'm being jolted around in my polyester coffin. There's very little asphalt here and you just turned sharply and made the suitcase swing over the potholes.

"I'm rolling you over the stones. I don't know if I have the right to venture out here, beyond the boat, but I always felt like it, and today I couldn't care less about what's not allowed."

That takes the cake. You just killed a man. Now you're developing a keen sense of transgression.

"I've always been so very good . . . This is a liberation proportionate to my former restraint. I've always wanted to explore that big, disintegrating structure, right there against the cliff. What a waste . . . It would have been beautiful cleared up, reconfigured, lived in. It could have been a place for you and me. To raise kids.

They would have built a cabin in the white boat. They would have measured themselves against the limestone, the low grass, the naked stone, against their fear of birds, which are not cute little jumping balls here but predators with beaks like drills. They would have learned not to trust their whiteness, their apparent gentleness, their claws as yellow as candy; it would have been a good school for learning to face life."

You're fantasizing. You never could have lived here. You're not made for islands. You would have wilted.

"For sure. But tonight I need to dream. And I want to keep on dreaming about the two of us and our past splendor, like the past splendor of that building."

Everything is surrounded by fences and No Entry signs . . . I never knew if it was because of the danger or a vestige of the military installations that practically covered the whole island.

"Forbidding people to do something never made anyone back off in this town. There's a hole in the fence. Hardly big enough for us to slip through."

I'm sure that house is a squat. It may not be prudent . . .

"Chicken! Do you know any squat as silent as this? No, there's nobody here. Just memories of illegal parties, of course . . . Murals, graffiti, rotten boards, stumps of doors and furniture . . . Some shit, maybe human. Greasy old papers. Empty cans. No worse than our street."

Thanks for thinking of giving me a little freedom. I'm feeling a bit cramped in my box. This breeze grazing my face feels good . . . So this is where you intend to leave me?

"No, of course not. I just want to look at you again before the hours pass and spoil what's left of your flesh."

But it's dark here.

"No big deal. I can taste you with my fingertips. I feel like imprisoning your skin in mine, so I can take the memory of a caress to where I'm going."

But you don't know where you're going.

"I won't go very far. We're on an island. It limits your options."

What do I look like?

"Still handsome. Hardly blue. It's just the smell that's starting to get unpleasant. Like here. It stinks. Dead rabbits and bird droppings. Decomposed vegetation and rotting wood."

Protect me from the flies.

"That's what I'm doing. I'm spreading my coat over your body, like the sheets on our bed. There, that's a lovely image. It brings back happy days. The moments when we fell asleep. When I curled up against you, when you said I was keeping you warm. The awakenings. Our faces all rumpled, not presentable yet. It made us laugh to see ourselves so ugly, before a trip to the bathroom made us radiant for one another again."

You're hurting yourself.

"That bothers you? You didn't have any scruples about hurting me."

What do you know about my scruples?

"You managed to look me straight in the eye every single day and act as casual as ever, throughout your affair with that woman. Not one eyelash expressing the slightest embarrassment. What esteem for me . . . I no longer existed. I was simply a nuisance, an obstacle between the two of you."

Caroline, I'm cold.

"You won't die from it, François. You're already cooled down."

I forgot. Everything . . . I just remember I was alive, and suddenly I had become nothing but my head in a suitcase. I don't even know how you killed me. Oh yes . . . I have a last memory . . . I know I was about to tell you something important. You were in the kitchen, very sexy, maybe a little too sexy. Very sexy and very sad. We'd spent the last two weeks making love day and night. No. You had spent the last two weeks making love to me, vamping me, making me lose all sense.

"So you had sense?"

I think I was kind of shaky when I left.

"Remember . . . I killed you just before you told me about her."

So that's it? And yet you knew. You had found out everything, I have no idea how.

"It happened in such an unexpected way . . . one of those chance events that humiliate you more than they get you down, because the first feeling that hits you in the gut is the sudden realization of your own stupidity . . . Asking yourself . . . how could I have been dumb enough not to see it? An accident that makes you feel like bursting with laughter like a scary clown with paint smudged all over your face—"

No digressions. Tell me how you found out.

"Shh! Be quiet! I just heard something . . . Little steps rattling the broken bricks and stones just behind that old wall . . ."

Rats. This island is a paradise for rats, seagulls, and rabbits. Here, the rats are kings. Here, they outwit the laws dictated by the capital . . . Here, they remember that their ancestors imported the Black Death. Boat people with poisoned fleas . . . And thousands of humans who died in abominable conditions because of a few precautions that were bypassed out of greed . . .

"You're insensitive enough to rehash your history books, here and now?"

Oh, because on top of it all I'm supposed to be sensitive? I should spare you? Plane off the rough spots? When I'm the one who's reduced to . . . this?

"This *what*, François? To an avatar of a dead human being, yes. To an imperfect dead man. I had no idea corpses could be so chatty, it wasn't part of the plan. Your death should have meant your silence. But you're still the way you always have been . . . Useless. Cerebral."

That's because I'm still full of gray matter. My brain is intact. If you had pulverized it, if you'd shot me in the head—

"I hear a noise . . . it's coming closer . . . Be quiet."

But you're the one who's talking all the time! Me, I'm just a heap of flesh, already soft and oozing into the lining of a suitcase on wheels. My voice is inside your head.

"They're coming closer!"

It's the smell of my corpse that's attracting them. Don't yell like that, for God's sake!

"A loud rustling of wings behind me . . . Those aren't rats . . . they're birds . . . There are lots of them . . . They're snatching up the last gleams of day, they're so white, so immaculate that they seem to be shining from inside, like children's phosphorescent toys . . . They look like an army of little ghosts moving toward us."

I think you should shut my lid. They're coming to devour me.

"I think I'd get the better of them."

Well, you're not thinking straight. You'll be no match for their beaks.

"They're so white . . . You can't be so cruel when you're so pure."

Bullshit. That's what you thought of love, and look where that got us.

"Right. I'm packing you up again. Onward."

Where to?

"You'll see. A spot that's more protected. The wind is beginning to rage. I want to go where we'll be more sheltered. From the wind and the creatures that want to tear you away from me. Today, I'm the one who's making the decisions. And it's out of the question that anyone else, man or beast, gets to decide what to do with you."

It's lighter outside. You were right: the full moon puts us in a very theatrical spotlight. We deserve at least that. What a tragedy, don't you think? Your dear Hamlet chatted with a skull too. You're very Shakespearean tonight.

"That's exactly what I was telling myself yesterday. You, on the other hand, floated around in an Éric Rohmer film, eaten away by a very noble dilemma—shall I kiss Jeanine or Monique?—while I was torturing myself with Elizabethan sorrows. It all comes down to this, you see. Wrong set."

You're having trouble moving uphill again. You'd be almost funny, blown around like this by the wind. Your hair like Medusa's snakes, your coat like a sail swollen by the storm, and that wind breaking in front of you rising like a wall.

"It burns my face. Don't be fooled, all right? These tears are due to the icy wind whipping at me, they aren't tears of sadness or remorse."

Look, you can't go forward anymore. It's comical. It reminds me of a scene in The Gold Rush, *when the cabin's leaning over and Charlie's skidding back and forth, sucked backward by gravity. I'm glad I can come up with something funny, considering the situation.*

"Happy man."

How did you find out? Caroline . . . you started to tell me, but we were interrupted.

"A mistake with our computer, François. I clicked on the wrong icon and I came upon your mailbox that you'd left open. Which didn't affect me one way or the other at first, since I never had the slightest curiosity about your contacts and messages. Never felt the urge to rummage through your private life, because you weren't supposed to have one . . . one apart from me, I mean. Another life. Everything had seemed so transparent to me for the last fifteen years . . . We were so close, like a real family . . . But my eye caught the first line of your inbox: *Me, Sonia (149).* And the first sentence of your last message: *My love. I can't wait to . . .* My love, I can't wait to. And Sonia's not me."

So you opened it and read it.

"Not right away. I remained planted there like a very old tree. I was so old, all of a sudden. No need to open it to realize that the catastrophe had happened. At that moment, I understood everything. Everything. The awareness of my idiocy overwhelmed me. A world had just ended. And that world was the one that kept me standing, the one that pushed me forward in life. And it was crumbling now, because of the wrong reflex of my forefinger on a mouse . . . like on the detonator of a bomb . . . You tell yourself that if you hadn't made that unfortunate little slip, the day would have continued along like all the other days, but it's too late . . . a whole life is called into question.

So I walked out of the study, I walked through the apartment, and, for a long time, I looked at the tangible traces of the two of us—objects, gifts, books, photos . . . the dirty dishes in the sink, your fingerprints on the glasses . . . That whole material pretense of love going down the drain before my eyes . . . I touched everything with my fingers. I went to sniff your clothes. I went to look at the hollow the ghost of your body left in our bed. A moment that seemed interminable, mute, paralyzed with stupidity, before making up my mind to go back to the computer and click on that infinite exchange of messages."

In short, you did the most masochistic thing possible.

"Coming from you, a despicable analysis like that doesn't surprise me. What would you have liked me to do? Close it all up fast, relegate the rest of my life to a personal access code and keep being cheated on without saying anything, pretending not to know? No, love, the end was on its way. The least I could do was try to understand why. So then, yes, at that moment I read it all. Months of nauseating messages, you and her bellowing out your stinking desire, weaving your schemes, organizing your disgusting double life, your dates, thrusting into each other in elevators, the justifications served up to your spouses when you came home a bit late, planning to break off and giving us ridiculous, revolting nicknames—both me and him. Rubberdick for him, The Nun for me, cooing novel words . . . Oh, my love . . . All the things you told her . . . told that stranger . . . words that even when we were at the height of our passion, you never said to me . . . Never . . ."

I'm not the type who pours out his feelings. I never was.

"Pours out, you say? *I love you.* Saying *I love you* to your wife is so hard to do? And the worst of it, you see, is this absence of words had never scandalized me. Until I discovered that another woman had been able to inspire you to use them. Or get them out of you with forceps, it hardly matters. And you want to know something? I closed my eyes . . . and I imagined, just for a minute, that you were saying all those wild things to me, all those silly teenage words, all those jokes bordering on pornography, those naughty whispers, those words of wonder, those compliments you say at the end of a party, the enamored or excited babble, those dissertations on her beauties, hidden or half-visible, those comments on the folds of her intimacy and the orifices of her body . . . and those whole pages of I LOVE YOU, yes, yes, in capital letters . . ."

Love isn't only in words. I shared fifteen years of my life with you. I was the first one to talk about getting married.

"No, that's true, not only in words. With me, you started with the principle that your presence alone, near me, that sleeping next to me, our common address for so many years, replaced words of love. Realizing in a fraction of a second that all those words, all that slightly silly or frankly dirty poetry you were serving her up on a trowel . . . flowery vomit that could have made me laugh, well, I would have loved so much to hear it . . . at least once . . . So I read and reread 149 messages like stabs to the heart, and with every line I could feel my body shrinking, melting, becoming as fleeting as a smoke ring . . ."

So that's when you decided to kill me.

"Not at all. At no time did I decide to kill you. Didn't even cross my mind. Ladies and gentlemen of the jury, that's my tragedy: no premeditation. I made the decision to reconquer you, you idiot. To fight. You have to fight for the things you hold dear, right?"

I remember now. One day I found you more tender, more catlike, more in love . . .

"More in love, no. I was never less in love. More giving, that's the word. Much more prosaic, in short. Sex. Sex as a weapon, not of mass destruction, but of sly reconquest. You wanted sex, I was going to give it to you. And then suddenly I dredged up all the little sexy underwear that had been sleeping in the drawers, the

sluttish paraphernalia I'd considered pathetic at my age, astonished that it still fit me fifteen years later and I could find myself
beautiful in it. Laces, ribbons, hooks that bite into the skin, truss-
ing up the body so expertly it takes your breath away; dresses that
don't allow you to sit, spike heels that scratch the floor—I threw
myself at your neck in all those frills I didn't think I needed anymore to get my soul to enter yours, because my God, I thought
that those flimsy garments, no matter how charming, were useless
when you were truly in love. Truly, you see. Going through beautiful landscapes together, hearts unfolding at the noise of a key
announcing a return, wanting to kiss every one of our scars, that
was more important than anything else for me. More important
than the various lickings, dunkings, and suckings whose pleasure,
after all, only lasts a moment. Telling myself that every day that
went by with our voices mingling more than our organs was a
multiple orgasm in itself."

You're digressing. Just tell me how it happened.

"By chance, love. Okay, I was talking about the lace."

*Nice moments you gave me then. I wondered why that dormant
sensuality had suddenly reemerged. But now I understand. It was a
sense of urgency. Panic.*

"You bastard. No. No urgency, no panic. Just howling out my
love differently. I wanted to be the ideal woman. Your little dream.
To make her fall back into the shadow, into the great nowhere she
came from. And you, into my lace, my waste-squeezers, my tight
bodices, my half-cup bras, my straps and my garters, you buried
yourself. You took. You hugged, squeezed, kneaded, licked, bit,
penetrated, you turned me over and flattened me out for weeks:
I was skinned, peeled, hollowed out, seeded, singed, buttered,
shredded, peppered, and grilled. Beat. With a wild heart, but not
yet satisfied. Thinking I could read in that body . . . penitence,
and your return . . . no woman was ever fucked like you fucked
me . . . those crazy days . . . Leave her right away. I . . . convinced
myself that everything had come back to me."

I was happy. My skin was in a state of bliss.

"Meanwhile, you . . . repaired your . . . confidentiality . . . access to your . . . you were dreaming . . . thought that . . . could convince myself . . . things were not so clear anymore . . ."

I can't hear you anymore. Everything is howling around us. The surf sounds like a highway, the wind is rushing into my capsule yelping like a mad beast. I'm bouncing around too much, I'm seasick. Can dead people vomit? It was crazy to take me here on a day when the mistral's blowing, Caroline. Nothing can stand up on the days when it's blowing. Even the trees drag along the ground, hoping to protect their limbs.

"SO THEY . . . HAVE A START ON YOU."

You're losing your breath . . . The gusts are hitting your thorax like uppercuts and making you catch your breath with the groans of an old woman with emphysema . . . I feel carried away . . . You'll end up dropping me and I'll fall to the foot of the rocks . . . Don't let that happen, Caroline. I deserve better than being dumped into a pit like an old fridge.

". . . NERVE TO TALK ABOUT . . . DESERVE."

Please, leave the road. Take me down to the beach. In the hollow of the cove we'll be sheltered. You'll be able to put us up against the rocky wall, where our huddled bodies won't run the risk of being ripped off the ground like wood chips. I'll be able to hear you again. You'll tell me everything. And then maybe you'll feel like leaving me there. The water will come and take me. I can't wait. I want to end it all. The very last thing I'll taste before meeting God knows what, God knows where, will be this sand sprinkled with so many pieces of brick polished by the sea that you'd think it was decorated with little orange eggs. And all around, like the edges of some porcelain basin, the white walls of the limestone cliffs twinkling under the moon. It will be beautiful. It will smell good. In fact, it will be better than the walls of a coffin . . . But you always were headstrong.

"For the moment, it's your head that's still strong. Oh, come on. One can laugh at anything."

You feel like laughing?

"Would that be so scandalous, François? Let's lighten up a little . . . I found us a den under this little overhang with two stone steps beneath it, where the wind doesn't blow in."

You're still laughing?

"Sorry. It's what you said awhile ago. *Can you hoist me up to the hospital, Caroline?*"

Yes, that's true, it's silly. Still, I avoided saying, You'll hoist me up to Caroline Hospital, Caroline? *For years we made those stupid plays on words. And now I'm being careful not to fall into that trap.*

"Because you'd still like to keep being dramatic. You want this moment to be solemn. You really have no sense of humor."

Let's say that in the situation we're in, I have a hard time feeling . . . detached.

"Not that I didn't help you do it. You know why you're pissed? Because you see me calm and peaceful. You would rather see me as a Sicilian mourner so you could tell yourself you were indispensable to me, irreplaceable."

And isn't that true? You killed me so I couldn't leave you.

"I think it was more to avenge the insult. To soothe the pain of disillusion. And I'm no longer so sure I feel like accompanying you."

Oh no. That's not fair. You're betraying me!

"That's exactly why I don't feel like it anymore. For fifteen years I thought you were a good guy. Two weeks ago I discovered you were a liar—scornful, calculating, and unfaithful. Tonight, I discover you're monstrously egotistical. I'm beginning to think I deserve better. I'm able to love gently, tenderly, deeply. I know how to build and not doubt. The love I can give isn't a tag on a wall, it's a tattoo that doesn't wash off even if the skin suffers for it. I have a magnificent ass and a brain that works. I can be maternal and bitchy, a saint and a whore. I can read and come at the same time. I think many men would be happy to find me on their path."

A pearl before swine?

"That's it. You just summed us up. You're the one who thought I was interchangeable. Into the scrap heap when there are problems. You found I wasn't hot or smooth enough, a little clogged up in the burners. So instead of making me shine again with a soft cloth and blowing on the fuse to create sparks, the whole shebang to revive lust—oh, it wouldn't have taken much . . . words that lubricate the eyes and the rest . . . looks that make us flow out of our clothes and into open arms . . . Well, no: you preferred to throw me into the garbage can and buy something all nice and new, something straight from the factory that starts right up . . . You couldn't understand why I wasn't greeting you in the evenings already on my knees with an open mouth and an avid cunt? You had lost the instructions. Perhaps others will find them."

You're being crude.

"It's not my fault. It's the island. You don't bother with amenities here, you're just above the rock and your flesh is prey to thorns and gusts of wind. Your layers of propriety are ripped away. Only the pulp remains. Look, you can see the city from here, illuminated and hysterical, you can sense the disorder and swarming of all those two-footed ants loving each other, hitting each other, boring each other, seducing each other, forgetting each other, devouring each other, falling asleep, counting their money, putting on makeup, multiplying, repenting, smearing themselves with civilization each at his own level, in any way they can. But us— we're here, standing in the darkness on the pebbles, swallowing the wind and dust, naked as rats, lured by the depths. We are less than human, we are in quarantine. Don't make me get out my history books too, you know it and you feel it, we're quarantined here, in a place to die, a lazaretto. We're in holy terror of having been contaminated, in the awful wait for the first signs of death throes. Here we have the memory of heads or tails, of croaking right here or being able to get to the other side of this arm of the sea and go on . . . So yes, I'm crude. I'm getting rid of my skin, I'm watching it fall off in shreds like the plague victims did and I'm stripping myself naked as a rock. And I'm waiting too. I'm waiting to see if the illness is crawling inside me. Or if I'm saved."

Caroline, I'm lonely . . .

"I've known that feeling—when I realized that the man living with me was no more than a body, because his heart was elsewhere."

It's because you're so hard. Because you're pushing me around. I have the feeling I don't exist anymore.

"My still loving you was convenient for you. Now you don't know anymore, and before you, there's a precipice. I know. I experienced that kind of pain and amputation."

It will soon be day. The island will start to fill up with people again. What will you look like when you walk past tourists and groups of schoolchildren with your stinking little suitcase?

"No one will come. On stormy days the shuttles don't leave the port. So we're condemned to stay for a few more hours or maybe two days here with the birds. You have nothing to worry about. Our fate will be settled by then. We're not going to hang around here forever."

Up to now I could still read into you a little, thanks to a strange omniscience, certainly due to my new state. But that's beginning to slip away from me too. Like you.

"Putrefaction holds many mysteries . . ."

You chose the steepest paths. You could have taken me down to the Morgeret inlet and sunk me cleanly. But you chose to climb farther up, to the very top of the cliff, to walk along the walls of the fort. I don't understand you anymore.

"You haven't understood me for a long time."

You want to throw me from the top of the cliff? It's not nice. That makes no sense.

"I haven't decided anything yet."

Birds make their nests up high. They're aggressive right now. Not

*only will they see you as an intruder, you'll tempt them with the choice
dish you're dragging after you. I think we're really in deep shit.*

"I'll watch them. It will surely do me good to see how you can
fight to protect your home and stop strangers from destroying what
you've patiently built up. Something I didn't succeed in doing."

Are you talking about her?

"Yes. I'm talking about that creature out of nowhere who
took everything away from me. It's all the more cruel, you know?
To be robbed of everything by a phantom. You don't need a ty-
phoon for citadels to collapse: a simple breeze is all it takes. At
one time, I thought I had gotten over it. There was so much mingling of flesh once again . . . But that was without taking last night
into account . . . when you came to see me in the kitchen without
hearing how hard my chest was thumping inside . . . coming to me
with your confessions while I was cutting up the chicken . . . You
just chose the moment when I was separating the flesh from the
bones and the head from the joints with the Japanese knife that
has that special blade—child's play!—wearing that dress with all
the cleavage, lost in the great hurricane of my thoughts, *he loves
me, he loves me, that appetite he has for me can only be mad love,* and
there you are, you come in and watch me with a worried look,
you seem to be beating around the bush and then, suddenly, after
a little cough, you dump that horror on me . . . *Caroline, I have to
talk to you. I'm in love with another woman . . .* But what came over
you? Why did you have to choose precisely that moment!"

*She'd just told me she threw her boyfriend out. I wanted to rise
to the situation. To accelerate the process and dive headfirst into our
promises. It was as if I was anesthetized. You could have been holding
a strainer, a skimmer, a whip, or a pepper mill and I couldn't have told
the difference.*

"At that moment, there was a kind of explosion. Is that what
hatred is? That blast, the whole inside of you shattering? I simply turned around. The hand that held the knife found its way
without my help . . . It went in with the sound of soft suction, a

special blade, yes, the precision of a scalpel . . . You rolled your eyes, wide with amazement, before you collapsed with your hands squeezing your abdomen and I just stood there, equally stupefied, and it all came back to me. I saw us again as we were during those two weeks when I knew, my days of struggle, my days of the dance of the seven veils, of purrs, of rapture, of tingling skin, and I suddenly realized that in that whole period, at no time did you hold your hand out to me, initiate a caress, or ask for an embrace. I had done all I could . . . I had given myself blindly, I had opened myself unconditionally like a fruit that cannot do otherwise than gush out of its skin, and you—all you had done was take, taste, and quench your thirst, but without desire, without love, without anything more than a rush of blood. On the floor, you were opening and closing your mouth like a fish that doesn't understand anything, and I looked at you, leaning over you, I watched you sinking into the great nowhere too, enjoying the way I was avenging my failure, my humiliation, and my disillusion. I loved watching you die, my dear. Oh yes, I loved so much telling myself that you would never live with her and I would remain your wife to the very end . . . And then came the time when you passed over to the other side."

Don't remember. No, no. Don't.

"It's better that way. You would have witnessed my collapse and it was not a pretty sight. The last image that you have of me is that of a pinup girl, although a slightly hollow-cheeked pinup girl, cutting up a chicken and perched on stilettos like nails anchoring her to the floor. But what happened afterward, that night huddled against you, trying to absorb your last warmth through the pores of my skin, kissing your face, murmuring words of farewell—you didn't witness that and it's much better that way. You would have been contemptuous of that scene, the image of your wife in tears next to your inert body . . . Much too soppy—the epilogue that's usually served up with funeral music in the background, just before the fadeout. Count yourself lucky."

Felt . . . nothing. Like the . . . darkness. Until . . . crossing.

"You seem to have a hard time talking. It's not my story that's upsetting you, I suppose."

My mind . . . blurred.

"At last a bit of rigor mortis! Soon you'll be reduced to silence, and that's good news. You'll be absent for real: I will be a widow at last. Not bad, that widow. Especially if she's merry and free. I feel so free! It must be because we're on a promontory and from the other side of the depths growling down below, the city continues to deploy its lights, vulgar but so alive, like a promise of continuity. I look at that constellation of small lamps and I think that there are so many men out there on the other side. So many men who will want to love me, to tell me the words that push girls' little buttons and give them back their desire to live. François, my man, if I can still call you that, I think it's the ideal moment to ask you for a divorce. That won't shock you too much, will it? It's what you were getting ready to do anyway."

Leave?

"Don't tempt me!"

. . . itch.

"Shh! It's so easy to insult someone. Keep your dignity. After all, you're the one who got us into this situation and I'm taking it rather well, right?"

Love.

"No, no. The end is unknitting your brain, that's all. Those are illusions brought on by the open air, by that geological purity that's blinding us; it's that apotheosis of rock and water, touched now by the first gleams of dawn, which passed over us like the blade of a knife and peeled the bark off us. It may be nothing more than panic and urgency. Remember panic and urgency? Easy to confuse them with love. You weren't able to tell the difference."

Ost. Don't know. What's . . . ?

"Well, François, you're getting soft up there."

Where are?

"Everything's slipping away from you, isn't it? I know. It's tragic to see life leaving us."

Oline.

"Yes, honeybun."

Oline. Not leave. Alone.

"Look at the last home I found for you! At the foot of those crosses that seem to stand there like an ancient premonition of our story. Those big metallic crosses pretending to look like a graveyard by the sea when in reality it's much more prosaic, just aborted plans for bunkers. That's life for you: you plan big things and it all comes to zilch. You want to build citadels, they end up as perches for seagulls. Speaking of which . . . you won't be alone. The birds are coming closer."

Shut.

"So sorry to disappoint you. I'm going to leave the suitcase open. As soon as I go away, as soon as I stop making a barrier with my body, you'll be the target of a cloud of giant wings, sugared beaks, and insatiable appetites. For the last few hours, they've been staring at you the way one looks at a chocolate éclair in the window of a pastry shop. Your aroma is the promise of a feast. You were good to love, good to kill, good to eat. You're just right, my beloved carrion."

Line. You.

"Me? Well, I'm going back down, my love. Look: I'm unzipping your plastic cover. The big white sails of birds are navigating closer and closer, and it won't be long before they are transformed into a rain of shears. I'm going to take the path back to the port and wait for the first shuttle as I listen to the mews of ecstasy of those flying ogres behind me. Their gullets will be your last home. And I'm going back home, where I'll take a long bath to get rid of your smell, and I'll make myself beautiful again. Then I'll go out and I'll meet someone. I don't think I'll miss you very much. I'm not contaminated; my life is ahead of me, out there, on the other side. I will leave, my love. I'll go away with the first man who isn't hurt by words. With the first one, François. The first man who says, *I love you.*

ON BORROWED TIME

BY EMMANUEL LOI

L'Estaque

I t was no accident and it couldn't have been a hallucination. An all-too-peaceful period. Miguel knew it: even after everything he'd tried for the ten years he'd been hanging around L'Estaque, he'd still wind up in deep shit.

When he first moved into the cabin he'd fixed up and covered with old boards, the neighbors confessed they were surprised that some joker out of nowhere could take root in the territory. He knew how to make himself handy, went out into the hillside, set up rabbit traps, and took on all kinds of odd jobs: repairing a fence, weeding a garden, cutting cords of wood for pizzerias. Never having idle conversations or trying to get close to people. This quiet stranger with a sad smile who didn't bother anybody. His mystery never lost its halo. Just about nobody ever entered his shack. Unknown, and he wanted to stay that way, practically off the grid.

Today, early in the morning as boats with their muffled motors start to drift in, there's a change. After ten years of this apparently inert way of life, two men land on L'Estaque and start combing street after street, store after store, asking about the soldier who knows how to do everything.

During that latency period—all those years undercover and not making waves—time had dug other tunnels. The two trackers with foreign accents couldn't have predicted that: this jack-of-all-trades was protected by his discretion, in a way. He'd been accepted without anyone giving it a thought and he'd managed to blend into the landscape. Here you don't squeal, you don't judge, you don't give out information to God knows what avenger. Talking about someone, informing on him, is betrayal. The past is the past, and past mistakes shouldn't influence your judgment. If someone's in hiding, he must have reasons for it. After four days, the whole village had identified the two thugs. Trackers, cops. Dogs who hunt deer in a pack.

Miguel's oldest neighbor, Pierrot, who lives two houses down, opens the gate, walks around the little shack. "Hey, Miguel, there are guys looking for you." No answer. He knocks on the door.

"Come in."

"Two guys are looking for you. They have funny accents."

Pierrot describes the missing little finger on the right hand and the abrupt manners of one of the two undertakers. "The other's wooly-headed. Looks like a guy from Martinique or Reunion, light-skinned black guy."

Miguel keeps whittling his piece of wood without raising his head.

Through the window, thirty feet away, Pierrot can see a gull trying to take off with a bloody rat dangling from its beak. He picks up the aluminum lid of a beat-up pot. The church bell rings three times.

"You checked your traps, Pierrot?"

"Yeah. Zero. I think there's too much traffic there or we're putting them too near the path."

"Not the only reason."

The neighbor realizes his curiosity won't be rewarded. The guy's tough as nails. It's been a long time since people stopped setting snares for rabbits.

"If those guys keep at it, what do we do?"

"Whack 'em."

Pierrot sits down and breaks off a piece of stale bread. He doesn't say the prowlers have ugly mugs. No, time has changed its rhythm, the hourglass has turned over. In the termite gallery, a whole crowd gets busy. They have no leaders, they're as old as the world. The calm of the quarry intrigues the retired fishing-boat pilot.

"You should come with me, see who they are."

Miguel eats the fish stew and dunks pieces of bread in the aioli, then pulls on a sweater full of holes and tucks a four-pound sledgehammer into his leather carpenter's kit.

As they walk, they avoid the terraces where pals might call out or intercept them. They know the labyrinth of dead ends and reach the jetty where Carasco rents out two rooms in his guest house. In the guidebooks, they say Cézanne used to walk here all the way from the Jas-de-Bouffan in Aix to paint and meet up with his mistress.

The landlady is reluctant to tell them where the bloodhounds went. "I don't follow my guests around."

Pierrot suggests they stay and wait for them. Night has fallen, there's less activity. The carrier pigeons are bound to come back to their base soon.

An hour goes by. The neighbor dozes off in an uncomfortable chair, but the thud of a body hitting the rug jerks him awake. The four-pound hammer has left a square imprint in the skull. The body twitches twice.

"This one won't see his islands again," Miguel says bluntly.

"How about the other guy?"

"He ran away."

They roll the body up in a frayed red rug, drag it out to a porch, and hide it behind a pile of cardboard boxes.

As they head back up to the cabin, Miguel discloses a few fragments of a past he would rather have left in darkness forever.

"It's a very old story, Pierrot. Does Ouvéa ring a bell?"

The fisherman just gapes at him.

"You probably don't remember. It was over twenty years ago . . . Twenty-three independence activists occupy a cave in New

Caledonia. French gendarmes storm the cave on the orders of that tough little doctor—the short guy with a crew cut Chirac sent over to take care of things . . ."

"Bernard Pons."

"Yeah, that's it. Their demands for a free Caledonia weren't going to get to first base. Uranium, precious minerals . . . The gendarmes smoked out the cave. It was a bottleneck with a vertical entrance, something like a stone chimney. I was part of the squad that bumped off the activists. Since I was the wiseguy who told the press we didn't give them a chance, they threw me in the brig . . . When I got out after two weeks, I beat the crap out of the master sergeant. The squad was dissolved, the whole thing was buried. That NCO was in league with two other guys. They've got to be the ones who're after me. They belonged to a movement, New Empire, the new Templars . . . Guys nostalgic for past grandeur."

They stop talking, listening for any suspicious noises that might indicate the return of the other guy. The night gets thicker and thicker, only letting through the sound of distant music.

"You think he'll be back?"

"I'd better be ahead of the game. Take him by surprise. These guys aren't gendarmes anymore. They're hit men, hired out as mercenaries in hot spots. They miss the good old days—good for them."

It takes them two days to sniff out the second thug. In Carnoux-en-Provence. He's hiding out in a convalescent home, wants to wrap up his mission.

Fearing accomplices inside the home, Miguel suggests they wait till the man returns to the village to finish the job. "Let him stew in his own juice."

Times goes by. Nothing. No prowler around. Three days and no weasel to be seen. Miguel agrees to go out fishing. They pick up their nets below the high path along the coast. A bream, a few sardines. As they peer at the houses up there over the sea, they decide to go as far as the local Valparaiso, a good cable's length from the port, a cascade of white shacks that tumble down to the sea, called by its inhabitants "Tortilla Flat."

"You know people there?" Miguel asks.

The pilot steers his boat over between the rocks and ties it to a buoy. They climb the steep slope in silence. In the gardens and on the terraces built on wooden pilings, people are sitting at tables, joking and chatting. Pierrot describes the thug to them. Nobody ran into anybody asking any questions. At the center of an orange-painted patio, a woman is hanging up her wash and asks about an old lady she hasn't seen in the village café for a while.

"Didn't see her," Pierrot says.

She offers them a glass of her homemade chartreuse, a mixture of thyme and herbs. Miguel tastes the concoction.

"A guy in a black turtleneck. Thin."

She shakes her head. "Ask Germaine."

She walks them to the hotel two houses farther up, a rendezvous for illegitimate couples. A stout woman with bleached hair opens the door of her den.

"Oh, it's you, honey, come on in."

They have a stunning view from her place; the virulence of the city loses its glitter. The traps of memory are assigned the same mission: burying the sediments of shame deeper and deeper. Crimes stuffed into a casket with their bones stripped from their flesh. A sea flat as glass, with the buildings of the Roy d'Espagne district on the horizon. Their windows send their ardent lights back to the sunset. Worthy of a lithograph.

After she hears the description of the ghost from the past, Germaine says she does remember getting a visit awhile ago from two men. They were nosy, a little too insistent. As the madam of a semi-legal brothel, she knows how to hold her tongue.

"They were turned away by Robert and Mario. You must've run into them down below."

"They didn't tell us anything."

Pierrot offers the fish to their hostess.

"You buying info now?"

Miguel decides to end the investigation right there. He knew he had to get rid of that old debt from the depths of time, had to free himself from it. An ax hanging over you that never falls, it puts a brake on your life. They stay there until nightfall, talking nonstop. Everything becomes easy and nice again.

Since the darkness is growing thicker and thicker, they leave the boat. It's not too long a walk back to L'Estaque. At the second crossroads, after they pass a beach and a few scooters with their lights turned off, a rock goes whistling by their ears.

The stone-throwing kids run away. The village is drifting off to sleep, the last restaurants folding up their tables. The wind is rumbling.

All night long, Miguel sleeps with one eye open, interpreting the slightest little rustling sound, a shutter banging, fearful dogs, the stir of the far-off city slowly burning off its last toxins. In a twisted dream that torments him till dawn, he's a lab rat trapped in a fenced-off tunnel, and then the waters rush in, green and muddy. Impossible to escape, twenty of them are going to be submerged but nobody screams.

When he wakes with a start, it's too late. The enemy is in the fort. Sitting at the kitchen table, a man in black is watching him, a dark revolver with a silencer in front of him on the peeling oilcloth.

"I could've killed you in your sleep. I didn't do it and I won't. You're worthless, you're not even worth hating . . . You're living in a dump, surrounded by losers. You—"

"Shut up."

The man gets up and stuffs the Colt back inside his belt. "Just remind yourself there's no hiding place, no protection. Somebody else will find you."

The man leaves the door open and the cool morning breeze drifts into Miguel's bedroom. With his hands crossed behind his head, he lies in bed and watches a white spider moving slowly toward its prey, a fly that's not moving anymore, all wrapped up in a deadly sarcophagus.

The ordinary sounds of day grow louder, everything is falling back into place. The storekeepers are opening up their shops, the school is waiting for the children, and the butcher is unloading carcasses of beef.

WHAT CAN I SAY?

BY REBECCA LIGHIERI

Longchamp

I was born on traverse de l'Observatoire, a street name that
will mean nothing to you. Who even remembers there was
an astronomical observatory in Marseille once, first in the
Accoules quarter and then on the Longchamp plateau?

Almost a dead-end street, traverse de l'Observatoire stops at
boulevard Camille Flammarion. And unless you want to consult
Esmée Villalonga, a fortune-teller and tarot reader who's been
at number 27 for years, there's no reason to go there, not you or
anyone else.

But I was born there, and that's different. And since my parents never left the three-room apartment where I grew up, naturally I have to go back, even though visiting them is no picnic—a
drag, more like.

There's nothing much to say about my childhood neighborhood, except that it doesn't look at all like the idea people have of
Marseille when they've never been there. Between place Leverrier and the square in front of the Jardin zoologique, you forget
pretty fast that the city is a port. The Palais Longchamp looks
like an enclave on the Danube with its lawns and cascades, its
dome, its colonnades, all green and cool, a thousand miles from
Luminy and L'Estaque, not to mention the Quartiers Nord, the
North End . . .

I'm not afraid to say that this "palace" was mine, my domain,
my fief, the enchanted kingdom I roamed ever since I was five,
under the watchful, sullen eye of my mother, who grew more and

more remote. She had better things to do than bring her son to the Jardin zoologique—the name the park kept despite the fact that there hasn't been the ghost of a bear or a giraffe there since the end of the eighties.

From the age of seven on, I went there alone, barely telling anyone I was going out. At any rate, when they weren't selling their stuff at the markets, my parents would sleep, tired of everything, of getting up at dawn, of loading their van, of working in all kinds of weather; tired of trying to sell their junk: imitation leather jackets, synthetic sweaters, fancy underwear, tight spandex or polyester dresses, a whole load of hideous clothes they wore themselves and dressed their three children in too.

I'm the oldest. After me, Salvatore, came Libero and Allegra. Even though both my parents grew up in Marseille without actually being born here, they wanted to remain faithful to their Italian origin by this choice of names while showing a certain optimism, a certain confidence in the world and their offspring. Optimism and confidence quickly defeated by reality, judging by the bitter sadness I've always seen in them, their ceaseless recriminations, and their indifference to anything that wasn't directly connected to mere survival: filling their shopping cart, paying their rent, and *basta*.

Salvatore—"the savior"—are you kidding? Yes, I did believe in this predestiny, but now that tragedy has struck, now that I killed the only woman I ever loved, I tell myself it would have been better to consult my neighbor Esmée Villalonga so she could have warned me, so she could have reminded me that in Marseille tarot, the Tower always meant doom.

Yes, but see, in 2001 I'm ten, doom is not in the picture yet, and besides, everything seems new and promising, gleaming under the June sun. The city hasn't given in to the torpor of summer yet, I've put my roller skates on and I'm speeding down the slope that connects the plateau of the Palais Longchamp to its arc de triomphe and the columns that line either side of the cascade. I burst onto the terrace with no problem, lean my elbows over the balustrade in the same movement, and look for my sign, Aquarius, sculpted on the frieze decorating the colonnade. It's a habit I've gotten into, among other childish rituals, to come here and run my fingers over the bas-relief: that muscular boy pouring water out of his vase with a huge splash always seemed a lucky sign, in this spot devoted to water, basins, and grottoes dripping artificial stalactites in the deafening noise of the cascade.

But today I'm out of luck: a girl's leaning back against my column and staring at me with a mocking look.

What can I say? When you're ten, how do you know you've just met the woman of your life, that she'll be the one and not someone else and your whole life won't be enough to know and love her—and in my case, that I'll sentence her to death?

What can I say? She's not even pretty the way I think of it at ten: a little plump, vaguely blond, with thick, heavy bangs that veil her blue eyes which don't have any particular sparkle. She's dressed the way I am: sweatpants and a T-shirt, black for me and pink for her, a color I hate because I'm a boy. Our resemblance stops at our dress, though: I have dark skin and dark hair, a curly mop on my head that still embarrasses me and I try to control with lots of gel. I have dark eyes that always look like I put on black eye shadow: they've given me my share of snide remarks and fights, because no way I'm going to let anybody call me a faggot without a fight.

What can I say? She's not my type, and as a matter of fact I don't care about girls, but on this fine June day, a shiver of pleasure goes through me, a very strong feeling, looking at her there and taking it as a sign that she's hiding the Aquarius on the frieze from my sight. She starts talking to me with remarkable ease and a touch of disapproval.

"You're lucky security didn't see you. No roller skates allowed here."

"I'm not scared of security."

"What's your name?"

"Salvatore, how about you?"

"Alice."

"In wonderland."

"You're only the thousandth guy who's said that."

The conversation could have stopped right there, at that little but unbearable humiliation to my young male pride, but no, contrary to all expectation, we keep on talking, we even spend the afternoon together, running from one end of the park to the other. Alice regularly dashes back to reassure her mother, who's reading on a bench while keeping an eye on her little brother, a fat baby named Quentin whose existence I instantly forget. I just tell myself—but it's not the first time—that all families are not alike and there are parents who're concerned about their children, afraid they might fall or run into the wrong people, while mine seem to have moved beyond parental concern long ago, just busy making ends meet and sleeping off their cheap wine or pastis.

What can I say? It continued. Alice became my friend, and wonderland was her, without my ever daring to tell her anything about my own wonder.

We would see each other in the park on Wednesday or Saturday afternoons for years. Together, we ran from the little kiosk selling drinks to the bandstand below; together, we beat countless bushes to flush out skinny cats, bums, or dazed junkies. If only I had known . . .

Together, we climbed over the balustrade separating the terrace from the monumental fountain and found ourselves wading in the stagnant water between the giant bulls that pull the chariot of the Durance, stamping impatiently with their hooves as if to make a triumphal entry into the city, then they'd run down boulevard Longchamp, take the Canebière, and end their cavalcade at the water's edge.

The first time, I'm the one who guides Alice, gives her a

hand, helps her climb up on the stony spine of one of the bulls as I'd occasionally been doing myself for a long time. Then we ride together, each on our mount, in the splashes that the wind brings back to us, in the glorious sun and toward a future that I still believe will be as radiant as that lovely day. With a satisfied look, Alice surveys the horned heads of our animals, the green water, the reeds, the moss.

"You'd think it was the Camargue."

"You've been there before?"

"Sure, lots of times. You haven't?"

I never go anywhere: my parents don't have the time and my school, Leverrier, doesn't go in for class trips. Too bad. I'll catch up later on with Alice and our kids.

We keep growing. At eleven, we enter sixth grade in the same junior high, Chartreux, but we make sure never to be seen together. When I run into her, her smile, that marvelous smile as frank as it is contagious, becomes evasive and distant, while her look goes right through me, even if she vaguely waves to me every once in a while.

That doesn't stop us from meeting from time to time, to explore the grottoes or the thickets, drink between the gilded caryatids of the Wallace fountain, or sit on the lawns next to the zoo where park security never comes after us with their strident whistles.

We keep growing, and growing up separates us. One day in January when strong winds are blowing through the city, I see her huddled up on the steps of the monumental staircase. I go down to join her and we sit next to each other for the last time in many years to come.

"What're you doing here?"

"Waiting for my girlfriends."

The wind tangles her hair, beats it down on her face and mine. She's changed the way she does her hair, freeing her forehead from the childish bangs that had made such an impression on me four or five years before, but she still has her enviable cheeks, and the mistral is bringing out their delicate pink. With a politeness that makes my heart sink, she asks about school: "What're you going to do after eighth grade?"

"Dunno. Maybe vocational school, become an electrician. I think. You?"

"Well . . . high school."

A new gust of wind brings us together and I breathe in, desperately, her dizzying girl smell, all freshness and lavender. From the pocket of her pretty navy-blue peacoat, a thousand miles from the loud down jackets my parents sell, she pulls out a playing card.

"Look, this just flew into my face. The wind brought it."

"What is it?"

"A tarot card. I'll give it to you."

Then she sees her friends and charges down the steps to meet them. All I can do is watch her gloomily as she leaves the palace and my life. If I had an ounce of sense, I'd double back to traverse de l'Observatoire and ask Esmée Villalonga to interpret that card Alice and the wind have drawn for me. But I do not. The card shows a crenelated tower with flames coming out of it. It also seems to suggest a fall, but how could I see my own fall coming when I'm only fifteen with plenty of rage in my heart—*la rabbia*, not to mention the rest: arrogance, confidence, and the urge to fight and make it?

I'm sixteen, then seventeen, eighteen, twenty. I didn't last long in school: I stopped as soon as I could, left my parents and the three-room apartment on traverse de l'Observatoire for a studio at the other side of the park, on rue Lacépède. I get by, doing odd jobs here and there, and mostly I do a lot of dealing: grass, coke, MDMA, a little of everything in fact. I adapt to the market, to the needs of my customers. I choose them carefully so I don't have to cope with real druggies—they disgust me and they're an endless pain in the ass.

In fact, the more time passes, the more bread I make from drugs. I must have a flair for business because I always manage to find the best product and deal it to the right people, the ones who aren't going to bug me with whining phone calls at three a.m. or trigger a raid on my studio. Its windows look out on the park, my wonderland of long ago, today disenchanted by the disaffection of my queen.

I go out, a lot. And I have as many girls as I like: sluts, not shy at all, but also bourgeois girls who remind me of Alice without being her. I fascinate them with my tough-guy demeanor, my dark curls, my eyes that always look like they're lined with kohl, and the casual way I pick them up at those parties where everybody waits for me because I dispense pleasure and dance, white powder, crystals, and multicolored, monogrammed pills.

If I didn't have moments of solitude where I can have a smoke at my window, waiting for the growl of the tigers, the cries of the monkeys, or the squawking of the parrots from the nearby zoo, I might lose myself completely in that futile life—a life not so different from my parents', when you come right down to it.

Sometimes I take the card Alice gave me years ago out of my wallet. I finally learned, without even trying, that it was the sixteenth Major Arcana card of Marseille tarot—in other words, the Tower, the most frightening card in the deck, the one that foreshadows the end. But when you're twenty, who can believe your end is near or even possible? I am immortal.

I lead a dangerous life all right, but I think I don't take useless risks. I never re-up in the projects, where they draw a gun on you at the drop of a hat for five kilos of grass or two thousand euros; I have regular customers in pretty unexpected spots, a village in the hills over Nice and another north of here in the Drôme: I do business with two fifty-somethings who look like ordinary folks, even if I suspect them of running their own drug deals that go way beyond the borders of the region. The less I know about them, the better.

Among other precautions, I take care to remain anonymous. Nobody knows me by my real name, since I call myself Ousmane, Nassim, or Farès: the bourgeois boys are flattered to buy their shit from an Arab. They feel like they're slumming it, like they have a foot in the North End through their dealer. They'd be very disappointed if I confessed that all I know about La Busserine or the Micocouliers projects is what I read in the papers, just like them—just like all those assholes excited by Kalashnikovs and Škorpions but who'll never get to see one up close.

I'm twenty. There's nothing exciting or glorious about my life, but all things considered, I like it better than my parents': I blow more money than they'll ever have, I don't have schedules to follow or loans to strangle me. I deal drugs, and if that doesn't exactly open up professional possibilities or prospects for the future, strictly speaking, nothing prevents me from transforming myself later in life, when I've put a little bread aside. We'll see what turns up.

One ordinary evening, I show up at Maël's, a regular customer. He's just a little older than I am and I like him. His parents have a beautiful house in La Pointe-Rouge and a boat somewhere or other, so they go sailing six months a year, leaving the key to the house with their son and feeding his bank account so generously that poor Maël spends his time throwing parties in Mom and Dad's triplex and flunking all his exams in architecture school.

He opens the door and his face lights up when he sees me. That's the way Maël is, always happy, always in a good mood, always polite and considerate. For him, I'm Farès, and we do business quickly in one of the rooms upstairs. He and his pals live on coke and MDMA and pay cash on the spot—never any fuck-ups.

"You want a drink? Anything you need is downstairs."

I appreciate his not throwing me out as soon as the transaction is over—after all, we're not buddies. I suspect he's one of those guys who thinks I'm a big shot in the projects and he enjoys showing me off a little at his parties.

"You didn't tell anybody who I am, right?"

"Relax. I'll say I know you from volleyball."

Yes, Maël drinks like a sieve, smokes a joint as soon as he gets up, and snorts line after line, but he's healthy as hell—plays sports and eats organic.

In the rooms on the ground floor, the party's going strong. People are sprawled out all over, the ashtrays are full and they're smoking like mad. Like all parties everywhere in the world, the girls are the only ones dancing, slowly, and without much enthusiasm. One of them turns around when I come in and stops rolling her hips: it's Alice, and she comes right over to me.

"Salvatore! Hey, what a surprise! What're you doing here?"

I can understand why she's surprised; so am I. Not about being here, but about her recognizing me, coming up to me, wanting to talk to me instead of acting remote the way she has been for the past four or five years on the rare occasions when I've bumped into her between Chartreux and Cinq-Avenues.

"I'm Farès, not Salvatore: you must be confusing me with someone else."

As she stares at me wide-eyed, I drag her toward an empty bedroom.

"You'd do me a favor if you didn't tell anybody what my real name is."

She bursts into joyous laughter. "Okay, now I know who you are: you're Maël's dealer. He told me you were going to come."

"What an asshole!"

"Nothing to worry about with me. You got any coke?"

"Go see your pal about that."

She laughs again, as if I'm the funniest guy in the world, while I look her over from head to toe. She's become slender, without losing her childish cheeks or rounded arms—not to mention an ample chest. She follows my look with amusement, adjusts her little top to cover her cleavage, and leaves me standing there.

I spend the rest of the evening watching her. She goes from one group to the other, relaxed and easy, with a glass in her hand and a cig in her lips. Given the size of her pupils, I suspect she went upstairs to do a few lines in Maël's parents' big bathroom, where the action seems to be. I don't care: that shit, I sell it, I don't use it, and this is the secret to my relative prosperity.

From time to time Alice comes over, talks to me, smiles, and exchanges banalities that make me feel good. I don't know if I can be fully objective about her, but I find her a hell of a lot classier than the other girls, less vampish, less zonked out: she doesn't kiss her girlfriends on the mouth, doesn't dance like a striptease artist, doesn't throw up in the sink, and doesn't pull me aside to assure me of her eternal friendship with that sentimentality of drunks and cokeheads that I've grown to loathe.

When it's five a.m. I finally decide to split. I don't want to know how she's going to end the evening, nor with whom. She catches up to me at the door: "Salvatore, wait a minute!"

"What?"

"Leave me your phone number."

"Okay, if you don't give it to anyone else."

"You really think I'm so stupid?"

At that, we part, and I go back home on my scooter, taking a few one-way streets the wrong way in the pink, glorious dawn, riding alongside the Corniche, passing les Catalans, the port, the Canebière, and ending up at the Cinq-Av' café, where I have a double espresso and a croissant—to celebrate the sunrise and play the film of last night over and over in my head, Alice's attentions to me, her smile, her breasts just begging to escape from her shirt, her way of dancing without showing off, aware of her effect on me. Alice . . .

Four days later she calls me. She wants some coke.

"I'm sick of going through Maël when I want something.

I'd rather deal directly with you. You understand, right?"

I understand, I *totally* understand, and I tell her to meet me at the Cinq-Av'. I'm a little disappointed, but at least it's a start: we need to reconnect, be like we were when we were childhood friends.

Before long I've become her official dealer, but I must say, to her credit, that she doesn't treat me that way. Every time she buys a gram of powder or crystal from me, she takes her time, we have a drink together, talk about everything under the sun, about what she's studying—literature, with little conviction—about her younger brother, the music she likes, the movies she's just seen. I share less about myself, but still, little by little, I tell her things: my parents, Italy, that Piedmont village where I spent every August from zero to sixteen, smack—something I absolutely don't want to touch—and my desire for a life that won't look like the ones I see sinking into the mud all around me.

What can I say, except that the promise we made when we were ten—unformulated, maybe not understood at all—is now being fully kept? The more I see Alice, the more I'm convinced that I was born to love her, her and no one else. I love the natural, spontaneous way she always is with me; I love her veiled beauty, her gray eyes, her straight hair with very slight curls in it, her fresh cheeks and the click of the bracelets on her forearms.

I also love that other Alice, the one she occasionally reveals when she looks at me with an almost wild despair and then pulls herself back immediately. Those days when her lips tremble slightly, when tears come to her eyes, wiped away too quickly for me to mention them, for me to ask her, *But what's wrong, Alice? Alice, please tell me* . . .

All I do is stiffen in my seat and look tough because I know she likes that—it's my Italian bad-boy side. I still have the Tower in my wallet but I don't think much about it. I should take it upon myself to burst the tight framework of our relationship, so strangely chaste, and try to learn more about that sadness, about what's driving her to take more and more drugs—coke, grass, and ecstasy.

One day, I happen to see three parallel scars on her wrist.

"What's that? You into scarification now?"

"Not anymore. I used to be."

"What do you get out of that?"

"Dunno. It's a teenage thing, you know: lots of girls do it. It relieves tension. After, you feel better: you can go on again."

"What tension?"

"Don't worry about it. It's over, I don't do it anymore, okay?"

A short time later, she asks me if I can get her some smack. And I can, of course.

"But what do you want smack for? Nobody does it anymore, you know."

"All the more reason. I just want to try it. They say it's not bad for a coke comedown."

"Except you'll have a smack downer and that can be mean."

"Fine, can you get me some or not?"

"Okay. But I want to be with you the first time you do it."

So she has her first sniff at my place. I tested it in advance, me who never takes anything, just to see if it's cut with too much crap. I've never trusted heroin. It's not something to party with, it's not something you have a nice evening with. Besides, Maël and his pals from Roucas-Blanc, La Pointe-Rouge, and the Périer heights never ask me for it. I have just a few customers who buy some, old people who look like they can handle it; otherwise, I wouldn't sell them any.

What can I say? I give in. I should tell Alice to stick with coke or go get her shit somewhere else. I should tell her: *Come on, let's get the car, I'm taking you to Italy. We'll walk around Vieux Nice, we'll swim on the beach at Menton and then, you'll see, it's the Roya Valley, you'll like it; we go over the Tende Pass, we go back down to Torino.*

I'll buy you ice cream on Piazza San Carlo, and then, I know a spot, a spot just for you, Alice, an inn under the pines in the mountains, one of my uncles runs it, come on . . .

But I don't say anything and she snorts the line I laid out for her on a corner of the table, leans back on the cushions of my folding couch, and says: "Wow! God, Salvatore, it's too good, you should try it! No comparison to coke!"

And then she gets very talkative because of the magic powder coursing through her veins. She talks a good part of the night, about everything, about adult life: she's afraid she won't be able to fit in, she always feels like she's somewhere else . . .

"What can I tell you, Salvatore? Everything's fine but nothing is."

The midsummer heat has dropped, it's nice out, we stand at the window and smoke in the summer night, the way I've done so by myself for years. I put my hand on her scarred wrist to quiet her and my fingers look for the little serrations of her three scars. "Shhh, be quiet for a minute, you'll hear them."

"Hear what?"

"The animals in the zoo. They howl all night."

She stares at me, stupefied. Unlike coke, heroin shrinks the size of the pupils, which makes her eyes look much lighter, astonishingly blue in her pale face.

"Hey, you're nuts, the zoo's closed. The animals left a long time ago!"

"That's what you think. Just listen."

She plays the game and listens hard in the direction of the chestnut trees in the park. Her face lights up and she smiles, like I just gave her a priceless gift. "Holy shit, you're right! I can hear them! I heard a lion! And a bird!"

"That must be a parrot, the birdcage is full of them."

What can I say? After that midsummer's night dream impossible to relate, that moment when I thought I'd gotten her to understand that life is sad for everybody but it's up to her to reenchant it a little, I keep selling her dope: less and less coke and more and more heroin.

She moves to shooting up, the first time under my guidance, in my studio on rue Lacépède, but the next times without me, and without my being able to say or do anything.

She changes, she gets thinner, loses her childish plumpness and the luster of her hair and the sparkle in her eyes. When I try to put a brake on her intake, she smiles: "Please, Salvatore."

"Alice, it's just that I don't want to see you destroy yourself. And it's my fault too!"

"Nothing's your fault. If you weren't here, I'd get it somewhere else. It's just that I need it, that's all—to get through a rough spot."

She always says that: it's temporary, she's going to stop. Unfortunately, I know druggies too well, their promises, their lies, and all their lousy little betrayals.

Since I ration her powder and cut it before selling it to her, she finds another dealer. And given the quantities she needs now, I suspect she's doing some shady things to get the bread. She stops going to classes. "That doesn't lead anywhere anyway."

We keep seeing each other. Sometimes she comes to shoot up at my place and I don't say anything because these days, it's the only chance I have of spending a little time with her.

"Alice, don't you see you're fucking up?"

"And you, you're *not* fucking up? Don't you think you're going to get busted one day?"

"It's not the same thing."

"Where are you going, Salvatore, with your crappy little drug business? You're going to do this till you're how old?"

"Yeah, but at least I'm not zonked out half the time."

"Right, you're clean, you're lucid, you're in control. And where does that get you?"

I'm not up to fighting with her, I give up right away. "Dunno, Alice. I just want . . . you to be okay. Less sad."

"But what if I want to be sad? What if being sad is what makes me who I am?"

I should laugh in her face and hug her, but I don't dare. Her absence of desire for me is too blatant to ignore. I want her, but she's the last woman in the world I would try to force myself on. I want her to love me, to admit that we're made for each other and the Palais Longchamp is the kingdom where we could reign for centuries to come.

All I do is watch the slow, methodical destruction of her body and soul, very much in accordance with what the Arcana number sixteen card predicted. Esmée Villalonga could warn me against it, if only I went back to traverse de l'Observatoire from time to time. But I don't, not anymore. My parents are losing it and vote far right now, not to mention that they've found their own weapon of mass destruction in liquor and I myself have enough destruction and waste to spare with Alice.

Still, one day when we're having coffee at the Cinq-Av' café and she's about to leave, I grab her by the arm, I look her in the eye, and forcing myself to control the trembling of my voice, even adding a hint of mockery to save us both from melodrama, I say: "Don't forget, you're the woman of my life."

She gets out of it with a little joke that saves us both from embarrassment, but I know she believes me.

Strangely enough, it's from that day on that she seems to get back on her feet. First I'm glad to see her put a bit of flesh on her bones, regain her curves and her color. She doesn't ask me to for dope anymore, she doesn't come shoot up at my place anymore, and our conversations in the café are evasive and cheerful. I'd be fully reassured if those same conversations weren't totally empty and pointless, as if she'd retreated to a place even more remote than where heroin took her. I'd be fully reassured if the look in her eyes wasn't so frightening, despite her beautiful smile, her cheeks full and pink again, and that sensational chest. Alice . . .

And then what had to happen happens: the network of my

quiet middle-aged guy in the Drôme is dismantled by the cops. I have to split, get rid of my cell phones, close my pad, and hit the road to Italy, the same one I would've liked so much to show Alice. I'm going to hole up in the country at my uncle's inn, wait till they forget about me, and see what happens.

Before leaving, I still have time to hide my stock—weed, coke, ecstasy, a little smack. You never know: when I come back, I might need it. On place Henry Dunant, there's a fence that's easy to climb, and bingo, there I am again in the green paradise of my childhood, not far from the terrace and the colonnade where I first met Alice. I bury the shit pretty deep under the thickets by the old observatory, in a place where in another time my queen and I had buried a whole treasure of marbles, taking an oath to come back and dig it out when we were all grown up. A forgotten oath, like so many others.

What can I say? Time goes by in the Piedmont, just like everywhere else. I work a little for my uncle. He's definitely not as much of an asshole as my father, but still. When I was in such a rush to get rid of my cell phones, I lost all my contacts, Alice's among them. At the time it seemed best, but six months later I'm beginning to miss her, and Marseille too.

Since the cops don't seem to have traced anything back to me, since nobody bothered my parents, since my studio on rue Lacépède wasn't searched, I finally return, and on the very first night I have a smoke at my window, my eyes lost in the swaying foliage of the chestnut trees, waiting in vain for the cries of the lions and parrots.

The next day and the days after that, I spend hours at the café where we used to hang out, but there's no sign of Alice. The waiters I ask about her don't even know who I'm talking about. They're new, they don't know her any more than they know me, and there's no lack of pretty girls with brown hair and blue eyes in Marseille.

So much for Alice. I won't give up looking for her but I have decisions to make: should I dig up my dope, start dealing again, or find myself a job as a waiter in a café by the port?

It's summer again, the season that suits my birthplace best, the season that shows it in its real light, its noble rot, and its smells, stronger than ever; the red dust left on cars by the southern wind, the glassy sea with just enough waves to lap the port with suction-like sounds that show its lassitude, the shrill screams of the girls, the loud boasts of the guys, a whole world I feel excluded from.

I start waiting tables at a restaurant on quai de Rive Neuve while hoping for something better to turn up. Waiting for . . . nothing much. For Alice to come back, for her to feel good without needing dope, for her eyes to look the way they did before, for us to be ten again with a whole palace just for the two of us, a whole kingdom to explore, with its stone bulls, its grottoes and cascades, its bandstand and phantom zoo.

And then one day, at the terrace of the restaurant where I work, I recognize Maël, my former customer. My heart leaps. "Maël?"

"Hey, Farès! How are you?"

"Okay, and you?"

He still has his pleasant face and his good manners, polite and all. And if I know him, he must be keeping up his jolly student life and shoving lots of coke into his nose every weekend.

"Like a drink?"

"No, I can't, actually, I work here. But I'll get you one. What do you want?"

"A Stella. Thanks. But sit down with me for a minute—look, there's no one out here."

"Okay, but I have to make it quick."

The heat is stifling. It won't go down for another two or three hours and Maël seems delighted to see his glass arrive all misted up. After exchanging a few slightly strained banalities, for we clearly have nothing to say to each other, I risk it: "Hey, Maël, you wouldn't have news of Alice by any chance?"

"Alice? Which Alice?"

"Alice T. I saw her at your place once."

"What, you knew Alice?"

"Yeah. We're childhood friends."

Maël, nice little Maël, suddenly looks distraught over his Stella. "Yo, dude, you mean you don't know?"

With me, Maël always thinks he has to talk like a guy from the projects. It irritates me right now but I don't let on, as I feel my anxiety rising.

"Well, no."

"She died, man."

"How?"

"OD."

"What? But she'd stopped!"

"Yeah, that's what everyone said. She'd been super-clean for three months at least. We partied together in April and she was in great shape—the Alice from before, see what I'm sayin'?"

The Alice from before, are you kidding me? The Alice from before had disappeared a long time ago, but I forgive Maël for his lack of insight and his *wesh mec*—yo, *dude*—and other annoying expressions, trying to make people forget where he comes from.

"So what happened?"

"Like I said, she OD'd. Except it might not have been an accident. You really don't know, bro?"

He's going to get a fist in his face if he keeps calling me "bro" or "dude," but I've got to know: "No, I really don't. Actually, I wasn't in Marseille. I just got back."

"They found her at the Palais Longchamp. She lived in the Cinq-Avenues, you know."

"Yeah, I know."

"Really weird. The newspapers talked about it, but if you weren't in Marseille . . ."

"No, I wasn't. Come on, spit it out!"

"Well, apparently she took all her stuff—the dope, the rig—and let herself be locked inside the park, or she somehow got in."

Alice knew the passage through place Henry Dunant, I'd showed it to her. We had climbed the fence to spend part of the evening in the grass, drinking and smoking. That was before I let her try the smack that killed her.

"Anyway, she did that at night, like around two months ago. You know where she chose to shoot up?"

Yes, I know, or I think I know, but I let him relish the macabre details. *Wesh mec*—yeah, right.

"She went into the fountain, you know, the big thing at the entrance to the park, over the cascade—there are bulls or something there, see. Actually, I never noticed them before. I never go that way, it's a bad neighborhood, dead, but okay, anyway, she climbed up on one of the bulls and she shot her shit into her veins, a crazy dose apparently, no way she could've survived, that's why they think it's suicide. Some kids found her the next day, can you imagine the shock? You're a kid, you're playing, and *bang*, you bump into a corpse with a rig still in her arm!"

I get up, knocking my chair over, I ditch Maël, the restaurant, and my new job, and I run away, I run like mad, I run up the Canebière, through le Chapitre, I take boulevard Longchamp still running, and so what if my heart is pounding, if my sides are aching and I'm gasping for breath? I get to the main entrance to the park, pass the statues of the lions devouring their prey, the fountains, the double ceremonial staircase, the chariot of the Durance triumphantly pulled by the stone bulls. And presto, like in the old days with Alice, I climb over the railing and get on my steed. The stone is still warm from the sun and I press my cheek against the colossal neck. From there I see what Alice must have seen before she died, the row of fountains, the flowering lawns, the trees on boulevard Longchamp, and that statue we loved and always saluted, a triton melancholically blowing into his conch for all eternity.

I cry, I talk to Alice, I draw her out of her incomprehensible sadness, I cradle her with tender words that would have restored her confidence in herself. Except that I'm too late, I get there after the game's over, I get there after she's met her fate, the point of no return predicted by the Arcana number sixteen that she reached before I did.

On boulevard Longchamp the light is dancing in the tree leaves and the trolleys are clanging their joyful bells. I pull the Tower card out of my wallet, tear it up into little pieces, and scatter them in the wind. They go fluttering over the steps of the monumental staircase, at the exact spot where Alice gave it to me one day. It was already the end, but we didn't know it.

PART III

Dirty & Rebellious

KATRINA

BY FRANÇOIS BEAUNE
La Belle de Mai

"It's crazy what happened to us on the 49 the other day," Alain tells me. "If I could've filmed the whole thing, YouTube would've flipped.

"You see, that bus, the 49, the one for pygmies dressed in plastic, you can't even sit in there, it goes through La Belle de Mai and down La Joliette. You get tossed all over the place. The driver works thirty-six faces of the city for you. With all the bumps and dead rats. You start sitting up front and you end up in the back with your head in the engine.

"What I'm saying, there's an asshole of the month every month. And if you're looking for him, nine times out of ten he's on the 49, trust me. That day I scored a bull's-eye, fate's always against you here, Allah really did his job.

"Bus 49, the whole cast of crabs moves sideways in there. A fucking aquarium. Sometimes even, as if we didn't have enough dickheads, tourists get on, like the other day, this couple from Mars: Is this the way to the MuCEM? they ask the driver. What the hell you take the 49 for to get to the MuCEM? I feel like telling them. You can't walk the Vieux-Port like everybody else? Besides, in Bavaria, all you got is MuCEMs, why you coming here to see what you got in your own country? Mr. Driver, we bought two tickets one way, make sure you tell us when to get off. Shit, if you miss the MuCEM you're not a tourist. The MuCEM, you know, that black thing there with its footbridge like a huge pipe, the coal shed, how can you miss it, you don't watch the documentary channel, that's for sure. Bavarians.

"Now that it's going through the docks, and past the whores who congregate on place de Lenche, it attracts an impressive bunch of losers—Krauts, Chinese. Not to mention the culture-vultures who stop at la Friche, with funny hair and Paris accents, a whole bunch of nuts all year round, not too cultured, believe you me; and also rich kids with problems, not totally hatched, going slumming with their skateboards and baseball caps. Boxer shorts. Jeans hanging down below their asses. They all join the competition to see who can bug us the most in our great neighborhood of La Belle de Mai. They send us their crappy offspring and then are surprised when their offspring sink the mayor's three-master (you know, the one he anchored in the Vieux-Port right in front of city hall that they once used as a restaurant).

"So anyway, the other day on the bus, there we are, like schmucks on the day they draw the lottery numbers, stuck at the Réformés Canebière stop for the last half hour, a nice gang of assholes who like to get fucked over, and frankly they're right not to hold back, they know we love it. We're sweating like monkeys in winter, smiling into the rearview mirror. It's fascinating to watch.

"The bus isn't moving, no A/C, more like the opposite. As if the city government had sprung for a microwave to defrost all the rotten meat of us pushovers of the 3rd arrondissement, with our greenhorn faces, a mixed dish of reheated frozen foods—the Picard chain but not from Picardy, all kinds of colors, polite assholes waiting nicely for the driver to deign to finish pissing. Seated standing, everybody. We scratch the time, we pick our snotballs. So we can make sense of our suffering, not die of suffocation. One day you begin to get used to it, accept your fate, and you end up choosing torture over death.

"I mean, it's a swimming pool here now. Sweat drips out of your hair and arms, right down into the smartphones—they now have the toilet bowl app, thanks to the satellites and all. Little kids slide their fingers along their screens. They've had this game for a while now. The short fat guy sitting next to me in Adidas sweatpants with his iPhone screen covered with watermelons and bananas that he bursts with his index finger—I tell myself it's getting worse and worse. That shitty little asshole's making a real shakshouka out of it. He smells like soap, so okay. Without saying a word he smashes up the whole Noailles market. You can bet he's not gonna go to one of those fancy schools up north. His father probably sells fruit and vegetables and when this kid has a break he screws watermelons to get rid of his Oedipus complex. I did an internship in psych recently, I know what I'm talking about. What can you do with this kind of kid when he grows up? You'll explain to him he shouldn't kill fruit?

"Me, I'm no spring chicken, I'm going on fifty-seven. Fifty-seven, that's an important number and I'm not gonna lie to you. For over twenty-five years I been working at the city hall for the 2nd and 3rd sectors. You hear me? The numbers. They mean something.

"Honestly, I work hard and I'm all for young people. I was fifteen when we came back to Marseille. I remember I had to readjust, find my place again—and it wasn't easy. My father couldn't live north of Valence in Givors anymore. My mother couldn't stand being so far from her mother, it was too painful for her.

"Now I know everybody here. But the problem nowadays is, we don't have kids anymore, just lunatics. I've been the moderator of the junior forum on the city hall website for a year now, and I see all kinds of crazy shit and every time I count their neurons, I can't believe they have so few of them, it's a Guinness record every time. Like the amount of sperm thrown away in our Marseille village of Les Goudes these last few years. You read the article, right? You realize the massacre? The Danes are the ones who counted them, they're serious up there and I trust them. Billions of tadpoles go into the wringer every night because of the pesticides, insecticides, and all the other fucking cides. So you can blame the same phenomenon on those kids' neurons. Today, aside from smashing fruit, there's zero motivation, they don't give a shit about all you're doing for them. The girls are a little better but really, they're no Rosa Luxemburg either.

"Since we're waiting to start, I look to my right through the burning window—a woman sitting under the bus shelter, a stroller, and a three-month old kid, crying. I feel sorry for her right away. Beautiful evasive blue eyes—Kabyle I'd say—but faded, lost, like they went through too many washes. The chador falling over a plastic sweater, you could almost see the bottles of Evian in it; same thing with the standard-model I'm-ashamed-of-my-body-and-I-want-to-hide-it djellaba dress—and anyway I'm finished, screwed, dead married. But you can imagine how hot it is under that thing? The girl's dressed for cross-country skiing—the poor version.

"She does look poor, the poor girl. Even the stroller's a piece of crap. The baby's howling like a Mediterranean ferry siren. I look in her eyes, she has fear inside her. How can I describe it, it's an all-purpose kind of fear. For the baby, fear he'll catch cold, deep-in-her-eyes fear of being in the city, fear something will happen, the husband will get mad, fear the little one will die because of a bad decision, not knowing how to manage, fear of making the slightest gesture, fear of being guilty when you never did anything bad.

"A guy sits down next to her on the bench. She looks elsewhere because she's on a public bus. Even if he weren't there she would probably just stare into space. Out of precaution, see. While waiting to dissolve, disappear into the aquarium of the wall-to-wall carpet, the baby wipes, the TV, and the smell of lamb's-neck stew the world has built for her. Waiting to go back to her stifling place. To be saved by Allah, who will close all the locks on the door behind her, from the highest to the lowest, and even the locks of her head to be on the safe side, that way it's all over.

"As for the guy, he's a pig, he doesn't know how to get her to notice him. He should have learned some other words than *your cunt* and *your breasts*. But with him it's very limited, you can see right away he's not gonna hit on her with a love sonnet by Ronsard.

"I look at her so much I start thinking like her. She must tell herself stuff like how can I get on the bus with the stroller? Should I sit or stand with the baby? If he cries do I keep him in my arms or do I restroller him once the bus starts moving? Stuff like that. Maybe she's thinking of Mohammed too. What he's going to bring her back tonight. Since he buys just about anything at all, stolen stuff that fell off the garbage truck, to get himself forgiven for being a shitty husband. What's he gonna bring back? One of those plastic games that help babies learn how to walk, I'll bet. Something to eat up the little living space they have.

"The pig's moving his head, with his starving eyes. She's still in her bubble, but she can feel his presence. She rocks the kid to make him understand he's going too far, he should be ashamed, but even without looking at him she knows he's got nothing left to lose anyway. There he goes, he dares talk to her. You should see the animal. He gets her to understand there's something, madam, that's falling out of your pocket. With all the thieves around here, she should watch out. She doesn't answer, takes a pack of chewing gum out of her pocket and puts it in the other pocket.

"I get a better look at him too, now. Not tall, and like her, dressed in plastic recycled from mineral water bottles, sneakers, the little imitation-leather jacket straight from the boonies, all for 1.99, and his eyes not evasive, no, more like unstable, fixed on the inside and speaking to him of asses and cunts, the ass to forget, the cunt on the horizon, a fuck to quiet his fatigue, stop walking around without knowing where to go in the city. What do you expect them to think about, those jerks? No encyclopedia up there.

"He looks beat; it's sex, see, it's liquor too telling him it'll do him good, smashed already even though it's not late. The heat, of course. Feel an ass, follow it, finally a goal, a little peace, an ass with a chador, it's something from here at least, and if she wants, right away, but how to do it he must be asking himself, with the kid? I don't want to screw her if he's crying. It's impressive to watch those guys: you can almost see them thinking. No, I'd have to catch her in the kitchen. She puts the kid to bed and then I put it into her. Here, bitch, and don't forget your five prayers facing Mecca, I spit on whores like you, or I drill her on the living room table, from behind. She's not Kate Moss, the sister. Too bad if she just had a baby, that'll put her ovaries back in place.

"We waited for so long the driver finally shows up, an Arab for a change, see. I don't know this one. We must've disturbed him in the middle of a video game, he looks irritated, but we don't blame him, we don't say anything, we don't say, okay, you done with your pee? You zipped up your fly all the way? No, we don't say anything, us jerks from the 3rd, we don't dare complain. Otherwise they'll serve us up even worse, a pygmy, a Martian, a Breton, anything they can unload ends up our way.

"The woman asks the driver to open the back door, to lift up the stroller. The pig offers to help her, she can't refuse. They find each other standing side by side. Me, I disconnect, I put on my headphones and my music, those two distract me too much.

"Right opposite me, sitting two rows down, there're two fat Jewish women, real Sephardic, stuff that fills up the whole seat. Actually, I notice, it's incredible, we're almost all obese on this bus. Every time you take the 49 it's a reality TV show. You never know the theme. Today the show is fat people: how do fat people deal with tsunamis?

"Me, I'm fat. I'm okay with it because I like good things. Except for the last time, I've always voted Communist, see, and I've always loved life. They're superb, those two women, and well-dressed too, big dark red scarves with maybe some green, some auburn, and then creased slacks and little boots. They're coming back loaded with their shopping from the Centre Bourse mall, all precious, happy, must be Moroccans, hairy like that, with big pulpy mouths, lipstick matching the scarf, the kind of detail that drives you wild. Impressive, the sweat streaming from their impeccable skin. Like a torrent in the middle of the two breasts! It's an equatorial forest. Niagara—not the rock group, the real one, the Falls.

"They're melting like popsicles. It's not just drops on their mustaches. I'm not exaggerating, there's practically as much sweat there as sauce on a Chinese spring roll. Chimneys like their cleavage must draw well, for sure. They're fountain-chimneys! Amazing. If they let me do it I'll change them into statues for Longchamp Park.

"And they're nice, good manners, good girls talking to each other in low voices, laughing into each other's ears, discretely even, Turkish delight syllables, smiling and happy, see, must've made two good arranged marriages; they're on their way to their mother-in-law's who has the A/C turned up to the max, and they sit down at the table and let-me-heat-up-the-meatballs and then they open their bags of lingerie to show everybody.

"Their breasts, let me tell you, there's enough to make four or six with them, the husbands have a feast and so do we. Hey, don't tell me we can't spend five minutes admiring the wonders of nature. My kids I moderate on the junior forum, they're not normal, they're like infected, formatted by their porn movies, they can't understand beauties like these.

"Last time, I'm not kidding, there's one who writes in the forum: *Hi everybody, so here's my problem, I egaculated into my hand the other day and then tree days later I penatrated my girlfriend with my fingers, does she have a chance of being pregnant?*

"What can you do with kids like that? And then the questions from his colleagues like: *How much time does sperm live in the open air?* And another: *Open air's like the normal air you have at home? Or like the air outside?*

"They don't know a thing, see, you got to explain what open air is! Lucky they know how to breathe. Me, I'm there for them, I answer, I explain, I say it's good to ask questions when you don't know something, but Jesus, that's not not-knowing even, it's something else, it's a whole other dimension. Two weeks I been explaining sperm while the Danes are telling us we don't have any left, and that's what's serious, the percentage of sperm per centi-liter, what's left of it compared to what we had before is nothing, and that asshole the other day with his stupid nickname, Angel of Darknitude, asking us: *So guys, here's my problem, I slept on my friends' living room couch and I came without realizing it, so my underwear was dirty, I didn't clean it and now I'm scared, if my girlfriend sits down on the couch naked and my sperm touches her vagina, is she going to get pregnant?*

"That drives me nuts, see. How do they bring them up, they invent stuff like that? And then, they're the ones who've gone to school. So just imagine the other ones, jerking off all over the Internet like total ignoramuses, going by their rule of three: blow-job, sodomy, and facial ejac. After that, don't be surprised if they get even dumber than us.

"Okay, finally, the bus is taking off from the Réformés Canebière stop. That is, it stops revving up. That sound drives me up the wall, but it stops when the bus moves. After twenty yards the mo-ron bus takes a sharp turn, making its way down rue des Abeilles to the Saint-Charles station. Parenthesis: the only station built on a hill. A real Marseille idea, that, just to brag a little, hey, you Parisians! Look how classy we are! You don't have stations like that up there in your Nord-Pas-de-Calais. Us, we put our trains way up and we think it looks good. Besides, we plan to build the next one up on Mount Sainte-Victoire, with money from the Norwegian mafia.

"I can't help looking at that nitwit pig, he keeps staring with his little snaky eyes, red from liquor, at the handles of the stroller so's not to stare at her panties. She's still holding the baby in her arms, maybe he's hungry, maybe he wants his mother's breast. What should I do, get up and smack him one as a preventive measure? I could, but people would get all worked up about it, they won't understand I have good reasons to act that way. You never know what to do in these situations. The guy may have a knife. Maybe she's coming back from tests, vaccinations for the kid. She's all white, like women back in the day, when it was the fashion to look like some shitty milkman.

"The problem is, actually, between the slut and the saint, what do you do, since there's only two models? Men and all my kids in the forum have to deal with that. Everything's too dirty inside their heads. When you look at a girl's mouth or eyes to make yourself come, you know there's a problem. To get to screw whores after that, those assholes rob other poor schmucks; I've been a civil servant for twenty-five years and I've never seen such a low level, the Gang of Barbarians—that anti-Semitic gang who tortured that Jewish boy to death—that's their mindset, there's no sense of right or wrong anymore, a porn film in each hand, a Lamborghini for the big family wedding on the Vieux-Port, you can see them on Saturdays all dressed up for the occasion, big bikes and Porsches for show when they don't have a penny in the bank.

"The other day I went to see Dire Straits at the Dôme to relax. Dire Straits, those guys never get old, that Mark Knopfler's still just as good, I'm telling you, the guy's a pro, short as he is with his bandanna, he's a giant. All the kids listening to their rap, they'd do better to listen to Dire Straits, there's no way you can't like them, impossible. Me, I'd be glad to take those kids to a concert, let them discover something different than their crappy music; I'd take them to the opera too, but who'd sign up if I posted the invitation on the site? Always the same ones, the ones who go already; I'm not particularly fond of faggots, but come on, guys like Sexion d'Assaut, they should put them in the slammer, that's all they deserve. Kids don't need that kind of example. With my wife, you know why we don't live in the neighborhood anymore? Let me tell you: when you keep hearing La Belle de Mai is the poorest neighborhood in Europe even counting Greece, shit, enough already, my wife doesn't want to be the poorest woman in Europe, me neither, and my children—you bet they don't.

"My grandfather arrived in La Belle de Mai without knowing where he landed. It was the 1920s, when there was still work in France, when there were still *workers*. Remember that? Ever saw real workers, or are you too young? Imagine men with real hands, perfectly adapted to hold pickaxes, peasants in fact, who moved to cities and never counted the hours. Hey, all they knew was the sun, none of that RMI or RSA crap, the handouts those bums get from the government, no, they worked out of pride, not to die of hunger, with real muscles, not muscles from the gym club, not that display to screw the missus like in the Saturday-night movie.

"My grandfather, he got himself a factory job. He came from Tuscany, from Capoliveri, on the Island of Elba where Napoleon took a little vacation. Twenty years later, he could send for his wife, a great cook. After twenty years, you hear me? He wasn't like the Kosovars and the gypsies from here. He didn't make it to Marseille like a dog, didn't send his kids out to beg or whore on the sidewalk, no, he worked hard, that's all, and he didn't buy the junk he needed at the Porte d'Aix market. And a long time after that he opened up a café, my father arrived, and here I am in front of you, and I can be proud, hold my head high.

"I'm telling you, the 49 is like the neighborhood. I don't lis-ten to the people who bitch about it anymore. On place Bernard Cadenat, the bus leans over and that's when Katrina, the big fat Comorian, the star of our story, gets on. I call her Katrina but she must have another name, she's a barrel, that woman, and in fact she has a barrel with her. Katrina's the kind who always has a bar-rel with her, see. In case it might come in handy. Close to six feet, huge arms, huge legs, a discus thrower who'd also dabbled with weights and the hammer-throw. She's all we needed! At least her man helps her hoist up her Jerrican. The bus sags with the new weight. The front tire no longer a rugby ball, but nearly the shape of a Frisbee. If the 49 was an elevator, with her, the Jerrican, and all of us, we'd break the Guinness record for excess weight.

"She elbows her way to the middle, sliding her Jerrican along, so the bus is balanced again. I don't know what she has in there, but it looks impressive. I tell myself right away it's food, some dish cooked in a special sauce maybe. I'm sitting in the back, the boat rocks, I put on a playlist that works for the 49, tailor-made. Dire Straits, Simple Minds, the Scorpions, Queen. Now that should be called classical music these days. In a thousand years they'll still be listening to Mark Knopfler. Maybe more than the Mozarts and the Ravels. Got nothing against them but I think they do a little too much Mozart and the rest. Make way for the young, for chrissake!

"My Sephardic friends get off at Jourdan Bonnardel, fine, but other people are getting on, shit, the bus is full, they're all standing, talking about their problems, and I can hear only the guitars. My ears aren't a garbage dump, I got myself Sony HD headphones, let them just try to rip them off, I'm well known here, they respect me, but sometimes they forget that this is the Italian neighborhood, don't piss us off. Pasolini, Antonioni, Rossellini, and Paolo Conte, all Italians, and Freddy Mercury who sings like an Italian, he's the English Luis Mariano.

"Dino Risi comedies! I can tell you, I didn't spend my time in junior forums, and as far as girls with strollers, just try to touch them. We were animals, but with principles. It was the time of the black leather jackets, me, my jacket was sort of dark gray, I remember. I loved that jacket. Anyone bugged me, I had brass knucks, Greek philosophers we were not.

"We all went out armed, that's what you did in those days. The kids today act like tough guys but they're just acting, they act tough to be tough, like the Sheetrock at Boulanger's. Real rough times, the eighties. They make me laugh now with their three stiffs a month. Just do the count again, son, back in the day it was a massacre, you wouldn't set foot or hand in Belsunce, and your daughter went all the way around through Cassis to avoid the center, and that was *before* six p.m.

"I had my technique down pat. I bombarded the girls with words. You might say I was the talker of the gang. I was the one who worked my tongue before enjoying our rewards. And I was the first to get it: just Mediterranean imports we got back then, black, Arab. No Chinese for chrissake. Back in the day we got only solid stuff with a ten-year guarantee.

"In nightclubs, the other Emilio, my buddy, he always wanted a blowjob before coming out with a complete sentence. Real muscle, we kept him, but God, you should've seen that ape, he caused problems, nothing serious, but the problems rubbed off on us, and that was more serious. He'd take out his dick before he said good evening, he'd screw up our plans; after that I'd spend days trying to fix things; I found ways, like in *Ridicule*. Did you see the movie? You didn't see it, you should. I'd talk their heads off, it made them all confused and the poor girls couldn't understand anything anymore, they ended up doing all the stuff that would make you blush, on the rocks, under a boat, under the tarp covering the propeller of a freighter. My sentences had no end. They were like a thing that drills you and enters deep into your skin, you can't get rid of it, an octopus or a giant sea urchin that sticks you where it hurts. On the Island of Elba the ancestors fished tuna and whales. But me, I'd adapted my instinct to rock sluts, and I had a feast, my arms were like fishnets.

"But at the same time I was going to school, I was serious, I stuck to it, I was sort of a hood, but a serious hood, respectful, mean in the good sense of the word. If I fucked up somebody, either he deserved it or it did him good, or both. Sometimes that puts things back in place. I even got my Bac that way, got my high school diploma while practicing all those extracurricular activities.

"My father programmed me to be a civil servant, he didn't want me to take over the café that was waiting for him when we came back, serving pastis to zombies, no, he didn't want that. His mother made him swear I'd be somebody. And since I was programmed by all of them and they all cared about me and were so supportive, not like my kids there who don't have help from their family, I managed to become a civil servant for the city of Marseille.

"It's all different now, trying to make something out of yourself. The assholes are in finance, in the big banks, the IMF fucks us on a daily basis, the kids get that all right, it makes them want to throw up and I can understand; when you're screwed by Goldman Sachs you don't exactly feel great about yourself, you don't tell yourself how you're gonna get revenge. You know you gotta get the hell out of here, but it's all globalized now, where can you go, everything's the same everywhere, same thing in every goddamn place, you're in their radar, where're you gonna go now so's not to get screwed? Senegal? Senegal's same as here, almost worse. You think it's better to get screwed by black capitalists? There are none so distant that fate cannot bring together.

"I thought I'd leave, not for Givors but Lyon for instance, bust out of this zoo, this pile of assholes. Marseille is a net that drags up everybody's shit. Nobody sorts it out. People turn round and round daily and they go crazy, of course. Frankly, if I didn't have a cushy job at city hall taking care of all those disadvantaged kids I would've packed my bags fast, let me tell you, I wouldn't be here anymore. But where, that's the thing. The colonies now, they're all corrupt, even for us there's no fun in the world anymore. La Belle de Mai, I like it, I'm telling you. I take my ride on the 49, I observe, I know it well, in fact I know it perfectly. Where do you want me to go that's better?

"The children left and they were right. I don't hold it against them, it's the way things are, I can tell you that as a Frenchman you're always an immigrant everywhere, we're all in the same boat. Me, I'm already on the other side of the tracks, see, it's progress, being in the Longchamp sideshows I made progress. They put those stupid giant arty plaques in the tunnel. Designed with our money by all those asshole artists from la Friche. That must have cost us morons a pretty penny. They think they're improving our reality with the black stuff from the exhaust. They think the plaques will distract us, make us think of something else. But me, ever since they've been up there in the tunnel, I can tell you I see the filth behind them five times more. I can smell it through every pore. All those jokers gathered together in what used to be our factory. Instead of giving work to the kids, they make us panels to hide the ugly stuff, so we shouldn't be so mad; but there's no jobs, I don't give a shit about your art, first get rid of those parasites, then put workers there instead. That's what you'll do if you want me to be happy, neighborhood kids who need a job, who want to work, and there're plenty of them for chrissake! Then you can do whatever you feel like, bring over bums from Vietnam to paint the tunnels, as many as you like for all I care.

"I'm not against art, I even like it, but hey, great art, real painting like in the Renaissance, not their vulturish concepts. Me, I'm as racist about that kind of bastard as about the riffraff that smashes up cars. My father was born here, my grandfather was not even twenty when he landed, and at that time the French government didn't lecture us with those Picassos who come show off at the factory. Artists had their dignity then, they respected work, and besides, they were all Communists, like us, they loved the people, and whether you were Italian or Spanish or Armenian you were the people first, but now there's no more people, no more solidarity, it's every man for himself because everybody talks on behalf of the people.

"Way things work now, I can see the multinationals decide what we get to eat. They don't give a shit about us, they just want to suck our blood, fuck us, and throw us into the sea. Back in the day there was respect, now you're constantly insulted, like on line at Mickey D's. Not that I don't like Mickey D's. Sometimes I even go to the one in Saint-Charles, it's convenient and you can eat outside. But I don't like being treated like a dog. Even if my kids in the forum are savages, which they are, I refuse to accept them being treated like dogs, I can't accept that, even if they don't deserve much and they're dumb as shit and they don't want to do anything—you can't leave them like that. Let's start by getting rid of the worst, all the new ones on the list, and try to take care of the ones who can be saved, the ones who speak a little French already and aren't surviving on scraps alone.

"Okay, we're arriving at Clovis Hugues, just in front of the bakery, you know, before the bus turns and goes back down. It's a very sharp turn, so the driver gives a big twist to his wheel, and to hold on, fat Katrina grabs the Jerrican, but it isn't heavy enough to hold her, I see everything like in slow motion, the can wants to stay flat on the floor but she grabs it as she falls, she grabs it like a treasure. And before collapsing like a crepe, a nice dark buckwheat crepe, her big body taking a good dive into space—normally only NASA sees stuff like this—the Jerrican goes bumping into one of the poles and now, fuck, the lid pops off, the thing opens, and now we're in the Philippines, the liquid spills out and there's a tidal wave on the bus! But not water, better than that, Comoros Katrina goes further than everybody, she beats all the Hurricane Cynthias, she cooks everything with oil.

"It spreads out, the first to go sliding is that pig, the one who was sniffing the chador, and that's nice to see. He does a whole figure-skating routine next to the stroller, incredible. He just discovered he has talent, he breaks his back and liquid spurts all over. After her dive, the Comorian next to him is now bleeding from the nose, she's emptying out, she apologizes to everybody, she says I'll clean it all up! I'll clean it all up! Mr. Driver, I'm a cleaning woman, don't worry! But how can you expect to clean up all that oil? You'd have to round up all the Ajax in the neighborhood. To top it all, an oil smelling of fish, all spotted with grease and veggie leftovers.

"Now the driver starts yelling: What's going on back there for chrissake? He turns around, see, and instead of heads all he sees are feet, sneakers, babouches, everybody ass over heels, a total massacre. And then I don't know what gets into him, he loses it. I see him opening the door of his cabin. I feel he doesn't understand what's happening but he wants to be with us, he wants to join the party. And now all it takes is a second of course, oooops, as soon as he sets a foot down, and it's even more violent, bang! Rabbit punch on the door, and smack down into the oil. Excuse me, driver! Katrina yells again. I'm so sorry! I'm gonna clean everything up! But he doesn't care anymore, he has slipped into the other world.

"When the firemen arrive they certify the death right away. There's fate for you, like I was telling you, how it makes fun of us, bides its time; whether it's God or Allah or another, when he wants to have a good laugh he goes for a little ride on the 49, it inspires him. That asshole, that moron of a driver, the only one who was really safe, really isolated from the oil. He had to be the one who croaked.

"Since that day nobody goes near the 49 bus. It's become a soapbox, too dangerous, even Nadia Comaneci couldn't stand in it. Only tourists take it because they don't know. Apparently, they arrive at the MuCEM with two broken ankles and a fractured jaw. They take off from Marignane with their crutches on the plane, and when they get back up there in their north, their friends ask, so how was Marseille? Was it fun? And they answer, yes, it was good but the city's kind of slippery. They put olive oil everywhere, even in the busses. From what I'd read, I thought the specialty there was the soap. Let me tell you, buddy, for us Bavarians, the culture of Marseille is very subtle, hard to figure out."

THE PROBLEM WITH THE ROTARY

BY PHILIPPE CARRESE

La Cayolle

Kevin's problem was the seven times table. Math in general but more specifically multiplication. The seven times table in particular. That's what his real problem was. He did okay with subtraction. For instance, lifting three doses on the sly from a dealer in the Paternelle housing projects and getting a return four times higher than the market price when he delivered the merchandise to his client on boulevard du Docteur Rodocanachi was math he could do more or less correctly. In that specific case, the four times table was no problem. Adding the price of the lines he sold during the day and counting the number of bills he had in his pocket, no problem either . . . But the seven times table was his current problem. The cops had dismantled his network of wholesalers in Castellane, at the other end of town. Kevin was forced to borrow great quantities of prime-quality coke from seven different retailers, and now he needed to repay them. Seven times. The figure was overwhelming and so was the situation. Kevin's other problem was his cowardliness. And also his limited vocabulary, but he was not aware of that.

Djawad's problem was the wheelie. He just couldn't do it. He'd hit the ground twice already and didn't dare accelerate too quickly on his super-powerful Booster. That drove him nuts. All his buddies in the Lauriers projects could do it: ride a whole street, a whole bus lane on the Prado from the first to the last stop, the whole width of the Grand Littoral parking lot, the whole

length of rue Tapis Vert. No problem. And on the very same stolen scooters pumped up by the same guy who specialized in mo-
torizing his neighborhood. Not him. Djawad's other problem was
the exorbitant price of his smuggled Booster. More specifically
how to repay it. But that problem was about to be settled. His
ride to the South End of the Phocaean city was supposed to allow
him to get rid of his debt, and even fill up a few times so he could
practice his wheelies.

Richard's problem was his mother. As is often the case with
Mediterranean adult males, Richard's problem was more material than psychological. He'd gotten rid of a large portion of his
Oedipus complex when he dumped his out-of-order progenitor
in a discreet retirement home, a chic place in the South End. But
that was precisely the problem with it: the glitzy die-in was all
too chic and was costing him a fortune. Richard's other problem
was his new BMW: flashy gray metallic—too flashy; a hands-free
rig with voice recognition optional, a ridiculous built-in refrig-
erator, memory leather seats (Alzheimer's brand), and golden
hubcaps—way too golden. His bedridden mother was costing
him, per year, the price of a Porsche Cayenne, an ideal vehicle
with all the indispensable accessories. Now Richard was riding
a BMW that was new, right, big, yes, metallic gray, right again,
but he raged at not being able to show off at the wheel. Driving
with your elbow leaning out the window, one foot above all those
Saint-Giniez hicks who need a loan to buy a lousy Mercedes sure
is something else.

Samantha's problem was her new beautician. To start with,
her name was Aïcha and the kid's Oriental origins were upsetting her. Samantha thought she'd been pretty clear; her cousin,
the owner of the beauty salon, was completely misguided: hiring
inexperienced girls from immigrant parents would lead to huge
problems one day or another, and faster than she thought. Samantha and her cousins were granddaughters of *pieds-noirs*, the
French from Algeria back then, so, understandably, some reflexes

are hard to get rid of. Samantha had painted an apocalyptic picture of what her cousin's salon would be like in a few months. A business with such a great location, at the edge of the last cool neighborhood in Marseille, a nail salon soon turned into an Islamic den run by women in burqas watched by bearded men in djellabas armed with Kalashnikovs. The discussion had stopped suddenly because Aïcha was back, carrying the coffee tray for the rich patrons of the salon, including an Arabica decaf from Peru for Samantha, very black with no foam and just a little sugar.

But more specifically, Sam's big problem was the loud red nail polish that she'd been wearing since midmorning. Not quite dry. But the time it took for the nail polish to dry was not the real problem. So damn red! And *that* kind of red, to top it off. Really . . . well, yes, red. It totally didn't match the body of her Fiat 500 (the red part of the Italian flag is completely different), it totally didn't match her iPhone case (she never should have picked one with glitter on it), it totally didn't match her Zara suit (sale season, the only one her size that was left: poppy red). A bright red that didn't match her present lipstick, which was a subtle red and outrageously expensive. She was trying to apply it to her lips while going over the many speed bumps of the Roy d'Espagne complex, her left knee wedged under the wheel to keep her driving more or less straight, her eyes riveted on the rearview mirror, on the delicate patches of her makeup. She *had* to look stunning. Because one of Samantha's other problems was Jan, her daughter Cindy's tennis teacher. Cindy! Another problem. The kid was only ten but a potential rival to her mother's career as a seducer.

The problem with Marseille's South End is how strangely mixed it is. Opulent homes stand alongside sordid housing projects, luxurious villas next to derelict cabins, and terraces with swimming pools look down on boat garages with rusty doors turned into summer dwellings. The beautiful Roy d'Espagne park spreads its lawns one alley away from the dilapidated Cayolle projects where the former shantytown that Le Corbusier had invented was razed to make way for a supermarket on permanent borrowed time, surrounded by local vandals. Baumettes prison is at the end of all the dead ends, the old stone mansions still shelter a handful of end-of-the-line aristocrats holding on to their ghosts and past glory, a few wealthy families are holed up in their famous architect-built houses, their windows stained with the sticky resin of the ever-present Aleppo pines. The nouveau riche and the old poor, the show-offs and the sluts. The sun weighs down on minds, the sea cools them off, the most beautiful streams in the whole world are within any tourist's reach, and the dealers are two bus stops away from the nearby junior high. Marseille, its pervasive mess, its generalized thoughtlessness. But is that really a problem . . . ?

The problem with the Beretta automatic are the bullet casings. Like with all automatic weapons. You shoot and you leave them everywhere. It looks more modern, true, but you don't exactly picture yourself as some experienced killer diving horizontally through a plate-glass window while emptying your charger with a piece from the last century. What's trendy now is the automatic pistol, especially the big-calibers, and especially all chrome and shiny. But if you don't know how to use it, it can jam, it's got a safety lock not to be confused with the safety of the charger, the casings make a loud noise when they scatter on the ground, they leave evidence for the crime lab, and it makes the cops' job incredibly easy: all they have to do is bend down to compare the number of bullets you've shot with the number of impacts on the stiff to evaluate very precisely the killer's expertise, his skill, or how near-sighted he is. The casings, that's the problem. Really. So Djawad's boss had equipped him with a Smith and Wesson, a .357 fitted with a four-inch barrel, black, inconspicuous, precise, and efficient, even in the hands of a novice. And when you shoot, the casings stay inside the cylinder.

The problem with the Smith and Wesson is the recoil. Especially in the hands of someone with no experience like Djawad.

Finding Kevin had been no problem at all: he was, as expected, in the basement of his building near the garbage room. And the Cayolle projects are not that big . . . Shooting had been no problem either. Djawad had come precisely for that and he was not about to go back like a shmuck to the North End after a failed mission. No way. There was bread involved, a scooter, and four tanks of gas. The first shot was no problem even though Djawad was killing one of his cronies for the first time. The problem was firing a second time, then a third, then firing a fourth time. Because of the recoil, yes, exactly. The first shot caught Kevin in the abdomen: he slumped to the ground right away. Djawad thought he could shoot his second bullet into the head of his boss's creditor just to be sure, but it got lost somewhere inside the garbage room. The third one landed on the windshield of an abandoned van, and the fourth went toward the hills out there, far away, in the limestone that borders the road toward Sormiou. With no consequences other than a deafening cannonade, the kind that doesn't impress anybody around here anymore. The South End is known as a hunting ground; it doesn't get as much media coverage as the neighborhoods that spread north of the Vieux-Port but it's just as deadly. Djawad was pissed. He took the trouble to get off his two-wheeler and stick the barrel of his gun to the dying Kevin's forehead. He fired, surprised once again by the recoil. Pissed off again. Because the problem with blood is that when it spurts out, it stains real bad.

Djawad wended his way home, extremely annoyed, his helmet not even fastened, as is customary in his project. His Adidas sweatshirt was all spotted with the blood of his first hit. He accelerated, found himself on the back wheel of his scooter, surprised to stay balanced. Wow! It was exhilarating. He accelerated some more. A wheelie! And one with staying power! So cool!

The problem with rotaries is they take you to several different roads. The other problem with these rotaries is that there is, after all, a certain system of right-of-way you must abide by and that's no small matter in the culture capital of cannabis and other herbs of Provence. Djawad's problem at that very moment had two very definite sources: the first was named Richard, the second liked to be called Sam, even though the nickname sounded more masculine than Samantha.

As he was entering the rotary at la Cayolle, Richard's problem was still an ego problem. He didn't have the Porsche Cayenne he deserved but his sedan was expensive enough to entitle him to all kinds of spectacular, bold actions: yielding right-of-way was for the underclasses, the nobodies, the proletariat used to obeying the narrow rules governing our society, a little like the traffic lights downtown and the handicapped parking spaces. So Richard accelerated. That was no problem. Man, he had power under his hood.

Samantha's problem was of a more domestic order. It took some hazardous research into her contacts but the touch screen finally displayed the picture and phone number of Jan, her daughter's new tennis instructor. Sam, already very frustrated by the color of her nail polish and the red smears around her Botoxed lips (not too Botoxed, but still), had to concentrate on the conversation she was planning to have with Jan. She took a deep breath, pushed the *Call* button, and kept on driving toward the rotary without paying attention to the signs saying she didn't have right-of-way. Her priority was Jan. Mostly how to arrange a date with him, if only to make clear to her daughter that the conceited little bitch didn't have what it takes to compete in the same league as her mother.

And then there was Francine. Francine had no problems of any kind. She was already in the rotary. She and her little Twingo had complete right-of-way.

Richard felt like a jerk with Francine's ridiculous car in front of his gleaming radiator grill. He accelerated, because he was a real man and had balls. Appearing suddenly on his right, and so happy to have finally mastered the wheelie, Djawad didn't even try to brake. He kept going straight ahead, thinking that if he drove through the flowers in the middle of the rotary, he'd manage to avoid that BMW which was accelerating in an attempt to avoid the Twingo.

"Hello? Jesus! Hey, I'm busy."

Completely taken by Jan's sexy voice, Samantha found herself right next to the metal body of Francine's Twingo, with not even the thickness of cigarette paper between the two cars. She didn't realize that the weird rustling sound she was hearing was not crackling on the line. Her Fiat 500 had cut into the Twingo all right. Richard wrenched his wheel, trying to skid to the side, but he controlled nothing. His axles smashed against the low concrete wall around the rotary right when Djawad was trying to fly over it. Fucking wall! The scooter took off, Djawad did not. His helmet, half sitting on his skull, the way the show-offs of his neighborhood wear it, seceded. It shot off like a cannonball and exploded Samantha's windshield, ending what sounded like a promising conversation with the handsome Jan.

"Hello? Hello? . . . I'm in the middle of a lesson here . . . Jesus. That woman's as dumb as her daughter . . ."

Samantha saw red. In fact, it's the last thing she saw. No time to seduce the handsome Jan, no time to find out that the tennis instructor was Kabyle—in other words, of Arab descent—something that would surely have put a damper on her desire to seduce him.

Djawad crashed onto Richard's hood before he ended up wedged between the left side of the Twingo and the right side of the Fiat 500. No luck. There was no room left for him between the two . . . The metal bodies acted like a press. The cracking of his bones was reminiscent of the irritating noise of a cockroach being crushed under a leather sole. Djawad's scooter landed heavily on the roof of the Twingo, which did not prove to be particularly resistant. Francine now had a real problem. As for Richard, he ended his trajectory embedded in a low wall after rolling over twice. This time he really had something under the hood, on the hood, and all around it. Richard cursed his mother once more. With a Porsche Cayenne, he might have survived the collision.

The paramedics' problem was deciding where to start: with the kid shot with a .357 next to his garbage cans, or with the mass grave at la Cayolle rotary. They started with the traffic fiasco, a problem definitely less common and more complex than drug dealers killing each other. Because in Marseille, the real problem is that it's easier to put a hit on someone than to drive a car.

THE PROSECUTION

BY PIA PETERSEN

Vieux-Port

Once upon a time there was a man sitting in a café drinking his beer, looking at the street and beyond the street, at the square and the port and the cars speeding between the street and the square and the port. He was in a very bad mood and he felt like insulting someone but he didn't know who, only that it could be anybody. He had been angry for so long.

He had made his decision and he intended to do exactly what he had written that very morning in his diary. If they wanted to know why, they could just read what was written there.

The why of the why was a murky and confused story and nobody would really understand the generosity of his act but that was not sufficient reason for giving up.

He had put the diary on his living room table so that everybody could see it. One day, someone would read it.

Once upon a time there was a man who landed in Marseille, a city that faced out toward the sea and turned its back on France. Marseille had changed names again and again because it was too rebellious said some, too much of a mess said others, but nobody really knew. The man had landed with a great deal of enthusiasm, with plans and even with money to last him awhile but a few years later he had no enthusiasm, no plans and no money at all and now he was too poor to leave the city. I'm stuck here, I'm stuck in this bitch of a city, he said to the few people he associated with.

He used to be a poet, a philosopher, a writer, a great reader and a humanist, that's what he replied when people asked him who he was. I like the proximity of seismic faults, he told his friends to explain why he was moving to Marseille, he said it was a logical poetic choice, even though he would have preferred the seismic fault of Los Angeles, it looked classier but it was too far away, too expensive, too dangerous, too complicated and he didn't know what an ESTA was, they had explained at the American Embassy that it was an Electronic System for Travel Authorization, which had seemed to him an insurmountable hurdle and so he landed in Marseille one fine morning to live in a little studio on rue Francis Davso at the Vieux-Port, right near the opera and its whores, or ladies of the night as they were sometimes called. He didn't know there weren't any seismic faults, Marseille felt like a city on the brink of disaster and everything else was just details. From his window, he could see the dumpsters from the fast-food restaurants on rue Glandèves and sometimes a rat would scoot out of the sewers to the garbage cans.

In Marseille nobody asked him for an ESTA, that would have been the last straw.

He could have settled in Haiti where they also had a major seismic fault. Or Japan where he could have lived right on the fault.

At first it was magical. Every day he would cross cours Honoré d'Estienne d'Orves, an Italian-style *mineral square*, a trendy concept a friend told him with a mysterious air but he saw only an empty concrete square, no lawn/trees/flowers. He would stroll along the Vieux-Port on one side and then on the other, taking the ferry that crossed the harbor several times a day and then walk back, passing under a strange roof that someone had built right in the middle of the port. Maybe it was built to shade people from the sun, he said to himself. But why there, why precisely that spot? He never got an answer. When he asked his friends who lounged around the neighborhood for hours on end, as he did, they would lean back and look at the roof but nobody knew. One of them said it was to reduce the smell of fish from the market where the early-morning catch was sold, a kind of lid but no one thought this a plausible answer.

He was living a cliché, having an aperitif right after lunch with his friends at Bar de la Marine, drinking pastis with relish while enjoying the life around the port, there was a tree on quai de Rive Neuve, just one, and the sun was always shining in a blue sky and the women walked with a slow and nonchalant gait. Bar de la Marine was famous thanks to Marcel Pagnol's film trilogy, which took place in an imaginary bar of the same name, so it was fortunate that such a place actually existed and Pagnol was Marseillais even though he was born in Aubagne, everybody knew that and as far as he was concerned he was having drinks in a literary environment and he liked that. The Vieux-Port wasn't just a port with boats, it was a place where people lived, it was the MuCEM and the Pharo and the rocks of Fort Saint-Jean from which kids would dive and swim, the place aux Huiles, rue Sainte with its restaurants and the suicidal Canebière that threw itself into the sea, that's what they said in guidebooks and often in novels, it was the café Olympique de Marseille and la Caravelle, a jazz restaurant-bar where the waiters always ignored him, city hall and the parking garage built at the spot where the César museum should have stood, the Eglise Saint-Ferréol les Augustins, the boats and especially the three-master that had sunk and was never brought up because it would have cost too much, they just cut off the masts, marked its outlines and that way they had a liquid public square, a mineral square *made in Marseille,* and there was the little blue train that went up to Notre-Dame-de-la-Garde, there was noise and tourists and sometimes strange gangster-looking guys and in the morning the fish market which was also the name of the theater on quai de Rive Neuve.

He would end his evenings right near his studio in the most fanciful and extravagant café in the neighborhood, l'Unic, where the bad boys erupted from time to time to kill each other, it was one of the only cafés that stayed open all night and as a regular he had his own barstool and if ever he was absent, which did happen once in a while, Dominique, the boss, would ask where he had been. She truly loved her customers and followed their latest news. She didn't say *latest news* because she never went online, she said she kept herself informed because her customers were long-term customers. She never used the expression *from way back*. Dominique was sensitive to this new era that transformed mankind into a mere economic vector, of value only until his *sell by* date or the expiration date for consumption.

A doll wearing glasses hung behind the bar, family snapshots and postcards were pasted to the wall, a little bear lay on the bottles and a disco ball rotated on the ceiling, reflecting the lights. On a shelf, an old photo of Edith Piaf and a pirate mask and several Enki Bilal reproductions. A fat dog slept on the bench seat.

Marseille was the city where anything was possible and they had been saying for a long time, for ages, that soon business would pick up and the city would become important, it was a city where the cards always had to be redealt, where everything was yet to be done, where nothing ever seemed finished or followed through to the end, a city of its time, rickety and unique because funds to bolster the economy were misappropriated by civil servants and politicians. In Marseille, it was all kept in the family.

At first he hadn't noticed it but then, little by little, that was all he could see.

The crack.

A rat who lived in his building saw him leaving one day, earlier than usual and saw him come back at night, later than usual, with his face somehow undone and an expression of disappointment in his eyes. The rat didn't know what the expression meant but he could see he was no longer the same man. Anyway, the rat couldn't care less about the man and his frustrations.

Something had happened, a veil had been rent and the man no

longer appreciated the sun and the blue sky, he observed the women walking and found them heavy and graceless, the pastis had lost its taste, the fish market no longer held any charm, discussions with friends were reduced to their most rudimentary form and besides soccer and a few shrugs, there was no communication. He tried to fight it and talked about literature, philosophy and even poetry in hopes of having an interesting conversation but they just looked at him and said stupid things. He was getting bored.

Dégun, engatser, cagole, boulègue, emboucaner, parler meilleur, pourrave, maronner, chourraver, zou, testard, emplâtre, rouscailler, c'est qu'une bouche. The famous Marseille slang, just a lot of chatter.

He saw the chipped, flaking walls, gray from pollution, dirty garbage containers with their lids always open stinking up the whole city, he saw plastic bags hanging on the branches of trees like Christmas decorations, shit from homeless people and dogs on the sidewalks, men pissing against doors and walls, he saw people littering the street instead of putting their trash into garbage cans, he saw metal posts in the middle of the sidewalk to prevent cars from parking on it, forcing people to walk single file to get around them, he saw a city adrift, up to its neck in filth and corruption and liking it, a city where anything was possible, a city drowning in bullshit and he was exasperated and he freaked out.

He thought of himself as a good and polite man, with a true civic sense. His glass was always half full but that evening, when he climbed the stairs to his place, he smelled the stench of urine, his fingers grazed the wall and the cracked paint peeled off, he felt the cold and the moisture because of a leak in the pipes and he remembered all the letters of complaint and then insults he had sent to the management company, to the real estate agency, to lawyers and city hall and how they had promised to fix things, a budget had been set aside and all they were waiting for were the workers but he was still waiting, nothing was ever done. His friends said he shouldn't be in such a rush, he had to give time some time, the time to be. His friends lived as slowly as they walked, they waited patiently for death, that's the way they saw themselves but he saw them otherwise, he saw the waste of life.

The rat didn't know what had happened, he couldn't discern what made sense and what didn't because he was a rat and he didn't follow the man wherever he went, nor did he think like him, he remained holed up under the garbage cans, under the dumpsters, that was his kingdom and from this roomy kingdom he saw the man go by, looking lost. The rat too was fat, he moved slowly, sure of himself, he ate a lot and had never known hunger, he was a rat *made in Marseille*.

A few days earlier, standing on a corner in the Vieux-Port where he had once again observed the lid they called a roof or a shade-giver or a gigantic upside-down mirror so people could see themselves and take a selfie, which was the irrefutable proof that Marseille was more or less experiencing modernity, the man forgot to verify if the cars had actually stopped at the light before he stepped off the curb. They had warned him when he arrived in Marseille that people were rebellious to the core and you couldn't cross even when the light was red without checking to make sure that cars had actually stopped, the issue wasn't really a lack of civic spirit but a sort of prideful disobedience, a matter of principle. They had said *nous, les Marseillais* and he had been proud. He had always seen himself as a rebel, so he liked this way of defining Marseille and when a car didn't stop at the light, he had just enough time to tell himself it was a city made for him, a perfect match, when he was thrown into the air, fell heavily onto the asphalt and banged his head as the car sped away. He was alive, he had been very lucky, too bad for him. When a paramedic shook him, his first reflex was to ask what happened and when the paramedic had stopped telling him about his adventures, his next reflex was to ask where the driver of the car that had practically killed him was. The police had closed off the area and were redirecting traffic while a crowd gathered. One of the policemen explained that there was no way for them to get their hands on the driver, he should try to forget the accident, he was okay and that was the main thing, being okay and he had to understand that the police were overwhelmed, so why press charges, no point wasting energy and anyway, with a good pastis, he would feel better. Shaken up by his accident, he agreed, of course.

Later, when he was having a drink with his friends, they told him that the car almost certainly belonged to a cop, they had recognized him. Hey, that's the way it is and they laughed stupidly.

He saw and became aware that their laughter was stupid and he lost his sense of humor.

Far from being rebellious, Marseille now appeared to him like a city where people got bogged down and grew dumber by the day. He tried to fight those wicked thoughts and prove to himself that the city didn't have that kind of influence on him, that it was all in his head and to avoid people, he went out for a walk early in the morning, probably too early since it was the time when the garbagemen having already cleaned the city gave themselves what they thought was a well-deserved cigarette break, leaving behind them a jumble of refuse and open garbage cans, the asphalt was slippery and dirty because they watered it down but never cleaned it and the detritus melted into a stinking paste. He would walk by them every morning and to show that he too was participating in cleaning the city, he would pick up trash from the ground, put it in the containers and close the lids and when the garbagemen did not react, he would ask them why they watered the asphalt like a garden when it was not a garden, why they didn't put the lids back on, why they didn't pick up the stuff, why they didn't clean and they made fun of him and turned their backs on him. He told them that this was no way to act, everybody suffered from the filth but the garbagemen responded with indifference and shrugs, they didn't care at all, they had work waiting for them at their cousin's place, their brother's, or a buddy of theirs. *Done and gone*, that's what you called the special treatment accorded to the garbagemen by city hall or perhaps the regional council, nobody really knew who was in charge of what in Marseille, things were often vague. The man went to see the driver of the little tourist train and explained that he should avoid the streets behind the Vieux-Port and their mountains of garbage so as not to frighten the tourists because, subsequently, the city would get even poorer and be swallowed up in the economic fault line but the driver merely shook his head.

In Haiti too they had a problem with the accumulating garbage which was understandable, they had nobody to clean it up, no garbage truck or men to pick it up and make it mysteriously disappear, no place to hide the trash, all they had was poetic words to name filth, they called it *fatras* and that wasn't so bad because in Marseille they didn't even have the poetic words, they had disappeared into a dumpster. He said to himself that it did not make him feel any better to know that it was worse in Haiti and that he had no desire to resemble this city but the dirt was getting under his skin and he washed his hands again and again.

He read Don DeLillo who had written magnificent pages on the accumulation of waste, of garbage, of everything man no longer wanted or needed, magnificent, disturbing pages but nobody ever talked about those pages, it was just literature.

He dragged himself along the streets, swearing and arguing with everybody and cursing the day he had moved here. Filth was everywhere despite all the signs saying *Do not leave garbage here. Violators will be prosecuted* and despite the cleanliness police who rode slowly around on their bikes, enjoying a bit of sun. He had nightmares, dreamed of dirt and filth and people who wallowed in it, enjoyed it and he spent hours and hours cleaning his apartment, the building, the street but there was always more of it and he could no longer put things in perspective. He kept washing his hands, over and over.

Once upon a time there was a city called Marseille and a man lived there, he was in a bad mood and was drinking beer on the Vieux-Port, he had made a decision and his eyes wandered off over to cours Honoré d'Estienne d'Orves and way beyond. Dominique, the owner, observed him, still grouchy, she said, tapping him on the shoulder. Three generations of men had come to her bar and she was sincerely attached to her customers, they were the apple of her eye, she said, which didn't stop her from occasionally throwing them out to teach them good manners.

It's not the way it used to be, she said as she sat down next to him. People don't know how to live anymore, they are so cautious, so reasonable. Can you believe it? Yesterday I served organic tomato juice and Diet Coke all day long. Not one bottle of champagne in a whole year. People are so uptight. The one leads to the other. Not like back in the day when they would down tequila while listening to rock and roll.

He didn't answer, he just looked at her and wondered if in those days people used to be that dirty and when she met his eyes, she kept quiet for a long time. Then she said. You know, you scare me. Are you okay? You look weird. He didn't say anything for a very long time and then, heavily, he stood up and said it was time for action, he said that from now on he would take care of everything, she had nothing to worry about and he walked out.

Sparing no efforts, he worked meticulously to put his plan in place, studied all the possibilities on the Internet, from how to make a homemade bomb to programming a detonator, and bit by bit he bought what was needed and slowly his apartment was transformed into a bomb kitchen. He was in no hurry, he had all the time he needed. He wanted to show the world that Marseille could become a clean city but first you had to get rid of the garbage.

And then he was ready. Taking advantage of National Heritage Day he entered city hall and walking from floor to floor he placed explosives everywhere he could without anyone noticing anything. He was a discreet man.

After spending the evening at l'Unic, he went home and wrote in his diary all night and when day broke and the garbagemen had left, he went out and prowled the neighborhood and stuck explosives under the dumpsters on rue Sainte, rue Glandèves, rue Molière, and rue Beauvau. On place Général-de-Gaulle he waved at the owner of the Brasserie de la Bourse, who, thanks to his cousin at city hall who had given him the keys to the city faucets, tapped into the water main every morning to clean his sidewalk. He set explosives there too.

The rat who often went shopping for food at the garbage heap on cours Jean Ballard near the newsstand saw the man bending down by the containers, one after the other and he, the rat, scuttled away fast. He didn't understand what was going on, only that something was going on, he could see that the man's expression had changed again and thought that this did not bode well. The rat had the instinct of a rat. As far as he was concerned, the existence of mankind was not inevitable, men were there one day, then maybe gone the next, it didn't matter but meanwhile the rat distrusted them. The rat lived in the present and, if possible, out of men's sight.

Late in the afternoon, the man strapped an explosive belt around his waist, he made sure his diary was in full view on the table, he took his phone and went for a last beer at Bar de la Marine and when he had finished his beer, he caught the last ferry and when the ferry was in the middle of the harbor, he took out his phone and triggered the explosives, they all went off at the same time, like the clamor that should have arisen during the inauguration of Marseille as the European Capital of Culture, although his own fireworks were more spectacular and blew him up too.

Some Marseillais were gathered around the Vieux-Port. It stinks worse than usual, said one of them. Yeah, we don't have any more garbage cans, said another. The guy who did that wasn't right in the head. Look, even a rat got obliterated. Jeez, said still another.

* * *

Once upon a time there was a city named Marseille and it was the dirtiest city in France until the day a man decided to sacrifice his life and since the day he blew up city hall and the dumpsters near the Vieux-Port as a protest against filth and corruption, the city has been cleaned up and kept clean because this is a tale and a tale always has a happy ending.

GREEN, SLIGHTLY GRAY

BY SERGE SCOTTO

La Plaine

I n Paris, it would be Montmartre. In Marseille, it's la Plaine. Where a mound of earth flattens out, attracting artists to it like flypaper. But if many a child of the Muse takes flight from the heights of Montmartre, in the underworld of la Plaine, all they do is get glued down. They should find the energy to leave . . . But la Plaine is a contagious disease you catch at bars where ill-fated artists make the world over, make the world over and over and over every single day with their mouths, and soon they can't do anything with their hands but lift their glasses, drowning their talent and good will in beer and pastis. And yet they thought they would lift the world up . . . Magnificent bums who think they're celebrated because they celebrate themselves and each other, who think they're powerful at the beginning of each month because they buy their colleagues a round with the little money they collect from the government, who think they're handsome because they appeal to drunks and druggies of the opposite sex, who think they're geniuses because they don't sell anything and think they're funny because they really are.

But if Montmartre is a beginning, la Plaine is an ending. We're near the end of the twentieth century and you still have to go up to Paris to make it? True, often the friends who've done that made out better than they did here, but you have to say they also slacked off a lot less . . . Their example isn't enough to motivate the majority of the troops. These indolent intellectuals have drawn a rebellious slogan from their laziness about succeeding: They want to "succeed here at home" and they're even capable of singing it to you in Provençal! A legitimate demand. The demand of an activist . . . But it's pathetic. A denial of reality: there's nothing to do in Marseille except go around it ten times over or take a high-speed train to Paris.

Maurice is one of those people who believes in la Plaine. It must be said that he fits right in—he's from La Belle de Mai, another neighborhood of people without a euro in their pockets. An equally working-class neighborhood, just more industrious. From there, this far-off paradise of artists seemed another world to him. When he plunked his bags down in la Plaine, he thought he'd arrived . . . and he still thinks so, for he has time, young blood runs in his veins and he has a head brimming with dreams well anchored to the ceiling. Maurice is convinced he'll become a rock star overnight, just like the legion of musicians who're invading the neighborhood by the hundreds. Rock bands form every day, rehearsing for a while in a cellar or a garage before playing in the local dives. They're acclaimed by the same people who played there the night before and the ones who'll play there the following night, giving them the illusion of an audience. They're not necessarily real bars, often makeshift places where liquor is sold without a license, pretending to be covered by the 1901 law regulating "nonprofit associations," which hardly even exist here. You can also find drugs there, a business transacted without a license anyway.

That's about all Maurice has done in the year he's lived in la Plaine—drank and smoked weed. He easily found a little apartment to rent in an old building. Two dark rooms on the second floor where sunlight never enters because the street is too narrow. It's not fancy, but for a coat of white paint slapped on quickly, the landlord gave him the first month free. The landlord is quite happy, because the portion of the rent covered by the government subsidy to low-income tenants goes directly to him. At least that part of the rent is guaranteed . . . You don't want to be too picky, it's hard to find a good tenant in Marseille, especially in this neighborhood that kind of scares people. The landlord would gladly sell the apartment—it's an inheritance from his grandmother—but it's not worth anything, or not much. Not even worth selling, really. That day will come—a promise from our elected officials. From one election to the next, there's always something to hope for; meanwhile, there's a high turnover of fairly unreliable tenants, evicted when necessary. Once spring has come, they pack up and go.

For the moment, all is well between Maurice and his landlord, a fifty-something who works "for the city." He's a road worker—that is, he pushes a broom over the streets while making his rounds to the cafés. Maurice has often seen him in his blue overalls sitting at a sidewalk café as soon as weather permits. From time to time, with his steel key, the municipal employee turns on the fire hydrants, releasing thousands of noisy liters through a plastic elbow in a powerful but almost useless spurt that flows into the gutter and turns into a measly stream slipping tortuously between the tires of the parked cars. When he decides it's clean, he thanks the owner for his coffee, turns off the faucet, and resumes his walk, making a few scattered sweeps with a new birch broom just to be on the safe side, hastily dispersing the biggest waste blockages.

Between his moonlighting in the piano bars and the sticks of hash he sells in aluminum foil, Maurice gets along okay. The first week of every month, he goes to a shop that sells jewelry and ethnic clothing, on a street perpendicular to cours Julien, the other emblematic square of the plateau. The "plateau" no more exists in the official registries than does its subsection la Plaine, but it's noteworthy: a mecca of Marseille life, la Plaine was in fact very officially baptized place Jean Jaurès long ago, after the socialist leader who was assassinated on the eve of the First World War, but the people of Marseille have always preferred to keep the traditional name of the huge agora, flouting the posthumous homage to the great man . . . Only the mailman and the locals know that it is really place Jean Jaurès. To someone looking for noise, black whores, or drugs, people will always suggest la Plaine; everybody knows how to get there even if the name can't be found on maps of the city.

Every Saturday, there's a young woman working in the jewelry store. She must be about the same age as Maurice. A superb redhead, natural or fake . . . Redheads are in fashion this year.

"Hi," she says, greeting him with a pretty smile, "how are you?"

They're formal, they address each other as *vous* to act like older people and keep their distance; mind you, she's the landlady's daughter and that deserves respect. She's the one to whom he gives the envelope with the rent check. In exchange, he gets his receipt.

"I saw you're a musician?" says the young saleslady. Finally, she's getting interested in him! "I'm Sarah."

"Matt . . ."

"Your name's not Maurice?"

How dumb can he get! She knows his first and last names as well as his address, of course. She laughs. He laughs.

"How do you know about my music?"

She shows him a photocopied poster pasted on the glass door. You can read it backward through the glass, *Sex Toys in concert at K-Foutch*, written with a felt-tip marker.

"Are you the guitarist?"

In the photo you can't see any instruments, only four stupid faces; rather than standing there looking glum, they'd do better to get a haircut.

"I'm the guitarist . . . *and* the singer." Maurice seems to take pride in it. "Matt's my stage name, it's . . . you have to in this job."

If he had announced that it was a directive given to the secret service to protect its agents, he couldn't have revealed it in a more modest tone . . .

"I'm okay with Matt."

* * *

Matt had always feigned indifference, same with Sarah: that's probably why they liked each other. Waiting with growing impatience every month for the moment they could see each other in the store. Maurice had seen her prancing around the street a few times, alone or with girlfriends, without even daring to approach her; ditto for Sarah. Time, fantasies, youth, and beauty did the rest: now they had a date! At Le Petit Nice, a respectable establishment run by a wise ex-boxer. You can read *Libération* there and you come across fewer cockroaches than in other cafés in the neighborhood.

Sarah trots in on red boots with open heels. Black miniskirt, tights—or stockings?—and matching diaphanous blouse, her bra brightly colored under the dark filmy fabric, and a purple-red leather jacket. As soon as he catches sight of her, Maurice mechanically folds up his newspaper. Seeing her dressed up like that, so desirable, he knows he has already won her over and she's offering herself to him.

Each one pretends not to know what will follow. They seduce each other. Sarah has ordered a Get, which mints up her breath. Sometimes their mouths happen to draw close, conversation becomes more intimate, but they don't kiss, not yet. Maurice is witty. Sarah cleverly lets him talk and laughs obligingly at his jokes; her smile is a weapon and she knows how to use it. Maurice puts his hand on the young woman's hand, as if inadvertently; she doesn't withdraw it . . .

"Wait for me," he says, "I just need two minutes, got to make a phone call!"

He gets up and leaves her there, crossing between the cars to get to the square where kids are playing soccer on the asphalt. One of the phones is out of order, vandalized for a few coins; in the other glass cabin right next to it, the phone works: in a few coded sentences, Maurice makes an appointment with his dealer to buy half a pound of hash, enough to cover his own consumption with plenty left over to sell—earning him a decent week's salary.

Back at the sidewalk café, he sits down and kisses Sarah directly on the mouth, by surprise. Their kiss lasts a few long seconds . . . A first kiss is important, you can't fake it: if it works, it will work!

Time passes so pleasantly that the two lovers didn't see night falling . . . Sarah remarks on this. Maurice asks her to dinner, to prolong the evening. Like a prince! His princess accepts without a fuss. The young man's eyes seem to stare at the horizon.

"Wait for me," he says again, "I just need two minutes."

Again he gets up, to meet a big guy "of North African appearance" according to the police description, twice as swarthy because of the darkness. The guy, in a white sweat suit, is balancing his scooter between his thighs. Once the brisk transaction is completed, the dealer starts the engine and disappears immediately with his helmet under his arm, leaving Maurice lit up for a second by the headlight of the roaring machine.

Meanwhile, Sarah has gotten up; she puts her leather jacket back on and lights up a Marlboro.

"Let's go!" Maurice says. "That was my dealer," he can't help boasting.

In Marseille, it is imperative to be a hood, even a little hood, it's basic . . . You boast of being a hood and kissing gang bosses as often as possible. In this town of paupers, where businessmen are the aristocracy and politicians are corrupt to the core, the hoodocracy is a way to climb the social ladder. All these fine people conduct business together.

At the Haunted House, the grub is homemade and cheap, you eat listening to hard rock in a cavernous light. One of those curious places covered with morbid frescoes, where a shady crowd of night people, owls, badgers, hyenas, and vampires come to meet. Behind the bar the owner looks like a barbarian Gaul, with his long blond hair, his bushy mustache, and his fringed vest; he seems to have a complete understanding of the world as it is, impassibly drawing his pints of beer. On the wall behind him there's a sign in capital letters: *CREDIT IS DEAD AND SO ARE YOU IF YOU DON'T PAY UP.* A pool table has replaced the stage ever since the old farts on the neighborhood committee complained about the cacophony of the live music, but you still have to talk loudly to be heard over the sound system. The place isn't very intimate, but it's pleasant, and the lovers manage to find a quiet table on the mezzanine. After the potato, bacon, and cheese tartlet and two dishes of stuffed beef rolls à la Provençal, Sarah is done telling her life story; Maurice pretended to be interested and listened attentively. She's going for a degree in commercial art at Saint Joseph les Maristes; the road worker's daughter is into infography, a new field he knows nothing about; apparently it's about drawing with a computer . . .

"Soon everyone will have their own personal computer at home," she prophesies.

I doubt it, Maurice thinks, without daring to contradict her; as if people have nothing else to do all day but deaden their minds in front of a screen—TV's quite enough for that. All he cares about is roaming the streets with his colleagues and making noise on the neck of his guitar.

All you have to do to is lean over the railing to order a beer; you grab your bottle between the cables of the railing so the owner doesn't have to climb the stairs. Time goes by fast when you drink beer, tongues loosen, intimacy becomes more pressing and lips soften in the dusky light. From time to time you do have to get up to go take a piss, which takes some courage because it's all the way downstairs . . .

The clock had struck midnight, the hour of crime, several hours earlier when the guitarist of the Sex Toys and his lady leave the hellhole on rue Vian.

In the sweetness of the night, Maurice has taken Sarah's hand.

Do they know where they're going? The municipal lighting gives a piss-colored shade to the dull façades of the old buildings which occupy most of the neighborhood, which is bathed in a uniformly pallid light, crossed by narrow streets, totally deserted at this ungodly hour. Their footsteps resound on the pavement. Suddenly the young buck pulls hard on his conquest's arm, dragging her under the entrance of a building . . . Sarah doesn't resist. Now she's backed against a scaly wall while Maurice is assailing her neck with kisses. They greedily attack each other's mouths amidst the smells of garbage cans. A soup of tongues in the stinking darkness disturbed only by the scurrying of the rats all around . . . Sarah can't get enough of those slobbery kisses. But Maurice quickly grows tired of them. He tells himself she's hot and it's high time to stick a finger in her; he's a methodical boy. He slips his right hand between the young woman's thighs. He did try to peek all evening, but in vain: stockings or tights? . . . Yes! He grazes the garter: the naughty girl is wearing the kind of stockings that attach to a garter belt, how convenient! Under his caresses, the satin of the little panties feels like the skin of an invisible animal, all feverish with desire. The fabric has come alive under his fingers, soon fusing with the juicy place it is no longer protecting. Sarah lifts a pink flamingo leg, planting one of her heels on the wall to open up to more pleasure, already moaning. All he has to do now is . . . That's when they hear the loud click of a timer switch turning on lights.

A bull's-eye lights up, revealing a massive wooden door behind Maurice. Sarah doesn't open her eyes right away, totally entranced by her own pleasure. But that ill-timed ray of light on her neck is enough to distract the young man, who suspends his activity. *They don't call it a switch for nothing,* he thinks, piqued. They hear shoes dragging over the hall. The door creaks open and Maurice turns around. Sarah closes back up like a flower. The fat guy looks more surprised than they do. A gelatinous colossus, evoking for the young woman, a former reader of fairy tales, the giant of the magic beanstalk. Something hairy shoots between her legs. A Yorkshire terrier, who makes straight for the rats . . .

"Hey, don't mind me, guys!" The master of the premises seems to be waxing indignant. He stands there, on his step, his garbage bag in his hand. In his underpants and slippers. The heavy door has closed slowly behind him.

"We're not doing anything wrong . . . We're leaving!" replies Maurice.

"Already?" The fat guy shoots forward with a speed that is astonishing for a pachyderm. In one bound, he's now blocking the passage. Without putting down his garbage bag.

The little window of light goes out, returning the entrance to the night. A medallion of light surrounds the dark silhouette of the fat guy blocking the exit; the street, just a step away, seems inaccessible, unless they walk through his body. Maurice feels Sarah's hand squeeze his own more tightly.

"Let us through, sir," he says without raising his voice, as calmly as possible, but with all the authority he can muster.

Facing him, silence. Their eyes get used to the darkness little by little, and in the whites of the fat guy's eyes, Maurice thinks he can see a lecherous gleam. His breath stinks of garlic and liquor, two things that spell solitude, not to mention the Yorkshire terrier.

"I don't want to harm you," the man finally declares with a sugary voice. "Just, couldn't we play together a little?" The bag thuds dully to the ground at his slippered feet. The fat guy extends his hand to them. "Just a little caress for the miss . . . It's my home here—to enter, you have to pay customs."

Sarah moves away, pulling Maurice backward. The fat guy steps forward.

"Don't be scared . . ."

The entrance is a dead end leading to closed doors. If the young people thought of it, all they'd have to do is grope for the doorbell to wake up the whole block. But they remain frozen there, wide-eyed and fascinated, with their backs to the wall, staring at a danger they can hardly see. A danger whose breath they can feel upon them, a danger whose animal movements they glimpse in the darkness.

"Don't play shy, baby, I know you're a little slut . . ." the voice murmurs softly. "And your boyfriend is cute too. You're young, you need some new experiences . . ."

Caressing, touching. The young man feels fingers running over his crotch. The obese heap of a man crushing them, those obscene tentacles squeezing them in, that smell—a mix of sweat and pastis. Terror paralyzing them . . . That hypnotic voice is advising them to just let themselves go, like a big snake wrapping itself around them . . .

"I'm sure you're going to like it," says the voice rubbing against him.

When Maurice finally reacts, he tries a blind knee-kick and only hits fat.

"Leave us alone!" Sarah begs without managing to scream.

"Come on, be good sports!" the voice orders.

The hand of a gorilla makes the skull of the Sex Toys' leader bounce against the wall. More than pain, vertigo instantly empties all Maurice's strength. As he faints, he can hear Sarah still begging . . .

When he comes to, a few seconds or a thousand years have gone by . . . He's lying on the floor, his nose in the garbage bags at the foot of a dumpster. It all comes back to him. Over his head, Sarah is struggling and sobbing. Words are no longer coming out of the girl's throat, which he guesses has been forced into silence. Maurice hears the giant whispering breathlessly, without understanding a word of the poison he's distilling into his victim's ear. The fat pig is completely absorbed. There's no light shining on the façades, just nothingness. Despite Sarah's coquetry in veiling herself in thin nylon, it's not yet the season for sleeping with the windows open. And anyway, in this neighborhood the silence is broken every night by the songs of drunks, the shouts from fights, and gunshots, when there's not an explosion a few streets over that makes your windows shake.

Something moist has just landed on his palm. Maurice jumps, but it's only the nose of the terrier. In the shadows that are quivering like some formless creature, he can sense the repugnant embrace of that tub of lard and his lovely girlfriend. In his effort to stand up, he finds under his hand something he identifies as the base of a metal lamp, heavy and cold. His strength returns. Despite his headache, he manages to stand up and in the same movement smashes down blindly on what he takes to be the guy's back.

"Ooof!" is the onomatopoeia the guy collapses with. His arms have released Sarah—she felt them withdraw like a moray eel going back into its hole. He has fallen like a boxer, and the thud didn't cover up the sound of a strange, plaintive crack . . .

"Sarah?" whispers Maurice softly.

The young woman's delicate hand finds him and lands on his cheek. Her imitation gold ring is rolling like a pearl on his lips and he's kissing those fingers in the air, his eyes closing briefly in the dark.

"He . . . he was going . . ." she stammers. Maurice draws her to him. She does not resist. Lets herself be hugged in someone's arms again, yes, but this time they're the right ones. She says thank you, she begins to cry, her head against Maurice's shoulder, pressing against him, hiccupping. She says again: "He was going to . . ." They're talking in low voices, as if someone might hear them . . . as if they were doing something bad by letting themselves be raped in a building entrance . . . They're in shock.

"We can't stay here."

"Did you . . . ?" She doesn't finish her sentence.

Maurice lets go of her—time to kneel down and check the body. He figures out the fat guy's lying on his belly. He gropes upward, toward the head; at the neck, thick as an ox's, Maurice feels a lukewarm, sticky substance on his fingers. "Blood . . ."

"He's dead?" Sarah whispers.

"I must've smashed his skull in . . . Come on, let's get out of here!"

They run. Hand in hand. The echo of their footsteps does not attract a single nose to a window . . . Why bother? Nothing to get excited about. In their beds, the insomniacs are watching documentaries about hunting and fishing in the bluish halo of their TV sets, other night owls are drinking alone or have gotten up to eat or drink a glass of milk, and others are grasping at one another, staining their sheets . . . and in the street, fugitives: the police or some other hoods are probably in pursuit, but by the time they arrive, the fugitives are already far away. Sirens would have to stop right under your windows for it to be worth checking out.

Maurice and Sarah don't stop running till they get to la Plaine. They catch their breath between two cars, bent over and panting, before they cross the huge square, which is transformed at night into a parking lot. Provoking the barks of a big dog forgotten in a van . . . they walk as naturally as possible, to fool people: a nice young couple nobody would suspect of being a modern Bonnie and Clyde.

At a street corner Maurice takes his keys out of his pocket. Only after he's double-locked his door do they both breathe again. They calm down little by little. Leaving the room in darkness, they remain hidden behind the half-closed shutters for the time being, watching the narrow street, pricking their ears for any unusual commotion, any police sirens heading in their direction.

Sarah wraps her arms around the young man, inhaling his sweat, while he feels the warmth of her breath on his neck. The joint is exchanged like a kiss, sticky from the lips of the other. They remain silent. He has his hand on hers and they stay there while time stands still, a thousand confused thoughts assail them, as if everything they just went through wasn't quite real . . . United more strongly by their shared nightmare than they could ever be by the parish priest.

They make love with the rising sun. Sarah is the first to fall asleep, wiped out by their lovemaking, after giving all she had; the sleep of a woman exorcised . . . After intermittently giving in to a restless half-sleep, he is now watching her.

She's beautiful. In peace. A soft light shines through the Venetian blinds, making the red wave of her hair gleam. Redheads are pretty . . . "Very classy," Maurice mumbles to himself, thinking of the flock of trashy women on rue Saint Ferréol traipsing around the shopping center on Saturdays, brunette by nature or blond against the will of God, shouting in their shrill voices. Little by little Sarah's distinct beauty has entered his heart and the troubadour begins to fear he's on the brink of falling in love; that's never advisable for a future rock star.

What color are her eyes? *Green,* he thinks, *slightly gray?* If he remembers the color of her eyes, it's a sign he's in love, he thinks: suspense . . .

From time to time, a little moan escapes from Sarah; he can't tell if it's from pleasure or fear, or from what she's dreaming about. She's sleeping on her stomach. Maurice has pulled the sheet down to her butt. He counts her beauty marks. Admires her freckles, light on her shoulders, assessing the velvet of her skin with a horse-trader's stroke that does not wake her. Sarah is a real redhead, he knows it now . . . He has her scent on the tip of his nose, so special, inebriating and sweet.

How many times has he opened his eyes, sober now, on a dog, white . . . or black? A complete stranger stretched out naked in his bed, a woman you have to get rid of as soon as possible. When you wake up Sunday morning it's all different: you went to sleep with a model, and it's a sea monster smiling at you as she says good morning. That's the price you pay for drinking. You should never go out on Saturday nights, Saturday night is an illusion, just a little makeup . . . And what about all those skanky groupies?

An eyelid lifts, then two. "Good morning," she grimaces. She has big green eyes, slightly gray, and they're having a hard time staying open . . .

"Good morning, Sarah." He takes pleasure in saying her name. She gives him a big smile, which suddenly shrivels up.

"Jesus, that disgusting fat guy . . . I'd forgotten him!"

The memories of the night before surface. That building entrance . . . her fear in the dark. The fat guy who wanted to rape her and Matt knocking him out, leaving him for dead. Their flight! The apartment as a refuge . . .

"It's over now," Maurice reassures her while combing her long hair with his hand. "You have nothing to fear now." He kisses her tenderly on the forehead.

"But what if you . . ."

"Who cares? Come into my arms . . ."

Sarah obeys and curls up in his embrace. With her ear against his torso, she hears her man's heart beating calmly. Like when she was a little girl, when she had the right to end her Sunday nights in her parents' bed and she would snuggle up to her daddy.

"If Daddy knew I slept here," she sighs.

"You think he'd raise the rent?"

They laugh nervously.

The morning stretches on as they go over the incident without leaving the sheets: Maurice and Sarah rewrite the story ten times over without managing to change the ending. The fat guy is almost certainly dead. But there's no reason why it should be traced back to them. It was dark and even if neighbors heard everything without showing themselves, how could they recognize them? The investigation will go nowhere, Maurice says. People get mugged every day in Marseille, corpses are found on the sidewalks, and there are unsolved crimes all over the city. In a week, the cops will move on to something else, and until then they'll just have to be careful: not see each other for a while, so as not to attract attention, avoid Le Petit Nice and the Haunted House, where they were seen together . . . And even if the police are looking for a young couple and make the rounds of local bars and restaurants, what would have distinguished them from hundreds of other couples aimlessly walking through the neighborhood?

"My red jacket!"

"Throw your red jacket in the trash."

"Are you crazy? It's too beautiful!"

"Into the closet then . . . I'll stash it away, you'll get it back later."

Silence means consent.

"I'll loan you my Perf when you leave. I bought it from a buddy, and anyway, it's too short for me. It'll fit you perfectly," says Maurice with what sounds like regret.

"What about my red hair?"

"We *so* don't care about your red hair! All you see are redheads these days! If you want me to, I can lend you a hat."

That afternoon, you can spot a slim silhouette in a Perfecto motorcycle jacket, wearing a Che cap, her face hidden by useless sunglasses as she slinks through the city hugging the walls.

If the fat guy's dead, we'll hear about it, Maurice tells himself. Consequently, he suffers through the local evening news on TV. Nothing.

The next morning, there's nothing in *Le Provençal* either. Maybe the fat guy didn't die after all? The following days he reads all the papers, even *La Marseillaise*, which is harder and harder to find in cafés, what with the decline of the Communist Party and all. During the week he calls the shop a number of times to reassure Sarah, but doesn't dare go there.

The young woman is sticking to her word, she doesn't say anything to anyone . . . In fact, what worries her more now is her red jacket: Maurice, prey to a fit of paranoia, hid it in the attic, where nobody ever disturbs the spiders, in the unlikely event that the police show up to search his place; that's what happens when you watch too many crime shows on TV . . .

Walking around as if nothing happened, he sees that nothing seems to have changed on the streets of Marseille. The pedestrians he passes don't seem to suspect in him the criminal he has become. Visibly, no one seems to care, from the baker who gives him back his change to the bum holding out his hand to ask for it. The mistral has begun to blow, cutting through bodies with its icy blade. Sarah has put away her miniskirts and open heels, once again wrapped up in her winter clothes.

In Marseille, you go from summer to Siberia as soon as the mistral blows. On market days in la Plaine, when the vendors have left, hundreds of abandoned plastic bags fly off in all directions and get stuck on branches, more decorated now than Christmas trees. The road workers do their best to fight the wind, and Sarah's father is struggling, his hands freezing despite his gloves. Backed up by the team of motorized sweepers that push heaps of trash toward the gutters with powerful jets of water, the sweepers on foot have to redouble their efforts to get to the end of it. Nonetheless collecting what can be recycled, like hangers for Sarah's shop: her boss likes them and Sarah likes to please her. But on those days, it's out of the question to make the rounds of the cafés to grab "a quick cup of coffee": it's not exactly a racket, more like a gift, renewed all year long by the café owners to thank the garbagemen for cleaning up out front.

During the day, la Plaine is a very lively neighborhood, with constant traffic jams, for the city's traffic plan was drafted by madmen. The incurable desynchronization of traffic lights doesn't help. At night it's just the opposite, it's a desert. And a paradise for rats and seagulls, who finish the road workers' job with such enthusiasm that it's obvious they're not members of the Force Ouvrière. Every evening, at the corner of rue des Trois Mages, faithful to her post, an old Eskimo woman in rags waits till it's past midnight. She's not there because of the snow—we get snow here once every ten years. She stands there at the red light offering bread and pastries stuffed in big plastic bags to the drivers. It's surplus from the nearby bakery which she sells these latecomers for next to nothing; what she doesn't sell, she distributes to the pigeons the next day, to the annoyance of the many neighborhood grouches.

Ever since the other night, because he's afraid of venturing any farther and because he can't be bothered to cook, Maurice has eaten lunch at Dirigible, a sandwich stand in the heart of the square. Among the bums waiting in line for their baguette stuffed with meatballs, how many know that this modest establishment owes its strange name to the takeoff, on this very spot, of a hot-air balloon which crossed the Mediterranean for the first time in 1886? The young man learned this by turning around to look at a girl and raising his eyes by chance to the plaque nobody ever notices that decorates the wall of the old post office building. Marseille is the oldest city in Europe, but you'd think it has no history . . . Under construction for the last 2,600 years, and nothing appears to be properly finished or durably built. It doesn't even have a historic downtown like you find in the smallest provincial sub-prefecture! The Yanks, our cousins in the New World, have some houses over there older than in Marseille, which permanently self-destructs rather than constructs, without the slightest respect for its old stones. For Marseille doesn't take care of itself, as it's been governed forever by a commercial aristocracy absorbed in its own business, which scorns the city and its working people, who've come here from all over the seven seas in search of a better life. And when, as bad luck would have it, Greek or Roman remains are discovered—something that happens at every strike of the pickax—there is only one pressing concern: bury them so as not to delay construction. Otherwise, the Phocaean city, as we call it, could live for a long time off the tourists who come to see its ancient monuments, like Pompeii . . . But here the concrete mixers turn like drums in a washing machine. Their main use is to launder cash.

Once, as he's getting ready to bite into a *tournedos* omelet, Maurice sees Sarah passing by in the distance . . . but he doesn't dare go meet her.

Maurice plunges ahead. He hesitated for a long time before he dared to cross his Rubicon. To cross la Plaine and venture back into the meandering little streets that separate it from cours Julien. To return to the scene of the crime. His beard has grown and with his dark glasses and his tuque, you'd take him for Serpico. He has to find out, he can't stand it anymore. For all this time, not one word in the papers; even at the neighborhood bar, he never heard a word about the incident. He finally told himself that if the fat guy was dead, he would have heard something, right? And yet there was all that blood . . . and that sound of broken bones when the colossus thudded facedown onto the ground. The light turns red, the pedestrian symbol turns green: *alea jacta est*, the die is cast!

On the other side of the crosswalk, he leaves his territory: an imaginary border traced inside his head, beyond which he's in trouble. First of all, la Plaine is his home, and then, there's plenty of space, it's bustling, and with market days and the line at the post office, there's all the animation an assassin might need to blend into the crowd and sink into anonymity. While in the narrow adjacent streets where few people walk by, you're careful to avoid the eyes of passersby; it immediately seems to him that everybody sees only him and he could be recognized. His heart starts beating hard, his throat tightens. He could still turn around but now he's already reached the next street. The fat guy's street. The entrance appears to be outlined with a dark border. Maurice breathes in deeply and resumes walking—he's aware he's going forward even though he no longer feels his legs beneath him. The doorway is getting nearer. A lady's rear end appears in the entranceway, moving backward. The door is growing larger in front of his very eyes; this time his heart actually stops beating, but he keeps moving forward. The fat guy is standing there, talking to the lady. The top of his head is bandaged. He doesn't seem to notice Maurice, who walks by like a zombie.

"It's horrible, why would anybody go after such a nice animal?" says the fat guy.

"You should get another one," she advises him. "Such a nice little dog!"

All the compassion in the world is expressed in the woman's voice, but from her very first words, Maurice understands that she would gladly bring back the death penalty for killers of little dogs and, as if the cold blade of the guillotine had landed on his neck, he feels a shiver pass through him—the Yorkshire terrier! The terrier is no longer around, running between his master's legs. It's the dog that died, crushed by its master's weight. That sinister crack . . .

"It's still too soon," laments the man with the bandaged head. "Later, maybe . . ."

Maurice can still hear the guy's voice without understanding his words any better. He walks away, amazed that no one stops him. The sun is shining at the other end of the street. He's almost there . . . He's there! He turns . . . and starts running like mad toward cours Julien, its fountain and its trees, the tables of the restaurants set for lunch, and toward all those people, toward life, this beautiful life, toward freedom!

The fat guy isn't dead and in a second it's ancient history in Maurice's head. God knows what version of his unfortunate four-legged companion's death the fat guy has invented for his neighbors . . . But that filthy asshole certainly won't have bragged about his attempted rape. It's no longer their concern. Maurice and Sarah are free.

PART IV

Always Outward Bound

THE RED MULE

BY MINNA SIF

Belsunce

Kevin posted the selfie with his head down and a big smile, squeezing the crotch of the green bull statue on display under the Ombrière—the polished steel sunroof in front of the Vieux-Port. He was enjoying the warm, springlike weather of this February afternoon in 2013. The city was the European Capital of Culture for the year. Herds of painted plastic animals lorded it all over the city. Kevin was a mule, working for the narco-jihad. One of thousands. He'd taken a certain pleasure in roaming through Europe for two years now, successfully trafficking cocaine and heroin, covering his traces for the anti-Jihadist cells as well as those of OCTRIS (the Central Office for the Repression of Trafficking Illicit Narcotics). The young man did good work. His predecessor's corpse had been found in a battered van converted into a whorehouse at the Belgian border. *That asshole!* He tried to outsmart everybody, Kevin sneered, as he posted self-portraits with a huge grin on his Facebook page. The mule before him, a cocaine addict, had begun to do business for himself and would subtract a few kilos of powder from the Organization to sell them off on the side. After slashing the guy's neck on the orders of his bosses, Kevin had relieved the guy of seventy-eight little packets, close to 568 grams of coke that the man had been planning to sneak into Belgium. He had a spasm of nausea when he recalled the scene of his disemboweling. So much shit in one body!

Kevin got high a lot, but he had a strict rule: never touch the employer's merchandise. This was his eighth mission and for the first time in his life he'd put a little money aside. Seventy thousand euros, to be exact, stashed in a plastered-up hole in the wall of his father's house in Roubaix. While waiting for better days, he lived an ordinary life as a tourist out for a good time, with his camera and videocam slung across his shoulder. He'd been recruited by a guy who called himself an imam in la Santé where Kevin had spent three years for armed robbery. To work in the narco-jihad, you had to convert to Islam, but it was a pure formality. The young man also took advantage of those missions to pay visits to the narco's branches—fly-by-night mosques, garages, or cellars in poor neighborhoods of the cities he passed through. Places run by ex-hoods turned apocalyptic preachers who rounded up young misfits dreaming of taking up arms in the name of God. Puny little runts on Rohypnol who trained for combat holed up in their rooms watching DVDs of guerillas in kaffiyehs. On those occasions Kevin would put on the traditional kashaba. He made a point of being scrupulous in all things.

Above all, he had a good time screwing as much as he could at the expense of his new employers. Sex had been his great passion since kindergarten, where he had taken advantage of his tender age to thrust his finger into plump-cheeked little girls. *None of those pink-ribboned babies ever complained,* Kevin remembered, as he stood under the sunroof at the Vieux-Port. *In exchange, I'd have them eat the scabs on my knees. I'm going to collect as much money as I can and get out of here, far away, Mexico or Venezuela. I could see myself with a cushy life as a gaucho on my steed, galloping over the pampa. A kickass horse with a leather saddle branded with my initials. I feel like fucking,* he said to himself as he scanned the lovers gathered under the Ombrière, busy taking pictures of themselves kissing. The Organization had forbidden him from approaching women in the street. Too risky. Abou Salem, his main contact, had told him many times that the sisters of the Revolution were there for that. Those women had girls whose main function was to satisfy the needs of the warrior brothers.

"If you want a war wife," Abou Salem had said, "the Organization will provide one for you."

I don't feel like having one of their girls, Kevin thought. *A bunch of pretentious females with martyr smiles on their faces. You listen to them, they're all saints. Talk about sexual jihad, they're all ass, and tits under their veils!*

In Alicante, after he'd sent a coded message to Abou Salem, the two women who came to see him at the hotel didn't speak a word of French. They were Bulgarians who'd come to the area to pick tomatoes. They would prostitute themselves from time to time. He'd done a line of coke and those whores had taken advantage, stealing a thousand euros from him.

Three days is a long time in this lousy place, Kevin said to himself. *Marseille is a dirty city and scares the shit out of you. They Kalash all over the place. You get whacked easy as a fly under a swatter,* he told himself, thinking of the gangland shootings that punctuated daily life in the Phocaean city. *Abou Salem lied to me when he promised it was a fun town. A fair under the smoke, are you kidding? A plastic zoo. Sunday outings for old people and if you're twenty, death at the foot of the hills. It's a lot more fun up north in Roubaix!*

He grimaced in disgust as he stepped out of the way to let a mother and her huge stroller go by. Clusters of parents were taking photos of kids perched on the fiberglass animals. Kevin stood there for a while, savoring the contagious excitement of the kids clutching the animals' necks. He, too, was excited at the idea of perching there with his legs hanging down, like on a merry-go-round. He promised himself a little nocturnal walk in front of city hall, to climb on the slanted back of the baby giraffe with red and orange spots. *The muzzle of that stupid horned beast with a red mouth is at least two yards above the ground,* he told himself, thrilled by the idea of mounting it. For a moment, he saw himself as a little boy of five wrapped up in his parka, squeezing the varnished neck of the wooden merry-go-round horse as hard as he could at the Christmas market in Roubaix. His dad, with his bloated face, would take big puffs on his Gitane as he encouraged him in his booming voice, holding his son's lollipop in one hand.

He spent the afternoon posting selfies on his Facebook page. Kevin, reflected under the high steel umbrella: short black hair, a thin, beardless face, small translucent gray eyes, a well-defined mouth with its thick upper lip, and the receding chin of a skinny kitten. He was twenty-five, hated his soft red mouth, too feminine for his taste. Kevin, snapped in front of the ferry station with the *Edmond Dantès* in the background ready to raise anchor for the Frioul archipelago. Kevin, in front of the Olympique de Marseille store, the selfie he liked best, posing proudly with his brand-new Adidas sports bag, its shoulder strap almost strangling him. Kevin, next to a seagull pecking away at the remains of his shish kebab. After taking that photo, he gave the animal a big kick and broke its wing. The gull tried to take off but fell back on its clawed feet with a shriek. Kevin instantly grabbed it by its broken wing and flung it into the water where it landed on beer cans and heaps of garbage floating on the surface.

He took the number 83 bus to see the ocean. He wanted a selfie with his feet in the sand. The bus driver pointed him to the beach called Plage du Prophète. "If you want sand, there's tons of it, don't worry," the guy said laughingly, with the vulgar accent they had around these parts. Kevin had his eyes on the man's thick, red neck sprinkled with black hairs. He suddenly felt like throwing up and squeezed the back of the seat in front of him as hard as he could. A strong mistral wind had arisen, sending torrents of water crashing against the rocks, shiny with seafoam. The beach seemed less beautiful to him than the one in Alicante, where he'd been barely a week ago. Not one walker on the horizon. A row of magnificent homes gleamed on the hillside over the Corniche, the coast road. Kevin ran down the stairs that reeked of piss, making his way to the edge of the water. At the bottom, he shivered and closed his green parka, then thrust his hands into the pockets of his jeans. The place was deserted except for an old gentleman sitting on a raffia mat watching the waves, a fishing rod next to him. Kevin was surprised by the contrast between the heart of the swarming city with its permanent hubbub and this sandy stretch of land lost in the pounding waves. A feeling of fear took hold of him. This spot was turning him away from the world of the living. When he was a child, nightmares of haunted castles would wake him up and he'd run screaming into his parents' bed. His father would drive him out of the room. "You're nothing but a little sissy!" he'd yell, while his mother, huddled under the blanket, watched him with her gray eyes, paralyzed by fear.

The dark silhouette of the Château d'If, assailed by the storm, added to the impression of sinking into another dimension of darkness and terror. Kevin walked over to the man and touched his shoulder. The old guy turned around with a start, wide-eyed. Kevin raised his arm, plunged his box cutter down, and slashed the carotid artery. The blood spurted out like a geyser. The old man collapsed with all his weight. The young man knelt down beside him and gently brushed a little sand from the wet cheek of the old fellow whose eyelids were fluttering. He held up the man's head while taking out his cell phone. He didn't post this selfie; it went into his personal collection. He walked back, tormented by the desire to find himself a girl for the night.

He had reserved a room at the L'Hôtel Duc, formerly L'Hôtel de l'Oasis, in the heart of the Canebière. A plaque at the entrance said Louise Michel had died there on January 9, 1905. He had never heard of Louise Michel, the red virgin, the heroine of the Paris Commune. He was not an anarchist, still less a revolutionary. Just a bloodthirsty guy who was out to conquer the most impregnable city in France. Kevin dreamed of a submissive Marseille on her knees, sucking his dick. He was sure of it, he'd get free of this fucking place without too much trouble. His room was on the third floor, overlooking the street. When he'd arrived the night before he'd slept very badly, his sleep interrupted by the noises from the street and the incessant stampedes up and down the stairs. Adventurous customers, eager to dive into the narrow streets of the Vieux-Port. Kevin passed by the concierge, who shot him a quick look. Suddenly, he had the strong feeling that the man was reading his mind. The radio was droning on—a whole string of Koranic suras broadcasting through its tinny speakers.

A woman came charging down the corridor. A small creature with big eyes and dark eye shadow, a scarlet mouth, and a narrow chin. Her bleached-blond hair went down to her waist. Kevin told himself it was too long and silky to be real. He breathed in big, jerky breaths, his heart beating hard. His chest hurt and he was suddenly afraid of getting a nosebleed. The girl was dressed in a pink sweater and a short black skirt that stopped halfway up her thighs. She was wearing laced black boots and a thin gold chain around her right ankle. Her translucent pink plastic earrings were the shape of kittens. Kevin had never seen earrings like them. The kittens were sticking their little pink tongues out. Her nail polish was also pink. She held her small hand out to him and said in a singsong accent: "Hey, brother, go get me a beer and a chicken-and-fries sandwich."

He almost broke her arm but controlled himself, his jaw clenched in anger. The concierge burst out laughing and said: "Come on, boy! You can't refuse that. You're a hit with Maria."

The girl didn't take her eyes off him. She came up close enough to graze the fur of his hood. He breathed in her perfume like a madman: a mix of cinnamon and cloves. He almost ripped the bill out of her hands and slammed the door on the way out, his cheeks flushed, pursued by the mocking laugh of the concierge. That woman had treated him like a little child. *This city is a shithole,* Kevin raged, humiliated. He tapped a number on his cell and screamed more than he spoke: "Brother, I swear, you threw me into the lion's den! You lied to me! You were lying all along. I'm so fuckin' mad I could burst. This city's a shithole!"

Abou Salem replied calmly: "You were warned. It's not a city, it's a mouth. Make sure you don't get swallowed up. Tomorrow, be at the place known as Porte d'Aix, a kind of open-air junk market. Our contact will be waiting there for you."

Kevin was dying for a beer as he walked along boulevard d'Athènes. He turned onto rue Nationale and walked into the first café he saw. Two men were sitting at a table playing dice and sipping whiskey-Cokes. A flat screen was showing a muted soccer game. He paid for his beer with the money Maria had given him and went to jerk off in the bathroom while thinking of her. He imagined her ass while he was screwing her. Kevin's naked butt was rubbing against the filthy walls, covered with drawings of cunts peppered with telephone numbers. Cheikha Rimitti's hoarse voice was coming out of an ancient stereo. A bitter *raï* song about a dark-haired girl who loved a man but made fun of him. The man went crazy with desire and sliced his rival's nose with a razor blade.

Kevin couldn't stand those burning laments, just as he hated Marseille rap. A rush of protest lyrics that were meant to be political. Those rappers weren't afraid of words. They grabbed syllables in their fists and gave you an uppercut to the chin. He'd tried to listen to some of them last night in his room at the L'Hôtel Duc and had ended up with his head hanging over the sink, his face twisted by tears, vomiting. He'd rather listen to rap in English; that way he was sure not to understand a thing.

The next day, Kevin stationed himself at Café Mauresque on place Jules Guesde in Porte d'Aix. As he drank his Coke, his eyes searched the swarming semi-legal market. Confusion reigned in the square from one end to the other. The putrid belly of Marseille, its contaminated face. The lawn of the arc de triomphe was a seedy disaster, wretched rags scattered in all four corners.

Battered sets of pots, burnt frying pans. Paperbacks with dog-eared covers and pages stained with tomato sauce. Mangy goatskin boots, trench coats in threadbare, imitation leather, fur coats moth-eaten at the armpits. A shambles of cracked dishes, handbags with their handles coming off, and old teddy bears piled up at the mouth of the gutters. Cars that couldn't brake fast enough drove over this stuff amid the curses of the enraged drivers. All this was the residue of dumpsters from L'Estaque to the Corniche, including the Canebière. The hideous debris of stuffed bellies, picked through tirelessly and sorted night after night by a whole army of needy souls before being resold on place Jules Guesde.

A man came up to Kevin and threw the daily paper on the table. He kept walking without stopping and turned left onto rue du Bon Pasteur. Kevin pretended to wait a moment before casting a distracted glance at the headline, quickly deciphering the address scribbled on the corner of the page. He paid for his drink and tried to make his way through the crowded sidewalks. He asked for directions from an old man sitting on a stool. The man stared at him and said: "Straight ahead on the other side of the street, son, but if I were you, I'd turn around and go back. I can see the ogress Aïcha Khandicha in her hairy clogs, holding you by the hand. You'd better go back home."

Kevin shook his head as he crossed the street, leaving the market behind him. The city had its professional lice-pickers. A galloping gangrene of illicit border crossers, of street people, of drunken bums, starving runaways, old men in furnished rooms, and families pushing shopping carts that swayed under the debris. These dark creatures roamed through the streets with their backpacks, armed with a twisted metal clothes hanger: the garbage reaper these men and women use to poke around in the heart of the trash. Crooks beware! Garbage was divided equitably by sector. People were on stir-duty every other night, airing out their fair share of refuse. By dawn, the filthy display would attract a whole crowd of sinister-looking characters along with the many

shoppers. Hoods would come to sell off the product of their rob-
beries, fighting over the territory occupied by the dirty kettles,
broken cups, and scratched vinyl records. A free-for-all where fits
of anger most often degenerated into knifings, under the fright-
ened eyes of the garbage-pickers. It was like an open manure hole
at the gates of the city. The rotting face of a horrible world displayed in broad daylight. The frightful foreboding of the coming
end. People with no rights, less-than-nothings appropriating the
scraps that had fallen off the tables. Folks put up with the wretched
of the earth, fed by the leftovers they had turned down. But they
raged against the ones in the garbage trade, for they attracted all
kinds of shady dealings. Terror loosened tongues. The sack of the
city was organized from this sinister spot where criminals mixed
with street peddlers. Among the latter, there were a handful of
runaways from the other bank of the Mediterranean. Not content with robbing open-air dumpsters, these wretched wetbacks
invited the worst villains to join the party. Pressure cookers sold
without lids, chipped coffee cups, and heaps of old shoes lay next
to the contents of recently stolen handbags.

Visitors would enter the city and bypass place Jules Guesde,
that crossroads of desolation. They would leave it the same
way, taking with them the spectacle of those men and women
in charge of cleaning out our garbage cans. Some inhabitants of
the city would gladly go cast stones at the devils on place Jules
Guesde, so much did they fear being confused with these seekers
of rancid crap. They threatened to beat them up. Officials made
a lot of noise denouncing depravity and murder.

"Roadblock, roadblock," men were whispering, caught by
surprise at the sudden arrival of the cops, panting as they fled
down boulevard des Dames dominated by the glass façade of the
Conseil Régional. The disorderly troupe was retreating toward
rue du Bon Pasteur, a little commercial street so narrow that the
disparate stampede bumped against passersby and knocked over
stalls in the bazaar before scattering into the adjacent streets.

The exhausted runners huddled in the doorways without dropping their stuff, loaded to hilt like a caravan of mules in the At-
las Mountains heading for the souk. Their loads stowed in total
disarray, as they had to pack in a rush. The bundles were coming
undone, revealing the black bottoms of pots and pans and vomiting a flow of old, sodden rags. Moldy clothes with sleeves frayed
at the wrist swept over the asphalt like the arms of hanged men
cut down in haste.

Utterly bewildered, Kevin escaped from the bedlam and left
to get the package of powder. He had to deliver the drugs to some
other European city. They would only tell him where when he
was just about to leave. *Tomorrow,* he told himself, *I'll get their
message and I can finally get the hell out of this cemetery under the
sun.*

He walked back to the hotel, threw himself on the bed,
and fell asleep fully dressed. At nightfall, Maria joined him in
his room. They drank beer, laughing like children. She began to
dance around the room with her long hair undone, after turning
the music up full blast. Then she threw herself on the bed and
wrapped her naked thighs around the young man's neck. Kevin
was groaning under Maria's greedy little bites. Her voracious
tongue was licking his penis and thrusting it deep into her mouth,
while strangling the base of it in a fist. The pleasure was so intense that he held out his hand and grabbed the girl's throat. She
pushed him away and placed herself on top of him. He exploded
in a whirlwind. When he woke up the next morning, his room
had been ransacked from top to bottom. The packet of powder
had disappeared too.

Consumed with rage, he rushed down the stairs, went out the
entrance like a gust of wind, and ran across boulevard d'Athènes.
No one on the street paid any attention to him. Men were smoking, sitting at tables on the sidewalks. He took rue Thubaneau,
dashed onto rue du Baignoir, and stumbled, panting, over a pile
of blankets for sale on the sidewalk in front of the entrance to a

bazaar. The shopkeeper cursed him with every word in the book. Kevin ran up rue des Petites Maries. He knew he was a dead man. Abou Salem would send his pack of killers after him. That man had zero tolerance for failure.

Kevin's phone rang. He ran his eyes madly over the text displayed on the screen: *Berlin, Ylmaz Grocery. 22409.* He was living on borrowed time now. He would not go to Berlin. His life was ending right here, in this city of white hills. He made a split-second decision: he wouldn't wait for Abou Salem's thugs to pick him up in some alley. *I won't let myself be Kalashed like a canary at the Foire du Trône*, the young man thought. He would kill himself on Plage du Prophète. No need to explain. Smiling, Kevin imagined the selfie that would make. He clenched his fist on the box cutter in his pocket and walked toward the staircase going up to the Saint-Charles metro station.

THE WAREHOUSE FOR PEOPLE FROM BEFORE

BY SALIM HATUBOU

La Solidarité

For my Comorian friend,
the poet-gendarme Mab Elhad

La Solidarité, a housing project in the North End of Marseille, is like a gap-toothed woman. Only a few buildings are still standing. Like a powerful cyclone, a program of the Agence Nationale pour la Rénovation Urbaine reduced some high-rises to dust and rubble while promising the tenants new apartments that must have needed a coal train to build, considering how long they've taken to come. This project is mine. I was born there. I grew up there. I live there.

This morning, from the tenth floor of building L-11, I look out on the stretch of villas that cover the hills as I enjoy my coffee. When I was a boy, I used to build cardboard cabins on those hills with my friends, but all that is far away, for today developers have put in private houses and built a wall to separate the new neighborhood from our apartment buildings.

I'm Sambafoum. Lieutenant Sambafoum. My parents left the Comoros archipelago to live in the Phocaean city. In kindergarten at La Solidarité or in the afterschool program, when we played cops-and-robbers, they always gave me the role of the robber, and even when we switched roles I remained the robber, despite my protests. So when I grew up, I became a cop in the game of life. I became a cop. My father was a construction worker. He died while working on the site of the metro between Sainte-

Marguerite and Bougainville. At dawn one February, when far right groups murdered a kid of Comorian origin in cold blood, my mother packed her things in a suitcase. When the far right won the elections in three cities in the south, my mother put on her jacket. When the far right took the fourth city in the south, my mother put on her shoes. And when the far right made it to the second round of the presidential elections one April evening, my mother split, destination: her native archipelago.

My cell rings. It's my boss. I pick up.

"Yes, hello!"

"Samba, did you read this morning's paper?"

"No! What's up, Chief?"

"They killed Radhia!" he announces.

The cup of coffee falls from my hand and splashes on the sidewalk. Radhia! I rush into the living room and turn on the TV. I stand there paralyzed before the images looping on the screen: on an ordinary road, a car is riddled with bullets. On the ground lies a body covered with a white sheet. And a commentary: "*The killers were extremely determined and didn't give their victim a chance. She was at the wheel of this convertible. Twenty-nine holes were found, twenty-nine bullets fired from a submachine gun. It's the first time a woman has been shot in these killings that continue to cast a shadow over Marseille.*"

With my jaws clenched, I slam my fist into the wall and collapse in tears like a little kid. Out there on the asphalt, under the makeshift sheet, lies Radhia, the love of my childhood and adolescence. My Radhia!

With a pistol pointed at his forehead, his back against the wall, and his eyes bulging, the redhead is stammering: "I swear I don't know anything! I haven't seen your Radhia for years."

All the customers in the café at the entrance to the Savine projects are holding their breath. Nobody moves. They all know me here and they know that whoever puts in his two cents might make some dentist rich.

"Listen up. You're going to tell me, nice and easy, who's connected to Radhia's death or I'll blow your head off."

"Okay, okay, put down your piece and I'll tell you everything I know. I've seen her hanging out with a Comorian guy a lot. He had a scar on his cheek and—"

I push him into the bathroom.

When I come out, I find the place empty. Everybody split. The redhead staggers out, covered with blood.

"Sorry for the disturbance," I say to Jo, the master of the house.

"Christ, Samba, I'll have to clean up everything now."

"Clean up your customers, that'll save you from having to mop up every time," I tell him as I walk out.

He's there with his nose almost glued to mine. We're standing in his office at the Évêché. Police headquarters. Right behind the building is Le Panier, where my father, like many Comorians, set down his suitcase when he landed in France before the law allowed him to send for his family and before he went to live in the North End where the high-rises were emerging from the concrete.

"Unacceptable, Samba. Unacceptable. Terrorizing a whole café. You're really off your rocker."

"I already told you the circumstances, Chief. I explained the whole thing from A to Z."

Chief holds his head and screams: "That's all they're talking about, Samba: a cop making mincemeat of a guy in some café. You know what? I'm going to tell you something, you asshole—what the hell business is it of yours, huh? When you asked me to give you the investigation into Radhia's death, I said no. And what do you do? You circumvent the official investigation."

"You put clock-watchers on the case, real jerkoffs, and you want me to stand there while Radhia's murderers are walking around free? You're screwing this up big time. And I'm being polite, Chief."

"Shut up!" Chief holds out his hand and says: "Okay, hand them over. Your badge and your weapon. You're suspended."

I throw them in his face and split. Avenue Robert Schuman. Traffic is heavy. I turn right on boulevard des Dames. At the entrance to the highway, I see a girl crossing the street. She looks like Radhia. No, it's not her. My Radhia is dead. The last time I saw her she was dancing in low-waisted jeans in the middle of my living room, eating strawberries. She'd come to tell me she was leaving and my tears wouldn't change anything, as Serge Gainsbourg says so well. She was someone else now. Jesus. When people have changed so completely, is there a warehouse to store what they were, like bags in a checkroom?

Night is falling. I drive to Plan d'Aou. The Plan d'Aou of my childhood no longer exists. New low buildings have replaced the old high-rises and construction is still in progress. I'm going to see Fadhul, one of my father's brothers. That is, one of his former co-workers he thought of as his brother. I've always called him uncle. I ring the doorbell. My uncle's wife opens the door and gives me a big hug. She invites me to sit on the couch. Her husband comes in.

"Uncle, I'm looking for a Comorian who has a scar on his left cheek. Does that ring a bell?"

He thinks for a long time and scratches his chin before he answers: "Yes, of course. I saw him twice. His name is Said Mhiba. He was with Hamda Karibedja, who lives in building A, fourth floor, in the Félix Pyat housing project."

I leave Plan d'Aou and head for Félix Pyat, which they call the Bellevue projects. When I find building A, the elevator's not working. The mailboxes are smashed in and the walls covered with tags. The staircase smells of piss. I walk up to the fourth floor and knock on the door. A boy of around twelve opens it and says "*Kwezi*" to me, a Comorian word to express respect. I ask to see his father and he tells me to come in. I find a man sitting on the couch listening to the radio. I'm walking over to say hello when he tells me to wait. So I can't help pricking up my ears and listening to the radio too. It's RFI, Radio France International:

"In the Comoros, President Said Mohamed Karim passed away at the age of sixty-two early Friday morning. The President of the Republic died of natural causes, according to a radio announcement by the Grand Mufti of Moroni. A source close to the president told us that the cause of death was a heart attack at three a.m. local time. We'll soon hear from our correspondent in . . ."

The man lowers the volume, stands up, and says hello.

"I'm sorry to bother you but I'm looking for Said Mhiba and I was told I might find him here," I say.

"He's my cousin, but he left for the Comoros last week."

"Do you know how I can reach him?"

"I don't know. Sorry . . ."

"No problem, uncle. Good night."

I leave the Félix Pyat projects and this man to his grief. The Comorian president is dead and I don't give a damn. And God knows how deeply I'm attached to the native archipelago of my parents.

I drive to La Solidarité. A few guys are loitering in front of the concrete bus shelter facing the mall that has only two stores and a pharmacy. I drive around the rotary. To the right, the two phone booths of my childhood have resisted the invasion of cell phones. I park next to the trash cans and go into my building. The elevator is out of order. At the tenth floor a man is smoking a cigarette, sitting on the steps. He gets up when he sees me.

"Good evening, dickhead!" he says.

I don't say anything. He throws his cigarette on the floor and stamps it out nervously. I keep walking upstairs; he follows me. I open the door and go in. He follows me and closes the door behind him. He walks into the living room, sits down on the couch, and puts his weapon down on the low table. I turn on the halogen lamp, a present from Radhia, and sit facing the man.

"So, you kidding me or what?" he says.

"Coffee or orange juice, Chief? That's all I have."

"Nothing." He holds two photos out to me. A man riddled with bullets in each one. "You recognize them?"

"Of course, Chief. This one's a stoolie. That one's the redhead I pushed around a little in the bar."

"One was whacked two hours after the other, today. But that's not why I'm here. I'm not going to beat around the bush. I'm giving you back your badge and your weapon. Here's why: the president of the Comoros is dead. As you know, our country has always been involved in destabilizing Africa and particularly the Comoros. Our new government wants to put an end to what's called Françafrique. So to show we have nothing to do with the death of this president, the prime minister is asking us to investigate, either to confirm the heart attack or find the possible murderers. We need the best person for this mission and that's you. If you agree, I'll give you the Radhia case. You've got my word."

"Chief, for Radhia I'd go all the way to the North Pole. When do I leave?"

The Comoros. Hahaya Airport. On the tarmac, a man is holding up a sign with my name on it. When I introduce myself, he asks me to follow him without saying who he is. We don't go the same way as the other passengers.

Now we're in an air-conditioned room with leather armchairs. The VIP lounge. The man takes my passport, goes out, and comes back. He had it stamped. A smiling girl comes to ask me if I want a glass of fresh orange juice, saying: "Welcome to the Comoros, sir." I thank her. They bring my suitcase back into the room.

"Let's go," the man says.

I still don't know his name. A chauffeured car is waiting for us. We get in the back. I watch the landscape go by in silence. A half hour later we're in Moroni, the capital. We park in a hotel lot and get out.

"Lieutenant, leave your suitcase here and we'll go for lunch."

We're at the Itsandra Beach Hotel's restaurant, facing the sea. Young people are playing beach volleyball on the sand. We move to a private spot in a corner of the terrace. While waiting for the waitress to take our orders, my host finally opens his mouth and introduces himself: "My name is Bam, Lieutenant Bam."

"I suppose that's a nickname," I retort.

"Just the initials of part of my real name, which goes on for miles. My name is Bourhane Ahmed Mohamed Kardjae Mzimba Ntsi."

"Right, I get it," I say, laughing.

But Bam doesn't laugh, he stares at me.

"Lieutenant, I have the feeling you're not exactly thrilled to see me here in the Comoros!"

"Listen, you have nothing to do with it, but your country is exasperating. Our president died and we're quite capable of investigating his death without France's help. And you have the nerve to tell us that interference—Françafrique—is over with? Who are they kidding? Lieutenant, if . . ."

He doesn't have time to finish his sentence, as a lovely waitress comes over to take our orders. Bam goes on nonetheless, really furious that France is interfering in the internal affairs of a former colony. I listen to him in silence.

"Listen, brother," I finally say, "you may not like France's foreign policy and I get it. But you and I are in the same boat here. We have to find out if the president was murdered or if he really died of a heart attack. Frankly, I couldn't care less. I accepted this mission so they would give me another investigation in Marseille. To learn who knocked off the love of my life. Period. So let's get down to work right away. Now, regarding your criticisms, why don't you tie them up in a little bundle, take them to the French Embassy, and give them to the ambassador who will forward them on to the French Ministry of Foreign Affairs, okay? Bon appétit, brother."

Bam opens his eyes wide and smiles. After the meal, he says: "Either we stay here to work, or we go to my office. Which do you want?"

"Here, no question."

He lays a file down on the table. I move my chair over and sit next to him. He explains the situation: "As you know, the president came back from a trip in the morning and seemed in good health. He died around three a.m., from a heart attack, we've been told."

"I suppose there was no autopsy?"

"No. He was buried the same day, of course."

"And who might want him dead, in your opinion?" I ask.

"Besides the people of this country, you mean? There's no shortage of enemies: the country is going through a big crisis. Anjouan, one of the Comoros islands, seceded and considers itself an independent state, although it's not recognized by the international community. The president sent in the army to bring the island back into the fold, but the separatists beat him badly. The president demoted General Mkouboi, the head of the operation. And of course that made him so mad he resigned. The separatist movement is supported and armed by the far right in France. And now it seems there's oil off the Comorian coast. The president supposedly gave the drilling market to the Ukrainians, to the dismay of the Russians. Then a colorful character comes on the scene: Colonel Madjomba. He controls the army now. As soon as the president's death was reported, he fanned his troops out all over the city. He's a friend of the famous French mercenary Bob Denard."

"And who's taking over during the interim?"

"According to the constitution, it's supposed to be the president of the high council of the republic, a certain M'hadjou Ben M'sa. But as he was going home after the president's funeral, his driver lost control of his car. Died on the spot. So the interim went to Madjid Ben Mawlana, the oldest member of the high council."

"And do you know anything about this man?"

"Well, he lived in Marseille for a long time and had kids there. He was a dishwasher in a restaurant on the Vieux-Port and after twenty-six years he was promoted to fish scaler. Comes back home and goes into politics. When they wanted to give him a ministerial position he refused and asked to be appointed to the high council, just three months ago. To sum up: when the president of the republic dies he's replaced by the president of the high council of the republic, who has sixty days to organize elections. If he dies too, he's replaced by the oldest member of that institution who takes his place with the same mission. But I have a feeling he has no intention of giving up power anytime soon."

"Well, lieutenant, they're really at each other's throats, aren't they? The problem is, we don't have much time," I say.

"So how do we start?"

"With coffee. It clears out the cobwebs. I'll go get it."

I walk to the bar. A man is drinking pastis and smoking a Gauloise, as he leans against the counter. I order two coffees. I'm about to go back but I turn around for a moment. Something strikes me about this man. I return to Bam.

"You see that guy at the bar . . ."

"The one who's leaving?"

"Jesus, quick. We've got to follow him."

Bam gets up without saying a word, picks up his things, and pays the check fast. We run to the car. We see the man get into a 4x4 parked opposite the Itsandra mosque.

"Why should we follow him?" Bam asks as he turns the key in the ignition.

"Because he has a scar on his left cheek."

"That's not a crime here, you know," he laughs.

"Very funny. Come on, go!"

We discreetly follow the man with the scar. He takes a path

lined with coconut trees and turns left. And we lose sight of him. We stop and get out. Suddenly, a car comes up and stops right behind ours. A young man in Bermuda shorts, stripped to the waist, gets out with a gun in his hand. He shoots off a round and we flatten ourselves on the ground.

"You're dead, motherfuckers! Mind your own business!"

I see him taking aim at Bam so I whip out my gun and shoot a bullet into his forehead. Welcome to my mother's country. In my head I can still hear the young man's words; there was such a contrast between this tropical landscape and his voice. We had something in common: a Marseille accent. He's dead, with his Kalashnikov in his hands and white, wet sand on the soles of his sandals. He was one of the young people playing volleyball on the beach; the little prick was watching us. He's wearing a bag slung across his shoulder. Bam opens it and waves his papers in the air: a French passport. Our young man is from Marseille. As for the man with the scar, he's still nowhere to be found.

"Thanks, you saved my life," says Bam.

"No thank yous between us, lieutenant."

"I know who the man in the 4x4 is."

"The guy with the scar?"

"Yes, yes. He's a rich local merchant. Come on, we're leaving for Moroni."

The sun is a golden ball casting a reddish glow on the horizon. It's one of the most beautiful sunsets I've ever seen. A few hours ago, I almost died under the bullets of a Kalashnikov, far from the Marseille projects where I live. Bam hands me his phone and I call Chief.

"What news?" he asks.

"Everything's fine, don't worry, Chief. But I need some info, urgent. Take a look at the records and please find me the file of a certain Swamadou Alhadhur. Born in Marseille. Call me back at this number."

"Okay, I'll call you back within half an hour."

While I'm talking, Bam's reading a book of poems. He writes poetry. He's published three collections already. In fact, he's been nicknamed the poet-lieutenant. Moreover—and this is rare—an excerpt from one of his poems is printed on a Comorian bank note. The phone rings.

"Yes, Chief, I'm listening."

"Here you go. I've got your little hood in the files. He has a record, mostly because of an armed robbery at Hard Discount. We haven't heard from him since the last time he got out, a few months ago."

"Okay. No risk of hearing about him anymore. I wasted him."

"So things are heating up over there. Be careful, and come home in one piece."

"Don't worry, Chief." I hang up.

"You don't just supply us with Marseille sardines. Shark too, I see," Bam says to me. "The guy with the scar has a big warehouse downtown where he organizes goods for his different stores. How about going there and having a little look around?"

"I like your style. Let's go," I say, standing up.

Moroni, the capital of the Comoros, is plunged in deafening nocturnal silence. We drive up to a big shed guarded by two uniformed men.

"Are they soldiers?" I ask.

"No, security guards. Listen, go talk to them. You speak good Comorian so that won't be a problem. Meanwhile, I'll walk around the building and go into the yard through the back."

"Okay, boss," I say, chuckling.

We park the car at a good distance and get out. While we're walking toward the shed, a pickup truck with a dozen soldiers stops alongside us. Their chief recognizes Bam and they salute each other. The soldier is talkative and Bam doesn't dare send him packing. I feign an urgent need to urinate and excuse myself.

I go around the shed, climb over the wall, and land in a poorly lit yard. I manage to get into the shed, which is full of bags of rice, cement, sugar—boxes and boxes of goods . . . Fifty-odd wooden crates in one corner attract my attention. I open one and there, before my eyes, are hundreds and hundreds of brand-new Kalashnikovs. I hear a noise and slip behind a pile of cardboard boxes stamped *Savon de Marseille*.

"Lieutenant, lieutenant!" a voice is whispering.

It's Bam, and he's staring wide-eyed at the crates. We close everything back up and leave.

"It's late. I'll drop you off at the hotel," Bam says.

A beautiful moon is illuminating the city. This archipelago really deserves its name: Juzur al-Qamar, the islands of the moon.

At dawn, the phone in my hotel room rings. It's Lieutenant Bam.

"You have to get up, brother, it's urgent!"

I take a quick shower, get dressed, and go downstairs. Bam is having coffee.

"Yesterday, after I left you here, I tracked down the scarred guy on the coast road. So I went to his place. I found a bunch of things. I've got two pieces of news for you, one good and one bad. The bad one is, you won't have time to go to Milevani to visit your mother—you're taking a flight back to Marseille in two hours. The guy with the scar will be on board and you have to keep an eye on him over there. I have lots of evidence connecting him to the death of the president of the high council of the republic so his fish-scaler friend can take power."

"So the president's heart attack was an attack after all, but it wasn't his heart that did it. And what's the good news?"

"You'll find out when you get on the plane," Bam says.

"Okay, I'll go pack. You're sure things'll be all right here?"

"Yes, don't worry, I've got the situation under control . . ."

At the airport, Bam gives me a signed book of his poems. Then

212 // Marseille Noir

he holds out a big envelope and says: "Open it on the plane, the good news is inside."

We say goodbye and promise to meet again. Each of us tells the other to dodge the bullets and do what it takes to stay alive. I'm in economy class, the guy with the scar's in first class. The plane takes off. The islands of the Comoros get farther and farther away. I'll be back. I open the envelope and . . .

Marseille. I trail the guy with the scar who doesn't appear to suspect a thing. Night covers the city. Sitting in my car parked on rue de Lyon, I see the guy quickly pull up to the curb and park his red Clio. He gets out and goes into number 6. I follow him, walking very softly. He goes up to the fourth floor and enters an apartment. I hear him talking with another man.

"You're a loser. I asked you to come to the Comoros with real men and all you can do is send me some asshole who can't even use a Kalash!"

"Lower your voice, will you? You know who you're talking to?"

"Of course. Your father may be the interim president, but you seem to be forgetting that he is where he is because of me. So if you want him to croak like all the others, and you with them, just keep talking to me like that. I lift my little finger and you go straight to hell."

The guy with the scar doesn't kid around. I kick the door in with my gun in my hand. The interim president's son pulls out his weapon but my Sig Sauer SP2022 is watching him with its cyclops eye, ready to spit fire like the Ngazidja volcano.

"Hi, guys, I came to have a cup of coffee or maybe eat some *mayele*, whichever you like," I say.

The guy with the scar crosses his arms and puts on a funny smile. He glances at his associate, who fires. I duck quickly and empty my chamber into his stomach. He doesn't seem to appreciate this five-bullet meal and collapses into a pool of blood. The scarred guy panics, tries to run out of the apartment, but I jump on him, tackle him to the floor, and cuff him. I make him sit down on a chair and plant myself in front of him.

"Welcome to Marseille, you son of a bitch. You wanted to knock me off back in the old country, but now the game's here at home. Let's have a little chat."

I open the envelope and take out papers, photos, and a French passport.

"Let's not waste time, because when you come down to it, things aren't so complicated: to enable Madjid Ben Mawlana to take power without a coup d'état, you had the president killed. But there's a problem: your boy wasn't the president of the high council so he couldn't take over. No big deal, you cut the brake lines in M'hadjou Ben M'sa's car. And according to the constitution, the position goes directly to your pal. I must say, your Marseille fish scaler was pretty clever. They thought he was a fool when he refused to become a minister and asked to be appointed to the high council. A good move, I must admit . . . I've got it right so far?"

"Yeah, and so what?" sighs the scarred guy.

"So what? I have photos here of you with a certain Radhia, and her passport was found in your house in Moroni. It's covered with a lot of visas. Radhia sure got around. And knowing her, I don't think she was traveling as a tourist. She belonged to your network and you're going to tell me why you had to get rid of her."

"What will you give me if I talk?" he asks.

"We lay everything on your friend, the interim president, and you get the hell out of here and go far, far away. I don't know you and you don't know me."

He peers at me and asks: "How do I know you'll keep your word?"

"*Hayi, wemkomori mi mkomori na mbe kali mbe!*" (Hey, you're Comorian and I'm Comorian. An ox never eats an ox.)

The fact that I spoke in his native tongue reassures him. So he starts talking: "Radhia was a very beautiful girl. After she got out of school, she couldn't see herself earning pennies at some boring office job. I recruited her. She went on lots of missions. When we had to kill the president, I sent Radhia to seduce him because no one was ever able to resist her charms. When he was in Marseille, the president invited Radhia to lunch, just him and her, at a restaurant on the Vieux-Port, where the man who is our interim president had been a dishwasher. Then, like in the movies, she poisoned the president's coffee while he was out answering a phone call from one of our accomplices. And that was that."

"Classic. So if he was poisoned here, how come he didn't die in Marseille?"

"No way. The president of the Comoros dies suddenly in France, can you imagine what a diplomatic mess that would make? We simply used a poison that doesn't take effect right away. After accompanying the president to the airport, Radhia was filled with remorse. She came to see me and told me she wanted to end all this, find the love of her younger days, ask for forgiveness, get married. But she knew far too much, especially state secrets. It wasn't safe to let her live. So I put out a hit on her, and the next morning two men on motorcycles took care of her."

"Give me the killers' names."

"You wasted the first one in the Comoros and you just killed the second. That's the whole story. Now it's your turn to keep your word."

I pick up my cell and say, "Oh shit, my phone recorded the whole thing. You're screwed. By the way, your boy the fish scaler was dismissed from his post. Lieutenant Bam read him a long poem before he arrested him. Your network has been dismantled."

I slip Radhia's passport into my pocket.

It's raining. It's night. I'm pacing back and forth in my apartment. I look out my window at La Solidarité. A boring housing project is just great. Far off, I see Radhia out there in the hills. I run down

the stairs and follow her. She goes into a huge warehouse. She
says to a lady: "I came to pick up what I was before and return
what I have become!"

The woman taps away at a keyboard and answers: "Hah! Too
late, mademoiselle. You missed the expiration date. You are sen-
tenced to remain what you became."

Radhia weeps. She didn't know that in the warehouse for
people from before, you have to read every clause of the contract
very carefully. And she evaporates.

I need rest. Monday, I'll fly back to the Comoros. Milevani.
My mother's little village is waiting for me.

JOLIETTE SOUND SYSTEM
BY CÉDRIC FABRE
La Joliette

He had the confident, greedy eyes, keen and dark, of those who have known for a long time, without having ever read a book, that the flesh is sad, as Mallarmé said. He was bald, had no eyebrows, and his own flesh was wounded, shriveled, and crushed in many spots on his arms and face. A scar ran from one ear to the other, as if his skull had been split in two. He wore a T-shirt advertising some exotic island. I clenched my fists as I watched the feet of the three huge guys sitting at the gaming table, each of their faces agitated by a nervous twitch as if they were synchronically beating out some kind of rhythm. They must have been listening to the same heavy metal song in their heads. No less than 160 bpm, I would have said.

Despite the cool wind coming in through one side of the double door, we were all sweating: the walls of the container they used for this dive had heated up in the sun all afternoon. The bar was made of a board resting on two oilcans, and cases of beer were piled up behind it. The fat guy had been introduced to me as both the manager of this improvised drinking joint and a kind of leader for the community that had cropped up on the docks in the last few weeks. Gypsies, gangsters on the run, dealers who had fallen out of favor, refugees, antiglobalization activists, and punks with dogs, but also ordinary families expelled from their homes occupied these abandoned containers converted into temporary shelters. Dozens of "boxes," as maritime transportation professionals referred to them, spread out between esplanade J4 and the silo d'Arenc. A whole makeshift village that had mushroomed up on the docks of the industrial port.

The fat guy pointed to my ring with the skull on it. I'd been trying to do business with him for the last ten minutes.

"Keith Richards's ring, right?" he said.

"Exactly. Lifted from his dressing room in Marseille during the last Stones tour."

He wanted the ring. He was ready to swallow anything with his gaping mouth. His breath stank of hash. He was flying high and I kept my distance, careful not to violate his air space. He had a piece of information I needed.

"You really think Keith snorted his father's ashes?" he asked.

"They say he even snorted the ashes of Mick Jagger's mother and that's why they hate each other."

"Can I trust you? You from Marseille? You don't have no accent."

"Depends on the day. I'm bilingual and bipolar."

He didn't laugh. Me neither. The container was plunged in semidarkness. Sprawled out in a corner, a woman I hadn't noticed till then coughed in her sleep. She was curled up on herself with her neck twisted, her head resting on her naked shoulder, her clasped hands holding her dress between her thighs, ripped net stockings and Dr. Martens on her feet. The fat guy pointed to her with his head.

"For that wheat-sucker, you got to wait a little. She had a hard day. What about the projectionist, what do you want from her?"

"I'd like to interview her," I said, frowning at the strange expression he used for the woman.

He ripped out a page from *La Provence*, blew his nose in it, crumpled it up, and threw it on the floor.

"Artists—it's all about them, these days. I never respected them. They make a mess out of workers' work. Look at César, he busted up cars and compressed them to make big cubes that still sell for millions. No wonder nobody respects work and industry in this town anymore."

"Yeah, the world's going down the drain . . . Can you help me or not?"

I took off the ring and held it out to him. He examined it. Tried to put it on his middle finger, grimaced as he forced it. In vain. He shrugged and stuffed the junk ring into his pocket.

"The girl you're looking for—the projectionist—her name's Phocéa."

He walked behind the bar, opened two cans of beer and gave me one. It was warm. He raised his can for a toast.

"That's it? What about Phocéa, where am I supposed to find her?"

"Just hang around here and there and she'll find you. I never knew what she meant to tell us with her improvised screenings. You seen them already?"

I nodded. I'd been told that every day a little before dawn, a film was projected on the side of a ferry. That morning, since I couldn't sleep in my shabby hotel on place de la Joliette, I'd gone out for a walk along the port as the streetlamps were turning off. A few destitute people sitting on the edge of a wharf with their feet hanging over the filthy water were looking at the pictures. They were black-and-white shots of the death throes of the *Costa Concordia*. Blurry images, as the distance between the source of the beam of light—impossible to locate—and the white hull that served as a screen must have been very big.

I absolutely had to meet the woman who was projecting those images. I had questioned a kid with wolfish eyes. He'd only said: "Ask the fat guy at the Cité Phocéenne, the dive in the container on esplanade J4. You can't miss it."

True enough. On one side of the container, there was an inscription in red paint: *Cité fausse et haine*—a pun on Marseille's nickname, *la cité phocéenne*.

The fat guy's gaze wandered off into space.

"That doesn't seem like a fair deal to me," I said.

"I know where she'll be tonight."

I turned around. It was the girl who'd said these words in a gravelly voice. She had just gotten up and was stretching.

"I could've gotten this info without you, it's not exactly worth my Keith's ring, is it?"

"Take the wheat-sucker with you, she's yours . . ."

I sighed and left. The mistral had risen. The girl caught up to me.

"Why does he refer to you as the wheat-sucker?" I asked.

"That's what they called the pipes that pumped the grain directly into the holds of ships to transfer it into the silo. Like thick metal straws."

"You live in a container too?"

"Here and there. I get by."

Ever since city hall announced the shutdown two months back, there had been no public services. The unemployed no longer got their benefits, landlords evicted them, and in a matter of days there'd been hundreds of them flocking from the three cardinal points of the city; the fourth was the west, the horizon. Because if disaster was on the way, salvation was always the sea, they thought. Whole families had moved into those containers that a street-art company had placed there for some kind of event. The boxes had served as restaurants, bars, venues for art shows, even a hairdresser's salon. Once the event had ended, everybody cleared out, but the cranes never showed up; the containers stayed and then were squatted and transformed into real pads, complete with mattresses, sometimes a table, and even knickknacks. I had even seen ex-votos hanging inside as decoration, probably stolen from the Cathédrale de la Major. Between the boxes, in the alleys, the residents would meet around improvised tables to drink pastis, gossip, or rail against continental Europe. There was a recent announcement that an early municipal election was coming. Perpetually drenched in sweat, the opposition candidate was out campaigning, mingling with the crowd, promising jobs and clean sidewalks. He wanted to be the mayor of Marseille so badly that he never failed to mention his Italian roots. I thought to myself, *In this country it's always the children of immigrants who get the worst jobs.*

I had been hanging around the "village" for three days, between the esplanade, the site of the new museums—including the MuCEM, closed like all the others—and the cathedral, and also between the docks and place de la Joliette. I had to get my hands on that video they wanted me to find.

"They" had called me directly at the paper where I wrote the culture column. It was one guy, actually, but he was only the messenger, as I quickly realized. A wheezing voice, slow speech. A threatening tone, an allusion to my poor mother who was losing her memory little by little in an old people's home.

"A videotape's going around the docks, from VCR to VCR. It's in the hands of a woman, an artist. You can see two well-known soccer players on it. You have four days to get hold of it. We'll call back."

I objected that I was neither an investigator nor a private detective and they were mistaking me for someone else, but the guy insisted, emphasizing my excellent "networks" in the world of culture and art. I had resigned myself to it, thinking of my mother and telling myself that it wouldn't be the first time in this city that a guy did a job for which he was neither qualified nor competent. I had vaguely deduced that the people behind this had their eyes on city hall too, or interests to defend. And the contents of the tape would help them, or ruin their ambitions if it fell—or had already fallen—into the wrong hands.

A man with a black eye was stationed in front of the half-open door of a container, guarding the entrance. You could hear children crying inside. I saw black marks on his knuckles, crusts of dried blood. He must have fought for the container. Shoes, stoles, caps, dolls, and gutted handbags were strewn around the waterfront.

"You could at least answer me. What's your name?"

The wheat-sucker. I'd almost forgotten her. I was walking mechanically toward place de la Joliette. She took my hand.

"I'm going with you. You'll have a hard time finding Phocéa. She's in hiding."

"Thanks for your help. Just call me the olive-pitter and we'll be even."

She laughed and squeezed my arm until I stopped walking. She drew her face near mine and put her hands on my shoulders. I felt her warm breath in my ear and on the nape of my neck.

"I know where Phocéa's going to be this evening," she whispered. "In the silo d'Arenc for the big multicultural party. Can I take you there? You're not a fucking racist, are you?"

"Just a bit, like everyone else: if we could choose, we'd all rather be Thai and invent the massage rather than English and invent the muffin, right? But it never came up: I'm from la Treille."

Marseille was supposedly made up of 111 villages that in reality never quite managed to get together and form a city; the village of la Treille was the gateway to Provence. Hills and scrubland. All through my childhood, I'd trapped rabbits and shot farm pheasants that the hunters had missed. A real Pagnol childhood. Except that "the glory of my father," to use Pagnol's title, could be summed up by the fact that he disappeared one day, dumping us, my mother and me, with a note of apology. His garage had failed and he chose to run away rather than commit suicide, he wrote. In short, adventure and the open sea: I could read between the lines. He had always preferred the beat poets and psychedelic rock to Provençal writers and Occitan folk musicians. I learned later that he had shipped out on a freighter and I never saw him again. After that, I discovered the punk scene, which led me to the university, probably due to misunderstanding the words of The Clash's "Career Opportunities."

But even immersed in the world of art galleries and the rock and theater scenes, I had still remained a kid from the land at heart: I hated the sea, I never ventured into the neighborhoods around the port, never went to the beach, and I still didn't know how to swim. For me, the port was the last frontier. Beyond, toward the horizon, lay a wild and hostile world.

"The port used to be the heart of the city back in the day," said the sucker, as if she had been reading my thoughts. "The nucleus of the atom of the planet Mars, to quote the famous rap song. A multimodal terminal for all the human odysseys of the Mediterranean."

A bit farther, you could see the huge construction site, the cluster of cranes and machines—a perfect square that already had a name: Les Terrasses du Port. It was a future mall, part of a plan aimed at "giving the sea back to the people of Marseille." Who took it away from them? I turned my head toward the open sea, toward that dark mass on which the dazzling white foam stood out; it seemed to jump up and bite before the swell swallowed it up again. The sea was anything but a symbol of freedom, it had always been nothing but a grave filled with wrecks and the only islands you could make out from here were the Château d'If, where the Count of Monte Cristo had been imprisoned, and the Frioul archipelago, which had been used to quarantine ships for centuries.

For the last few days, I had been sensing a sort of pressure under my feet. The port was giving me the feeling of a tragic ending. Too many trials and tribulations that wouldn't find their end here, I imagined. People came from the other end of the Mediterranean and crashed here. The piers looked like ramparts, everything was fenced off, it was a closed space that had stolen longshoremen's lives day after day, grinding down the guys they called "waterfront dogs." It was a sick tangle of rails and footbridges that went nowhere, a kind of spiral, a siphon that would bring everything back to the sea and empty itself into it.

The sun was stuck behind the horizon, leaving shreds of orange-tinted clouds in the sky, torn by the wind. The night seemed to have surged out of the bowels of the city, out of the depths of Le Panier, to spread over the port and swallow up, one by one, the metallic reflections on the gates and the belly of the ships. The cranes had just been lit up, dressed now in their blue and green lights, suggesting that the postindustrial age could also be a promise of celebration.

The wheat-sucker quickened her step. "Come on, let's move it."

I let go of her hand. I had never been relaxed with women, especially women like her, with their pungent perfume of freedom, even if the wheat-sucker was mostly trailing a sour smell of iodine, moldy seaweed, and rust.

All around us I could make out silhouettes trotting toward the north. They were coming out from all over—from sheds, from behind the low walls and containers, from the roofs of buildings, and from footbridges. They dropped from there, supple as cats, and landed on heaps of sand before starting to run. Dozens of shadows converging in silence, like us, toward the silo.

"We are all shadows," whispered the wheat-sucker. "The docks have never been well lit. A problem merchants used to gripe about whenever they weren't complaining about the scarcity of weighers on the waterfront. A weird profession, those weighers had: the guys had to know how to read and do arithmetic, but mostly prove they were honest. But us, we're light. We don't weigh anything—we're not worth anything and we're not a weight on anyone's shoulders."

I nodded dully. I was out of breath and my lungs were on fire.

"You're not into sports, clearly. The longshoremen carried fifty-kilo bags, so at the end of the day they'd lifted close to forty tons . . ."

"I don't know a thing about the life of the longshoremen. When they tell me about working at an ungodly pace I only think of Jimi Hendrix solos."

She shrugged and quickened her step still more.

The shadows were going through the wire fences and jump-ing over obstacles. Nothing stopped their progress. We scaled concrete barriers, hoisted ourselves onto the hoods of cars wait-ing in line for the ferry to Algeria: soon, it would open its hull like an ulcerous mouth under the astonished eyes of the drivers smoking cigs at the wheel. We then followed railroad tracks and I almost tripped over the rails embedded in the asphalt.

"Why's everybody running? Couldn't we walk there at a nor-mal pace?"

"We'll get there late and it might be packed. Most of the people running around you have no place to sleep and the silo's a warm place to spend the night. A storm's coming."

The silo d'Arenc was the emblem of the port. When you came into Marseille by car across the bridges and over the docks, it hit you right in the face. Over sixty feet high, the silo stood out in stark contrast to this dizzying horizontal landscape. It marked the entrance to the city, just before you dove into the tunnel and emerged a few hundred yards later onto the Vieux-Port—the yachtsman's paradise. The old silo had finally been rehabilitated and was now a theater. It became clear that its rich history as a major trading and shipping port was over when the ruins of its industrial past were converted into cultural venues: a tobacco factory had become a multicultural multimedia center in La Belle de Mai and old warehouses were now harboring music stages at Dock des Suds. Museums had sprung from the earth, from the Archives to the MuCEM, the Frac and the J1; now they defined the neighborhood of the port. Recently, people had started talking of Marseille as a "world city" and you couldn't help wondering—so out of it did the place seem—if it would one day be included in that other concept the north had created to reassure and flatter the south: the "global village." All I could see here was *No Future*. In fact, during the last French tour by the Ramones, in 1977, Marseille was the only city where they hadn't been able to play. The power supply couldn't handle the sound system and the amplifiers.

The sucker slowed down at the foot of the silo, where the crowd was forming an orderly line at the entrance. They were wearing clothes from all four corners of the earth. There were the inevitable Rastas, of course, in Peruvian toques; a group of guys wearing Scottish kilts, and flip-flops; a whole bunch of people sporting Olympique de Marseille T-shirts, but also teenagers wearing animal prints. I followed the sucker inside and had barely made it into the hall with its huge ceiling when I began feeling as oppressed by the dancing as I was by the shouting and the chaotic beams of the projectors. Upstairs, on the two balconies that stretched over the whole length of the hall on each side, some people were screaming to attract attention to themselves. The bass was pulsating throughout my body. On stage, the group's guitarist was playing harsh riffs while the singer screamed out aggressive slogans in English: *"No people! No fun! No football! No feelings! No me! No dock! No sea! No food! No city!"*

In one of the recesses under the first mezzanine, I could make out windows illuminated by blue, white, and red neon lights. Groups of onlookers had clustered in front of them. Some of them were making monkey calls, with their hands flattened on the window panes. I walked over to them. A sign read, *(post-)Colonial (un)Fair*. Behind the panes stood men and women in traditional Provençal garb: a woman in a recreated old-style kitchen wearing a white lace bonnet, a black corset, and a flowery dress was cutting vegetables on an oak table in front of a big copper pot sitting on an old stove top. Next to it, in another enclosed space of a few square yards, a hunter in a red shirt and scarf, short pants, and big clumpy shoes stood motionless with one eye shut, aiming at a stuffed rabbit in a scrubland décor that recreated the Provence garrigue; in the background, a child with his hands in the air was acting delighted. It looked like a live Provençal crèche except for the last tableau, where you saw an old man in jeans and a T-shirt mowing the lawn of his modern villa, depicted on a mural.

I heard a voice behind me and turned around. An old artist

with a pipe in his mouth wearing a cap and a sailor's sweater was making a speech in a thick voice with a northern French accent: "In 1906, Marseille held a phenomenal colonial exhibition where France put on a display of its colonies and their natives. We never should have stopped that tradition, so we have concocted a fine one here for you, with real natives from Aubagne and Aix, from the foot of Mount Sainte-Victoire to the foot of Sainte-Baume. Look at that kitchen, it's totally period. Provence, for us Marseille people—first-rate citizens in a third-worldized urban mess—it's the Promised Land, a pioneer utopia, it's the Jeffersonian American Dream in the valleys of the Arc and the Huveaune rivers."

I shuddered. "You should display some Marseille people in your windows. Marseille is our true colony, our own far-off, foreign country, our ultimate dream of exoticism."

"You don't like it?"

"Not really. I grew up near the Garlaban—you know, the 'lonely moorland that stretches from Aubagne to Aix' as Pagnol said. Mule paths, wild rosemary, and savory, does that ring a bell?"

"You're oversensitive." The sucker pulled me by the arm. "Come on, relax. They're actors, don't worry, no peasants have been harmed."

"Why're you following me like this, what do you want from me?"

"I'm your guide. You're lost and there's something you have to do. When you're done with your mission, you'll take care of me."

"It's this goddamned port. Nothing seems to make sense. I've been seasick for the past three days. Right now, it's Phocéa I'm interested in."

"She's here. She's the one who puts on those screenings." She pointed to the long curtain hanging behind the stage. Three different films were superimposed on it and seemed to melt into each other. A documentary about animals, a Disney movie, and an X-rated film. "Great summary of the history of the world, right?"

"Phocéa—do you know her?"

"We just keep the myth going: she's supposedly a former artivist who put subversive messages into commercials. I'm not even sure she actually has a message to communicate—she's having fun, that's all. Nothing's more exhilarating than belonging to the shadows while you play with the light, don't you think?"

"Exhilarating, like you say."

Each portion of the walls and ceiling was now covered with fragments of moving images. Several beams of light were going through the big hall; you could see dust and curling smoke dancing in them. I could make out boats—fishing boats—on the roofs of apartment buildings, fish thrashing around in a net on a bed where a couple was making love, as if they, too, had been caught in the mesh; pictures of the Nazi destruction of the "reserved quarter" of Marseille in 1943. Another film was projected on the dancing crowd. Faces were deformed and the floor seemed to move. It looked to me like images of a violent storm at sea.

On the curtain you could now see a film showing Zinedine Zidane and Eric Cantona. Without the sound. The two soccer players were speaking alternately, side by side, pointing fingers at the camera. On stage, the group had launched into an instrumental piece. It was a psychedelic version of an Olympique de Marseille anthem. The people stopped dancing, fascinated by the film. My employers had told me: "Soccer. In this city, soccer is the key to everything. Find the film."

The two soccer stars seemed to be talking very seriously, almost vehemently. Then they stopped talking and pointed their fingers again, perhaps at the spectators. Their lips still moved, synchronized. They were probably saying the same thing. They raised their fists in the air and froze. Fade-out. Sequences from films of demonstrations followed the clip.

Zidane and Cantona. Together. The two most popular Marseille players, although Zidane had never been with the

Olympique de Marseille and the latter had hung up his uniform in a fit of anger.

They had disappeared from the media over the past few days. In fact they had disappeared altogether, according to rumors; their families and friends allegedly hadn't heard from them.

"Not such a great duet, right?" the sucker said. "Apparently *they* like it . . ."

The crowd had launched into a furious pogo dance. The group had come up with their own wild version of Alibert's old Marseille standard "Un petit cabanon," complete with chorus and distorted lyrics.

"Wait for me here."

I walked toward the stairs that led to the upper mezzanine where a beam of light seemed to have its source. I climbed the stairs two by two. In the middle of the platform, a few punks who could hardly stand were hanging out around a bar. In one corner, a kind of booth made of hanging black cloths: the projector. As I was moving toward it, one of the punks bumped into me; I was pulled into a corner and suddenly there she was in front of me in a Medusa wig with latex octopus tentacles dancing on her shoulders.

"Phocéa."

"You were looking for me, right?"

"The film . . . what's so special about it?"

"They sent you to get it back, is that it?"

"You stole it from them?"

"From the ones who made it, yes. But it doesn't belong to your employers, who would like to steal it from me. What will be, will be, with or without the film. Two soccer stars speaking subversively enough to unleash total mayhem . . ."

"What are they saying?"

"They're icons and they're speaking with one voice. They could say anything at all and it would be gospel."

"Are there any copies?"

"No. The film was shot on video and the only existing tape is the one I have. Here, have a drink, you look pale and it's not just because of the purple lighting."

I took the glass she held out to me and emptied it in one gulp. A spritzer. I made a face at the bitter taste.

"I'm really sorry but I have to get that film back . . ."

I headed toward the improvised projection booth but she blocked my way. I took hold of her forearm to move her away but she freed herself with a quick, supple movement, grabbed my wrist, and twisted it until she could read my astonishment in my eyes. Then she broke her hold.

"Relax. You've got nothing to fear here, we're not downtown."

Downtown. The expression brought a smile to my face.

"Since this morning, I've been wondering whether I should give the film to your employers—well, to you actually—or destroy it."

Shouts of hate and insults reached us from below. I leaned over the railing. A fight had broken out in front of the windows of their goddamn colonial exhibition. It was bound to happen. The rock group had left. A deejay was wriggling around in front of the turntables. A hammering of industrial sounds. The labor unions, not to mention Isaac Asimov, had warned us that one day robots would replace humans—and now machines had already taken control of music.

When I turned around, Phocéa had disappeared. I felt like my brain was spinning around on itself. Down below, people were whistling to me. Around me, guys were patting me on the back, as if to congratulate me. On the curtain I saw a black-and-white film in sped-up motion. It was a close-up of a face. It was happening right here, perhaps at this very moment. That face was mine.

I heard a laugh behind me. Phocéa.

My legs suddenly gave way; I was held up by the armpits and my eyes blurred over. The last image I saw was the wheat-sucker walking in front of me, pushing aside the crowd to make way for the men who were carrying me. The ocean swell . . . it had caught up with me. Then everything went dark and silent as that fucking sea.

When I came to, the first thing I noticed was that I was drenched in sweat. I looked around for Phocéa; there was only the wheat-sucker wrapped in a pagne, asleep, with a hand on my belly. We were lying on an old mattress in a container. I shook her and she lurched back before drawing me to her.

"Where's Phocéa?" I asked.

She gave me a sad smile. "You in love with her? What were you thinking? They brought you here, so I tucked you in and watched over you. You might thank me."

"By the way, don't you have a first name?"

"Aurore. Thanks for finally striking up a conversation with me."

"Did we sleep together?"

"Not yet, no. You weren't in good shape last night."

"There was a pill in the drink Phocéa gave me. I never could stand those things."

I got up and pushed the heavy door open. The sun was hardly up, but it was already stiflingly hot. The mistral was blowing, making the cables and container doors clack loudly. Bare-chested kids were coming and going between the alleys, carrying boxes of fruit. Gypsy women were pushing children of six or seven in strollers, asking for change from the old men seated around a folding table drinking coffee; the gypsies took their insults for a while without flinching, then went digging through the heaps of garbage that filled the open trenches in the street. On the other side of the road there was the daily round of teenage girls with empty eyes coming out of the cathedral, candles stashed in their pockets—pockets big enough for the girls themselves to disappear in, bury themselves inside, erase themselves from the surface of the earth. I had a headache; my thoughts were confused and sounds felt as if they were amplified.

"I really need a cup of coffee, Aurore. Please."

She sighed, then went down the alley and disappeared around the corner of a container.

Small groups had gathered, people who were talking in low voices with clenched jaws. They looked worried.

Aurore soon reappeared with a tray. Steaming coffee and buttered slices of baguette. She walked into the container and came out with a big straw mat she put down in a spot shielded from the wind. She placed the tray on it and sat down without a word.

"You look funny. So do those people. What's going on?"

"All hell broke loose last night after we left the silo. That's what the mama who gave me the coffee just told me. Armed men came in and there were shots. Some people were wounded. We don't know what they wanted. Downtown, there've been demonstrations since dawn and they've turned into street fights. They destroyed the animal sculptures at the Vieux-Port and looted the cardboard buildings of the artists—you know, what they called the Ephemeral City." Cell phones were useless; they hadn't been working for the last few days.

She lowered her head and blew on her coffee, then looked into my eyes. "And something happened to Phocéa."

"How do you know?"

"This morning at dawn, there was the usual crowd on the waterfront. They were waiting for the screening, the images of the day. But there weren't any. It's the first time, in a whole month."

She threw her paper cup in front of her, got up, and held out her hand to help me up too. "You'll find her in J1; she has a hideout at the back of the building. Go there fast, do what you have to do, then meet me at La Joliette and we'll get the hell out of here. We'll leave this fucking port, our purgatory, our aborted dreams."

The seagulls were sniggering over our heads. I hated those birds; their droppings polluted the drinking water. My mother always told me that the real catastrophe would come the day they closed the huge open-air garbage dumps all around Marseille that the gulls used as a food cupboard. *Then they'll move inland, loot the planted fields, and destroy the hothouses. Like a plague of Egypt.*

I stared at Aurore. Realizing that she was actually quite beautiful. She motioned to me to get moving.

I ran to the J1. When I reached the cathedral, I heard noises that seemed to be coming from the Vieux-Port; following the gaze of the passersby standing there, frozen on the spot, I saw black smoke rising over the buildings. I heard a mailman who'd just stepped off his scooter say to the people surrounding him: "They stormed the city halls in all the sectors . . ."

I stepped up my pace. Once in front of the building, I climbed over the fence and went up the metal stairs. I almost slipped on the wet footbridge. The sea was lashing the dikes, but I was no longer afraid of that mass of water spilling all over, with its dips, its waves, its wounds. The glass door was closed. Behind it, I saw someone point to a guy who then lifted the metal bar barricading the entrance. Someone pulled me inside. I rushed toward the big hall and slowed down when I discovered dozens of photos pinned up on panels that created a guided path. I knew I would find her not far from there: all I had to do was follow the exhibit, go around the panels covered with vacation snapshots and family portraits donated by anonymous people in Marseille—children with shrimping nets on a rock, a woman in a black dress fishing from a small boat, a bunch of brothers and sisters all wearing ribboned straw hats standing in front of a Citroën Ami 8 . . .

She was lying there between the last panel and the window that looked over the Arenc basin, stretched out on a mattress on the floor. A woman with a serious face and a tense mouth was kneeling over her, doing something; bloody cloths were scattered around Phocéa. I squatted down, noticed a wound on her chest, and turned my eyes away immediately.

"They got me. They took their tape back . . . Your employers must be furious. I don't work for anyone, I hope you understood that, right? I only show true images, pictures we need to make sense. That's all." Her face tightened. "I'm ready now. I'm not afraid."

I thought of Louis Brauquier's line: *Marseille, tragic and always consenting.* "Did you call an ambulance?"

"They say they're coming but they're overwhelmed, it's a real mess downtown." Phocéa closed her eyes. "I won't make it, anyway . . . Do you hear the shouts outside, you see the smoke? It's started . . . chaos. We deserved it. We, the artists, abandoned our city. Culture capitulated. The video was posted on the Internet at five this morning. An hour later, it had been viewed a hundred thousand times and men started going out into the streets with flags in the city's colors, wearing Olympique de Marseille T-shirts, sometimes with their wives and children. First they forced open the doors of the city hall of the third sector and then all the others. People say they smashed the emblem of the Republic: the busts of Marianne were replaced by replicas of the 1993 European Cup. They built barricades in the streets, they're surrounding the police stations; some of them have weapons."

"The video? You mean the clip with Zidane and Cantona? How can that be responsible for what's happening in the streets?"

"They're calling on fans to drive out the politicians and occupy the city halls of all the sectors. They say the citizens have become cowards. They're asking the fans what they're waiting for to take everything over by force, since in reality they already have: they're the ones who made Marseille a city that wins, in the eyes of the world. They're telling them to go out into the streets and they're promising to become the new coaches of the Olympique de Marseille. And lift the city out of its depression . . ."

I was stupefied. Local identity was sometimes summed up by the soccer slogan *Proud to be Marseillais.* The Olympique de Marseille was a whole economic system founded on the revenge of the working classes, in addition to being a commercial enterprise with its suppliers, its customers, and occasional strikes by its fans.

"That's the only thing people want here. The future of the

city was sabotaged by the politicians, but when Marseille stops being a blighted city and the capital of delinquency, if only for the duration of one game, it will be thanks to the Olympique de Marseille. It's not just an outlet, it's the collective unconscious of Marseille, its share of light. Only soccer can ward off the failure of a whole city and its inhabitants."

"And because two soccer stars incite them to do it, they destroy the city?"

"Apparently, you don't really understand this place."

I'd screwed up my mission and my employers were going to demand an explanation; I had to split. The image of my mother appeared at the back of my mind. "It doesn't matter. I'm going to leave. Goodbye, Phocéa."

I kissed her on the forehead. She winked back at me and then had a coughing fit that brought up blood. I took the opportunity to walk away.

On the port, cars were flooding in to board the ferry, creating a mammoth traffic jam. Columns of people were walking in, loaded with luggage. Some of them were running around shouting.

Aurore called out to me: "Are you ready? This ferry's leaving in an hour."

"I have to go back to my hotel first."

I charged ahead and she followed closely behind. At the reception desk, the concierge was busy stuffing clothes and books in a bag on the counter. He stopped, searched his desk, and gave me a piece of paper.

"There were two calls for you. I'm sorry. One came from the director of an old people's home and he said your mother died this morning. A heart attack. She didn't suffer. And the other one . . . said the same thing. But the person who called didn't tell me who he was."

I felt nauseous. I took Aurore by the arm and pulled her outside. "Let's split, they'll probably show up here soon."

"The ferry. Follow me."

We ran right past the line of cars. At the ticket checkpoint Aurore talked to a guy in a white shirt and tie. She pulled a wad of bills out of her pocket and the guy stuffed it in his; then he gave Aurore two boarding tickets and let us through.

We rushed onto the open mouth of the ferry, climbed narrow stairs, and found ourselves on the deck, where we dashed to the front of the boat.

I sat down on a metal bench facing the horizon and grabbed the armrests. The mistral and spray were slapping at me and I realized to my surprise that I wasn't feeling at all seasick. Aurore was grasping the railing and her eyes were closed. She had a smile on her lips and seemed to be drinking in the salt air.

A young man walked by in front of me. The back of his Olympique de Marseille T-shirt read, *Marseille Too Powerful*. He approached a group of passengers who seemed to be in the middle of an argument. Because of the wind whistling through the rigging, I only caught fragments of the conversation. One of them seemed to be explaining that the two former soccer players had been taken hostage and made this clip under duress. Then they all went back inside the boat.

I tried to accept the absurdity of what was happening to me, what was happening to all of us. That this was the way the world worked, with guys who came out of nowhere ordering us to do things that seemed meaningless, and we obeyed from fear of punishment or through simple habit. I felt a little ashamed not to be in mourning for my mother. I was almost relieved. It's when I thought of Phocéa that I felt sad.

Aurore came over to sit next to me and took my hand. "I was a whore for years, and that was in a port. I held up sailors who started staggering as soon as they set foot on the ground. So there are things I can feel. This is my time. To raise anchor. And for you too, it's time."

The ship bellowed and started moving. When it went past the last dike, I saw them on the open sea: dozens of kiteboarders shooting across the crests of the waves with cries of victory, while columns of smoke rose from every corner of Marseille. As if it were their last ride.

For me, it was a first crossing. Everything could begin at last.

ABOUT THE CONTRIBUTORS

DAVID AND NICOLE BALL have translated six novels and one book-length essay together, stories in Akashic's *Paris Noir* and *Haiti Noir*, and many poems and stories elsewhere. Their work has twice been awarded grants from the French Cultural Service in New York. David's translation of Jean Guéhenno's *Diary of the Dark Years, 1940–1944* won the French-American Foundation's Translation Prize for nonfiction in 2015. David and Nicole divide their time between Northampton, Massachusetts and Paris.

FRANÇOIS BEAUNE was born in Clermont-Ferrand in 1978. He is the author of *Un homme louche* and *Un ange noir,* and the founder of the art journal *Louche,* the cabaret show Le Majestic Louche Palace, and the website *Loucheactu.* In partnership with Marseille-Provence 2013, he spent a year searching for "true stories from the Mediterranean" in a voyage that led him to twelve ports. The collection of these stories, *La Lune dans le puits,* was published in 2013. Beaune currently lives in Marseille.

PHILIPPE CARRESE was born in Marseille in 1956. Immersed in Mediterranean culture, he has written fifteen colorful novels and directed a number of well-received films for television and cinema. His most recent work, *Virtuoso Ostinato,* was published in 2014. In addition to his activities as a writer and director, Carrese is a music composer and sometimes indulges in creating political cartoons for newspapers.

PATRICK COULOMB was born in Marseille in 1958. Trained as a geographer, he is the author of several novels and short story volumes including, most recently, *L'inventeur de villes.* He is also the cofounder of the publishing house L'Écailler, and currently works as a journalist for the newspaper *La Provence.*

CÉDRIC FABRE lives and works in Marseille. He is a freelance journalist who also runs writing workshops. A lover of pop and rock cultures and of literary "subgenres," he has written novels that flirt with the fantastic (*La commune des minots*) and crime novels, the last of which, *Marseille's Burning,* came out in 2013, the year the city was named the European Capital of Culture.

C. Hélie

RENÉ FRÉGNI was born in Marseille in 1947. He deserted from the army at the age of nineteen and lived in Turkey under a false identity doing odd jobs. He was eventually found and spent six months in prison, where he began his career as a writer. He ran workshops in Baumettes prison, and has written close to a dozen novels, including his most recent publication, *Sous la ville rouge*. Currently working as a psychiatric nurse, he divides his time between Marseille and Manosque.

Serge Peri

CHRISTIAN GARCIN lives near Marseille, where he was born in 1959. His novels, short stories, poems, travel writing, and essays about literature and paintings have been published by Gallimard, Verdier, l'Escampette, and Stock. His most recent novel, *Selon Vincent*, takes place in France, Russia, and south Patagonia between the nineteenth century and the present day.

SALIM HATUBOU (1972–2015) was born in the Comoros. He arrived in Marseille at the age of ten and grew up in the Solidarité housing project in the North End. A novelist and storyteller, he was influenced by his second home as well as his native archipelago. He is one of the most prominent authors of Comorian literature in French. His last book was *Que sont nos cités devenues?* in collaboration with the photographer Jean-Pierre Vallorani.

Hélène Bamberger / P.O.L.

REBECCA LIGHIERI, a.k.a. Emmanuelle Bayamack-Tam, was born in Marseille and has lived there for twenty-three years. She is a founding member of the organization Autres et Pareils and codirector of the publishing company Contre-Pied. Lighieri is the author of two plays and eight novels, all published by P.O.L. Her latest novel, *Husbands*, came out in 2013.

Catherine Hélie

After being a Red Guard in the 1970s, **EMMANUEL LOI** went bad and began a life of literary crime. He is notorious for twenty-odd books, got mixed up in the world of theater, and did time on the radio. His punishment is now recognition, something he no longer flees like the plague. His most recent book, a despairing love song, is *Marseille amor*.

MARIE NEUSER was born in Marseille in 1970. She acquired a passion for writing very early on, while studying Italian in Aix-en-Provence. Her first novel, *Je tue les enfants français dans les jardins,* was published by l'Écailler in 2011; it was followed by *Un petit jouet mecanique* in 2012, which won the Prix de la Ville de Mauves-sur-Loire and the Prix Marseillais du Polar (the Marseille prize for a crime novel) in 2013.

PIA PETERSEN was born in Copenhagen, Denmark. She came to France when she was young, and learned the language while doing odd jobs and studying philosophy at the Sorbonne. Peterson is the author of more than ten novels, all written in French; her most recent publication is *Mon nom est Dieu.* She also contributes to the literary journals *l'Atelier du roman* and *La revue littéraire,* and splits her time between Marseille, Paris, and Los Angeles.

Catherine Droux

SERGE SCOTTO is a novelist, lyricist, graphic artist, illustrator, and journalist. His literature often alternates between humor and horror. His dog Saucisse became famous as a candidate in the 2001 Marseille municipal elections.

Nazareth Agopian

MINNA SIF was born in Corsica to a family from the south of Morocco. She lives in Marseille, where she writes and runs writing workshops. She has published two novels, *Massalia Blues* and *Méchamment Berbère,* and her short fiction has appeared in the anthologies *Scandale, Une enfance corse,* and *Le pays natal.*

FRANÇOIS THOMAZEAU was born in Lille in 1961 and grew up in Marseille. With Jean-Claude Izzo and Philippe Carrese, he was one of the pioneers of Marseille crime fiction. He published *La faute à Dégun* in 1995, followed by the *justiciers RMistes* series. As a publisher he cofounded L'Écailler, and as a sportswriter he has written several books on tennis, bicycle racing, and rugby. A bookseller in Paris and restaurateur in Marseille, he is also a musician.